Acclaim for Andrea Barrett's

THE MIDDLE KINGDOM

"AN AFFECTING NOVEL ABOUT AN AMERICAN WOMAN'S SELF-DISCOVERY. . . . Barrett here re-creates not China itself but, more reasonably, her heroine's fascination with it, and she manages to infuse her characters, Grace especially, with a psychic energy and charm. . . ."

—*Publishers Weekly*

■

"ENGAGING . . . By recapturing the powerful impact of the China experience, Andrea Barrett confronts us with the fickleness of our cultural affections, exhuming, as from a distant past, the lure of the Middle Kingdom. . . . Alternating scenes from past and present powerfully convey the awakening and renewal that have often characterized the unwitting foreigner's China passage."

—*Los Angeles Times Book Review*

■

"Every bit as bright as Barrett's *Lucid Stars* . . . an absorbing and complex portrait . . . Barrett spins Grace's story backwards, as one flashback leads to another. . . . It works naturally, even powerfully . . . [with] a compelling edge . . . EVOCATIVE, FUNNY, AND JUST MYSTERIOUS ENOUGH: BARRETT'S BEST YET."

—*Kirkus Reviews*

■

"I admired Andrea Barrett's previous novels, but I was somehow unprepared for the astonishing leap forward represented by this book, with its delicately interlocking worlds of personal and public politics, the vividly realized setting in China, and the spiral meaning that widens continually from the first page to the last."

—Jay Parini, author of *The Last Station*

A Literary Guild Alternate Selection

■

"I READ ANDREA BARRETT'S *THE MIDDLE KINGDOM* NONSTOP. IT'S AN EXHILARATING BOOK, WITH SUCH WONDERFUL AND GENEROUS INSIGHTS FROM THE VIEWPOINT OF THE OUTSIDER, THE INSIDER, THE OBSERVER AND THE OBSERVED, THE PERSON STANDING AT THE CENTER OF THE WORLD. MS. BARRETT HAS CAPTURED A TRULY AUTHENTIC BEIJING, SIGHTS, SMELLS, OUTER AND INNER TURMOIL."

—Amy Tan

■

"The sometimes disjointed exchange of information between two people of totally different cultures gives the novel its strength and authenticity. . . ."

—*ALA Booklist*

■

"FINELY HONED . . . A SUBTLE, LUMINOUS NOVEL."

—*Detroit News*

■

"Barrett expertly weaves together the disordered strands of an unfulfilled life. . . . Her new book is notable for its three-dimensional characters, accessible prose and unsparing yet warmly sympathetic examination of the struggle to create a meaningful existence. . . . It's a pleasure to follow the progress of a writer like Barrett, never satisfied to merely duplicate her achievements, reaching in each new novel to build on her strengths and deepen her approach."

—*Cleveland Plain Dealer*

■

"A GRACEFULLY CRAFTED, THICKLY EMBROIDERED NOVEL . . . IT GLITTERS WITH SENSITIVITY AND UNDERSTANDING. . . . The intermingling of Chinese culture and American attitudes, without denigrating either, infuses Barrett's novel with a textual richness. . . . Barrett opts for rich embroidery, for masterful twists of language. And she succeeds. She has woven a thick, glistening tapestry with so many sequins that we can see ourselves mirrored in them."

—*Rochester Democrat & Chronicle* (New York)

■

"A STUNNINGLY EFFECTIVE TOUR OF BEIJING IN THE DAYS OF TIANANMEN AND BEFORE, AS SEEN THROUGH THE REFRACTING GLASS OF AMERICAN LIFE. THIS PROSE IS LUMINOUS."

—Mark Childress, author of *Tender*

■

"Barrett's style of storytelling is engrossing."

—*Arkansas Gazette*

■

"Andrea Barrett's *THE MIDDLE KINGDOM* is so fully imagined that it communicates with the passion and revelation of memoir. It has the fevered quality of a dream and, at the same time, a dailiness so vivid and moving as to be almost overwhelming. Ms. Barrett knows the political geography of China, but more important, she knows the geography of the heart. THIS IS A WONDERFUL BOOK."

—Robert Nathan, author of *The White Tiger*

Also by Andrea Barrett

Secret Harmonies
Lucid Stars

THE MIDDLE KINGDOM

ANDREA BARRETT

WASHINGTON SQUARE PRESS
PUBLISHED BY POCKET BOOKS
New York London Toronto Sydney Tokyo Singapore

My thanks to fellow writers Tim J. Fox, James S. Gamble, Betsy Isbell, Laurence E. Keefe, Susan Keefe, John Strazzabosco, and Deborah C. Weiss, for their constant support and helpful criticism.

Thanks also to Yaddo and to the MacDowell Colony, where parts of this book were written.

A Washington Square Press Publication of
POCKET BOOKS, a division of Simon & Schuster Inc.
1230 Avenue of the Americas, New York, NY 10020

Library of Congress Cataloging-in-Publication Data
Barrett, Andrea.
The middle kingdom / Andrea Barrett.
p. cm.
Originally published: New York : Pocket Books, c1991.
ISBN 0-671-72961-6 : $8.00
I. Title.
[PS3552.A7327M5 1991b]
813'.54—dc20 91-35221
CIP

First Washington Square Press trade paperback printing March 1992

10 9 8 7 6 5 4 3 2 1

WASHINGTON SQUARE PRESS and colophon are registered trademarks of Simon & Schuster Inc.

Cover design by David Stevenson
Cover art by Gary Kelley

Printed in the U.S.A.

Contents

▪ I ▪

The Old Men

June 1989

Patient: *I've experienced a feeling of general malaise for quite a long time.*

Doctor: *Since when?*

Patient: *For nearly one year.*

Doctor: *How is your appetite?*

Patient: *I have no appetite at all. I have a feeling of fullness in the upper abdomen—often I really feel very heavy. My gums bleed and my tongue is coated with a thin layer of whitish fur.*

Doctor: *Have you lost any weight?*

Patient: *Yes, I have lost ten pounds since last year.*

Doctor: *Let me feel your pulse. Lay your wrist on the little pillow, like this.* (Patient puts his right wrist on the pillow with the palm facing upward.) *Your pulse is deep and thready.*

Patient: *What does it mean?*

Doctor: *It means there is a deficiency of vital energy.*

—*adapted from* A Dialogue in the Hospitals, English-Chinese *(a handbook designed to help Chinese physicians care for English-speaking patients)*

All of Beijing was blanketed with smoke and rumors. From midnight on Friday, when we first heard that soldiers were trying to jog down Changan Avenue, through the chaos of Saturday and the horrors of Sunday morning, those of us still on the Qinghua campus clustered around radios and televisions and ringing phones, relaying whatever we heard and trying frantically to understand what was going on. We heard that the soldiers were unarmed, armed, armed and pumped full of amphetamines. We heard they were crashing through Tiananmen Square, crushing the demonstrators and mowing them down with machine guns; then that workers were ambushing soldiers in the streets. Someone said a soldier had been disemboweled and hung from his burning truck. Someone said snipers had shot out the windows of the Beijing Hotel.

Deng was dead, we heard. The army was in charge. Li Peng had been shot in the leg and the statue of the Goddess of Democracy was down. There were two armies, six armies, the armies were fighting each other. Deng was alive and the armies were under his control. Ten thousand people had been killed, someone said. A hundred. None. In the square, someone said, the soldiers were burning bodies with blowtorches and flamethrowers. The students had captured some of the soldiers' guns and were shooting back. The soldiers were driving over the students' tents.

Jianming arrived wild-eyed on Sunday night and said she had seen the whole thing. Unbelievable, she said. A massacre. Worse than the worst days of the Cultural Revolution. She and a group of her friends had been huddled at the base of the Monument to the Revolutionary Heroes during the height of the shooting; at first the tracers had soared over their heads, she said, over the top of the obelisk, but then the ribbons of white light had moved lower, lower, until bullets were ringing off the granite. They'd fled then, she said; the streets were burning. She had ridden her bike north through the alleys and back roads, avoiding the columns of smoke. Smashed buses and trucks lay on their sides, and the intersections were blocked by barricades of twisted rubble. Troops guarded the square and were still firing at anyone who approached. A truck was making a mournful procession from campus to campus; in the back, Jianming said (and she was a thoughtful, quiet girl, not given to exaggeration), in the back the bodies of five students crushed by tanks had been packed in dry ice.

That night, on Beijing Radio, we heard the Mayor talking about how the brave soldiers had crushed the counterrevolutionary riot instigated by foreign influences and hooligans, but on Monday, a student from Beijing University arrived with an armload of posters and leaflets that contradicted everything the Mayor had said.

Jianming left Monday morning for her parents' home in Changsha, after hearing that soldiers and security men were beginning to sweep the campuses for troublemakers. She hadn't been deeply involved in the movement, nor had the other students I'd been living and working with for the past few years. But all of them had participated—they'd gone to the square in the late weeks of April, when the mood was festive, almost joyful; they'd marched in the big parade on May Fourth and had returned to the square for the demonstrations during Gorbachev's visit. But then they'd come back to campus, dismayed by the declaration of martial law and the growing rumors. And except for Jianming they'd stayed there, gathering in the courtyards and the empty rooms.

Now the professors left on campus urged the students to go home. Yan and Liren and Yuanguang left that afternoon; Yulong and Qingxin went on Tuesday. Wenwen was the last to go—Wenwen, who had tutored me in Mandarin after classes and who had proved to be the brightest of the students working in Dr. Yu Xiaomin's lab. Wenwen and I had dissected hundreds of fish together, shared a rowboat when we went to sample the lake, cobbled together a paper chromatography setup for a demonstration.

"I have to go," she said, after we'd heard that the student leaders had been ordered to turn themselves in, and after we'd seen some of the TV footage the government had spliced together from the tapes of the remote-control cameras mounted in the main streets and on the square. The military actions had been edited out; the images that repeated again and again were of protesters burning Army trucks, attacking soldiers, throwing bottles and bricks. Rioting, the voice-overs said. Threatening the city with chaos. Then we heard another rumor: that those cameras had been rolling quietly throughout the six weeks of demonstrations, photographing the ebullient marchers long before there was any trouble. The student who told us this warned that hundreds, maybe thousands of security men were combing those tapes now, blowing up pictures of individual demonstrators. Mug shots of the student leaders were already pasted all over the city, he said. Hot lines had been set up, so that people could turn in protesters they recognized.

"What if my face turns up?" Wenwen said. "I was carrying a banner when I was there on the eighteenth."

In Xiaomin's absence—Xiaomin had been gone since Friday, and no one knew whether she was at home, or with her husband at the hospital, or caught somewhere in between; no one even knew where to hope she was, since we'd all heard that the hospitals were full of troops and that the area where Xiaomin's apartment was had been particularly hard-hit—in Xiaomin's absence, I knew Wenwen was hoping I'd have some advice.

I was Xiaomin's assistant—not a professor, but not a student either—and the students looked up to me. I'd brought books and equipment into the lab that they'd never seen before, castoffs from my friends at home, which had turned into treasures here. I'd lectured to Wenwen and the others in the halting Mandarin they'd taught me, and I'd listened to their stories of the Qing Ming demonstrations and the Democracy Wall movement. But despite those tales, and despite all Xiaomin had told me about the other crackdowns and campaigns she'd survived, I didn't know what to tell Wenwen now.

"Why would they come for you?" I said. "You didn't do anything."

"Why would they do any of this?" she said.

From the window of my room, we could see students

milling around the latest batch of posters and the copies, faxed from Hong Kong, of photographs of the dead and wounded. Many were crying. Some stood frozen, as if they'd never move again. "Where would you go?" I asked.

"To find my brother," she said. "And if I find him, I'll take him to some friends we have in the country. It's too dangerous here."

She was the last person on campus that I knew well. "You should go too," she said, studying my face. "Home, I mean. You hear the radio—the government is blaming all this on foreign instigators. Americans are not safe here. Especially not women. Especially not a woman with a baby . . ."

"Jody," I said. "I know."

He'd been sleeping, but he woke when he heard his name—my son, whose second birthday had fallen on Friday, before our world collapsed. "*Muqin,*" he said then, smiling at me sleepily. Mother. He knew as many words in Mandarin as he did in English.

"*Juehan,*" Wenwen said, which was what she and the others called Jody—a rough translation of John, as close as we could get. Wenwen kissed Jody and me good-bye and we promised to keep in touch, although neither of us knew how we'd manage that.

"You'll go?" she asked.

"I'll see," I said. "I have to find Xiaomin, first." We said good-bye again, and then I gave Wenwen most of the money I had and watched as she made her way from the building and through the crowd below.

I took my passport, a few clothes, some food for Jody; Jody's passport and birth certificate, which Xiaomin and her husband had helped me get from the U.S. Embassy a few days after Jody's birth; and the contraption I used to carry Jody on my back. I left everything else behind—I still thought I might be coming back—and then I closed the door to the tiny room that Jody and I had shared, which despite its size had been luxurious compared to the dorms where the students piled four or six to a room. From the window in the stairwell I saw four trucks filled with soldiers head for the main courtyard. I moved the sheaf of Chinese documents that certified my right to be here, to teach, to live, from my bag to my jacket pocket, and then I ran down the stairs and headed for my bicycle. And then I turned around, spinning so sharply that Jody, on my back, giggled and cried, "Horsey!"

I raced around the building toward our lab. Jody had his hands on my shoulders, and he greeted every person we passed with high-pitched cries of *"ni hau!"*—hello. People who hadn't smiled in days smiled at him, at me, as they had since the day I'd first brought him here—he was something of a mascot, at least in the science wing, and in better days he'd been much fussed over in the nursery. *"Ni hau,* Grace," my colleagues said, after they'd smiled at Jody, and I tried to slow my steps and respond to them. But they were moving quickly too. Their greetings came to us from heads turned over their shoulders as their bodies rushed away, and my responses trailed me like a tail.

The lab door was open, but no one was inside. The long wooden table was littered with equipment from the experiments we'd been running before the demonstrations. The pH meter a scientist visiting from California had brought, the micropipette and the precious pipette tips I'd had Page send me from Massachusetts, the jars full of lake water, the dissecting trays, the slides and the workbooks and the stained filters and nets—all Xiaomin and I had worked so hard to assemble.

"Yu!" Jody called, tugging at my hair. Fish. Along the

wall the fish we'd kept as live specimens were still moving in slow circles through their murky tanks.

In the bottom drawer of Xiaomin's desk were the notebooks we'd kept for our project, and drafts of several papers we hadn't completed. Everything else in the lab could be replaced but these, the only records of our attempt to map the populations of the lake we'd studied in the Western Hills. A simple project—I'd worked on one similar to it when I was a student in Massachusetts, but then it hadn't meant anything to me. Then it had all been tied up with Walter, who had been my advisor; and after we got married I'd come to find the work tiresome and unimportant. But here I'd found the students' enthusiasm contagious, and I'd worked late into the night, trying to learn enough to stay ahead of them.

I slid the notebooks into the sack that held Jody, so that they were pressed between my back and his clinging chest. I fed the fish and stowed what I could in the cupboards, and then I tore off again and mounted my bicycle and pedaled along the edge of campus toward the north gate. Jianming had said that most of the fighting was concentrated along Changan Avenue and the areas south of it, and so I planned a circular, northern route. East on East Qinghua Road, I decided, studying my city map; and then south on Changping, east on Deshengmen, and south at the Lama Temple on Dongsi, which would turn into Dongdan and drop us—unnoticed, I hoped—east of Tiananmen Square and north of Changan, at the hospital where Xiaomin's husband worked.

Jody fell asleep on my back as I pedaled through the heat of the afternoon. Things were quiet up here, and the fields stretching along the road were green and soft. Only when we approached the northern end of Beihai Park did I begin to hear the occasional distant pop of gunfire. Jody woke up and tickled the back of my neck. I sang him a couple of songs. The soft popping might have been fireworks, rising into the air to celebrate a new year. The streets were empty, which seemed even eerier than it would have in Boston or New York; I'd grown used to bicycling as part of a moving wave of people, a particle massed so closely with the others that I almost didn't have to steer.

When we turned down Dongsi we began to see people again, clustered in knots around the posters and photographs pasted on trees and poles. They were crying, shouting, reading the posters out loud. I passed a burned-out bus and then a group of grim soldiers clearing away a heap of rubble at an intersection. The soldiers looked at us but didn't stop us; maybe Jody's smile disarmed them. I pedaled faster, toward the noise and smoke, and finally reached the gate to the hospital. The soldiers stopped me there.

"No admittance," one of them said to me. We spoke in his language, which had become one of mine. "And you are forbidden to be on the streets. Please return to your place of residence."

"My baby is sick," I said, but Jody, no help at all, reached for the soldier's cap and laughed.

"Not sick," the soldier said. "Go home."

"He has asthma," I lied. "His medicine is all gone. I have to get some before tomorrow, or he'll be sick."

Jody parroted me. *"You qichuan bing,"* he said gaily. Asthma. His accent was better than mine.

Despite himself, the soldier smiled. And then he looked at Jody's hair and eyes, which were nothing like mine. "Chinese baby?" he said. "Speaks Chinese."

"He's very smart," I said. "He learned from our neighbors."

"Nay-boors," Jody said in English.

"Let her go in," the other soldier said. "The doctors

are very busy, but maybe you will find someone to help you."

They let me pass, and in a second we were in. I threw my bike on the ground and ran up the steps.

It took me twenty minutes to find Xiaomin, and in that time I saw more than I'd ever wanted to of what had been going on. Worse than Jianming had said, worse than the rumors we'd heard—I took Jody off my back and pressed him to my chest, both to shield him from the sights and to comfort myself with his flesh. There were people everywhere, in the lobby, the halls, the rooms, on the stairs, people lying on the doors and planks on which they'd been carried in, people draped across chairs and on the dirty floor. Some were unconscious. Some groaned and bled. Some, who'd been treated already, lay on makeshift pallets and beds outside the overflowing rooms. Others were dead.

A medical student pulled me away from the door I'd opened, which led into a room packed with shrouded bodies. "The morgue is full," he said tightly. "Everyplace is full." And then he looked at my face again, as if seeing it for the first time. "Why are you here?"

Jody started crying; he'd caught my terror by then and was wailing and kicking in my arms, screaming at me to put him down. The medical student reached for him. "Is he hurt?" he said. "Even little babies . . ."

I held Jody tighter. "He's fine," I said. "He's just frightened."

"Everyone is frightened," the student said. "The soldiers have been in and out of here since Sunday. They forbid us to allow the relatives of the dead to claim the bodies, to talk to reporters—are you a reporter?"

"No," I said.

"Too bad. But you should go home. Go home and tell everyone what has happened here."

The air was dense with the smell of blood and disinfectant, and beside us someone groaned. A girl, no older than Wenwen, was using her right hand to support her left, which was bound in a green strip of cloth and missing two fingers. The student turned away from me and began murmuring to the girl. "Gunshot?" I heard him say. "This morning? Where?" But when I moved toward the elevator, he looked back over his shoulder and said, "You must go out."

"Dr. Zhang Meng," I said. "Do you know him? I have to find him or his wife. She's a biologist, Dr. Yu Xiaomin . . ."

The student nodded. "I know her," he said. "I know them. Dr. Yu has been helping her husband here since Sunday. Please—wait outside on the steps. I will send her to you."

I picked my way back through the wounded people until I reached the fresh air and could close the door on the sights and sounds I'd never meant Jody to see. Jody climbed down and grabbed one of the posts supporting the railing. When he saw me begin to cry he started kicking the post with one cloth-shoed foot.

"Don't cry," he said.

And so I stood silently. I had once spent a week in this hospital, which had been sleepy and quiet and clean. The halls had been empty except for the soft upholstered armchairs. The sun had shone on the smooth wooden floors. And when I'd returned the following June to have Jody, I'd had the same sun, the same quiet, and a roomful of smiling mothers for company. I'd had Xiaomin, who, as the door banged open now, stumbled into the light.

Jody looked up and called "Minmin!"—his name for her—and then ran up to her leg and seized it. Xiaomin was pale and drawn and her hands were shaking, but she bent down and smoothed Jody's hair while she greeted me.

"You're all right," she said. "We were so frightened. And the baby . . ."

"He's fine," I said. "He slept for most of our bike ride in."

She smiled at that. "You're fine," she said. "You're both fine. And the students?"

"They're all right," I said. "Some soldiers came to the campus earlier this afternoon, but almost everyone was gone by then. And then I thought I'd better come find you. I wasn't sure you'd be here, I was afraid you'd be at home . . ."

"I've been here with Meng the whole time," she said, and then she spread her hands in the air and turned them over and back, as if they were chickens at the market. "I assisted him," she said. "All the wounded people—he cut and I held what he told me to."

In the sun her hands looked transparent. "Have you slept?" I asked.

"A little," she said. "Not much." She looked down at Jody, who was fiddling with the hem of her pants.

"I brought our notebooks," I said. "And the drafts of the papers. What do you want to do with them?"

In the distance we heard a single sharp pop, which might have been a truck backfiring or another gun. "What does it matter now?" she said, but when I dug them out of my sack she took them and pressed them to her chest. "Thank you," she said. "But the important thing, the important thing is to get you out of here. Thank God Zaofan is gone."

We looked at each other then, and Jody looked up at us. Thank God indeed—Zaofan, Xiaomin's oldest son, had left China in the fall of 1986, and that was what

Xiaomin and I had said to each other the first winter he was gone, during the demonstrations that led to the downfall of Hu Yaobang. Those had involved a few thousand students, a handful of arrests, but both Xiaomin and I had been convinced that Zaofan would have been one of those detained. If he'd been here now, he might have been shot.

"He called Monday night," Xiaomin said. "From Massachusetts. Our phone was still working then. He was frantic—he'd heard that some doctors from our hospital had been killed trying to rescue students from the square. And he wanted to know if we'd heard from you. And then he said he was coming back—you know how he's been—and that I couldn't stop him. I had to put Meng on the phone. Meng told him no. No, absolutely. He said Zaofan could help us more by staying there."

"I'll call him," I promised. "As soon as I can. I'll make him stay."

She picked up Jody and carried him down the steps and onto the grass, where she gave him a length of rubber tubing she pulled from her pocket. "You can call him from there," she said, knotting the tubing into a sling. "You can see him. You must go home."

A gentle breeze blew, carrying with it odd hints of burning rubber and gasoline. "This *is* home," I said. I had never meant to stay here forever—three years, Xiaomin and I had decided. Maybe four. Just until we finished our project and Jody was ready for school. But I had no intention of leaving now.

"Zaofan begged us to come and join him," Xiaomin said. "I told him we might later on—what will be left for us after this? We have to stay now, at least until this is over. But I promised him I'd send you and Jody."

"That's ridiculous," I said. "We're staying here. I can help."

Jody looped the sling around his foot and pulled against it. Xiaomin struck the railing with her hand. "You have to go," she said sharply. "Now. Already there were soldiers this morning at Jinguomenwai, firing into the air around the British and American embassies. Your embassy is evacuating everyone. You have to go."

"No," I said, and I glared at her stubbornly. We had never argued. We had disagreed over many things, most of them having to do with Jody: she'd been appalled at what I'd let him eat, and at my failure to discipline him; I'd been annoyed that she'd sent pictures of him to Zaofan. But even our disagreements had worked out. Jody was at least as healthy and happy as the other children in his nursery, and as for the pictures—that hadn't been all bad. Zaofan had sent me a stilted, formal letter after he'd gotten the first one, congratulating me on Jody's birth. I'd sent another back, thanking him and avoiding any explanation of Jody's physical appearance. "I've given Jody my maiden name," I'd written. "Doerring—Jody Doerring. My father is pleased." And if Zaofan knew more about Jody's paternity than that, he never pressed it. Since then, we'd kept up an occasional correspondence in which I described how Jody was growing and Zaofan described his adjustments to life in Massachusetts.

"Think of Jody," Xiaomin said. "What if something happens to him?"

"No," I said again.

"You'll hurt us if you stay," she said softly. "You'll make things worse for us—I can't afford to have an American working in my lab. And you can't refuse me, not after all that Meng and I have done for you."

And that was the one argument I couldn't refute. She and Meng had done everything for me: arranged for me to stay in China, found me work in Xiaomin's lab, stood by me throughout my pregnancy and during my labor and then helped me through the awkwardness of registering Jody's birth when I had no husband. They'd helped me buy a bike. They'd taught me to find my way around the city. And, whether they'd meant to or not, they'd helped me discover how I fit into the world.

"I owe you," I told her. "I know I do. But don't make me repay you like this."

"I can't let you keep Jody here," she said. "He's all we have."

And so there we were. She sat down on the grass beside Jody and pulled me down beside her, and then she traced an imaginary map on the grass with her finger and explained how I should slip through the alleys to the back side of the diplomatic compound and the door to the American embassy. "Turn here," she said. "And then here." She couldn't look at my face.

"How can I go?" I said. Somewhere, I knew, Jianming was on a train or a truck, heading for Changsha. Wenwen was searching the city for her brother; parents were searching the morgues for the bodies of their children. People hid in their rooms and prepared to pull into themselves again, shuttering their eyes, closing down their faces. Chinese students working abroad faxed photographs and articles across the air to machines here, any machines, hoping someone might pick up the messages. In Shanghai, a bus was on fire. In secret buildings in the Western Hills, the old men who ruled China huddled together, massaging their legs and avoiding each other's eyes as they drafted statements couched in a rhetoric they'd worn out decades earlier.

"Wenwen and the others," I said to Xiaomin. "What's going to happen to them?"

"I don't know," she said. "But the old men can't last much longer, and the rest of us will still be here after they're gone. You have your passport? And Jody's?"

"They're in my pocket," I said. "I didn't think I should leave them in my room."

"That's all you need. I'll send you the rest later."

I was going, then. To the embassy, to rooms full of people I didn't know and had avoided during my stay; to a bus full of terrified tourists eager to flee this alien place. To a plane, to Hong Kong or Tokyo, across the ocean: home. What had once been home. For a minute I thought of Zillah, my first, lost friend, and I wondered if I was repeating what I'd done with her. But then I heard Zillah's voice, as clearly as if she stood there on the steps.

Don't confuse the situations, she said.

"Juice?" Jody said, looking at me expectantly. It was time for his snack and his nap.

"Let me say good-bye to Meng," I said to Xiaomin.

She shook her head. "He's operating," she said. "You can't go in. He'll understand."

When I rose she put Jody's pack over my shoulders and then picked him up and dropped him in. "You have a good trip," she said to him. "Remember your Minmin."

"See you later," Jody said. "Alligator."

Xiaomin had been in my room when I'd taught Jody that phrase; she loved to hear it and Jody loved to say it, because it always made her smile. She smiled now, and then she said to me, "Don't worry. I'll see you again."

I knew she was right: that for the rest of my life, she'd be with me wherever I went. "I'll miss you," she said, and then we both ran out of words. As I wheeled my bike away from the steps, I turned and saw her watching, the breeze blowing her graying hair away from her face.

▪ II ▪

Entering China

September 1986

Patient: *Doctor, I've come to you because I think I have a strange disease.*

Doctor: *What is it?*

Patient: *I have been afraid of noise and strong light for two years. When I'm exposed to these, I feel tense and restless.*

Doctor: *Do you have other symptoms?*

Patient: *Yes. At times I suffer from palpitations and shortness of breath. I sleep poorly and am troubled almost nightly by frightening dreams.*

Doctor: *What sort of dreams do you have?*

Patient: *They are different. For instance, once I dreamed that I fell down from a precipice. On another occasion I was chased by a wolf, and in other dreams I have lost my way in a desert.*

—*adapted from* A Dialogue in the Hospitals

The Fragrant Hills

> We must learn to look at problems all-sidedly, seeing the reverse as well as the obverse side of things. In given conditions a bad thing can lead to good results and a good thing to bad results.
>
> —Mao

When I was nine I had scarlatina, which was something like being boiled alive. A huge burning fever. Scalded skin. And a delirium so deep that, always after that, I believed in the possibility of another world.

My mother packed me in ice every few hours to knock my fever down, and afterward she never tired of recounting her trials. In a room full of friends and relatives she would draw me to her, stroke my head, and describe my rigid and trembling form, my burned lips and my rolled-back eyes. She'd tell how she had labored over me then, cooling, stroking, soothing; for years she drew on that capital, reproaching me each time I failed her with tales of her sleepless nights.

Maybe she stayed awake all those nights. Maybe she kept me alive. That doesn't sound like her, but maybe it's true—all I know of those lost days is what she told me. All that remains of my own from then is a memory of the voice that came to visit my head.

Eat your peas, the voice said at first. My mother, inside my skull.

Don't put your elbows on the table.

Sit up straight. Hold your stomach in. Don't bite your fingernails.

I had caught the fever from a girl named Zillah, who lived in the projects by the riverside and who had the habit of making whole worlds out of pebbles and feathers and pinecones and rice. She laid these out on the sand at the base of the gravel pit, where we were strictly forbidden to play, and once she'd finished we peopled the streets and spaces with the beings we saw in our heads. Stones that grew out of the earth like trees. Trees that sang like birds. Stars that wept and talking dogs and wheat that acted with one mind, moving like an army. I was forbidden to play with Zillah, but she drew me like fire and when she got sick I followed her right in.

She died. I lived. And on the night she died, the voice that had nagged me throughout my fever—low and trivial, admonitory, hardly a voice at all—took a sharp turn and started bringing me Zillah's life instead. Zillah's voice, all that Zillah had dreamed and thought unreeling inside my head; Zillah's family, Zillah's home, Zillah's plans for our lives. She gave me a glimpse, when I was too young to understand it, of what it was truly like to inhabit someone else's skin. And then she left.

I lost Zillah's voice as soon as my fever broke, and I didn't think about it for years—not until the fall of 1986, when I was on the last leg of a long journey from Massachusetts to China. I'd cried from Boston to Chicago: I was afraid of planes, I hated to fly. From Chicago to Seattle I'd slept. Some hours out of Seattle, the stewardess had woken me to point out the glaciated wonders of the arctic waters below, and from then until we reached Japan I'd sat in a tranquilizer haze, trying to smother my terrors with facts.

I knew about China what any other earnest, middle-aged visitor might: rather more than a billion people lived there, elbow to elbow, skin to skin. Beijing lay in the north and its name meant "Northern Capital." Two-thirds of the country was mountain or desert or bitter plateau, unfit for cultivation; the fertile plains were often flooded and famines were as common as snow. The names of Mao and Deng and Zhou Enlai rang a bell with me; also those of Sun Yatsen and Chiang Kaishek, Marco Polo and Genghis Khan, the missionaries and the Opium Wars, the Taiping and the Boxer Rebellions, coups and terrors and insurrections, the Long March, the Great Leap Forward, the Cultural Revolution and the Gang of Four, Democracy Wall, the Four Modernizations. I knew dates and proper names and phrases so worn they came dressed in capital letters; which is to say I knew nothing at all.

We flew from Japan to Beijing on a CAAC flight, and it was then that Zillah's voice came back to me. The flight attendents wore blue pants and tight-buttoned jackets and open sandals, and because they couldn't speak English they greeted us with a videotape instead. The picture was grainy and the background music wavered and crashed.

The English title flickered, pale and ghostly, along the screen: *In-Flight Annunciation*, I read. The annunciations I knew about were the sort where the angel Gabriel comes, pronouncements are made, preparations undertaken. Voices are heard and taken seriously.

Pay attention, Zillah said.

I didn't recognize her at first. I jumped and looked at the cabin attendant, wondering where she'd found that English phrase, but she looked at me blankly and gestured toward the screen. "For complete personal safeness," the next line read, "all lap belts securely fasten please."

I took the warning seriously. I fastened my seat belt so tightly I nearly cut myself in half, and still I was so scared by our jerky, hesitant flight that I added another tranquilizer to the pair I'd swallowed at the airport in Japan. When the cabin pressure dropped over the Yellow Sea and the crew rushed down the aisle to pound the plane's rear door and make sure the seal was set, I took another pill and then I heard Zillah again.

Don't worry, she said. *You're safe. Remember the day we tried to fly?*

This time I knew who she was, and I acted accordingly. I shut my ears, I threw her out of my mind. I pushed her back to that place where I'd pushed everything for years. And I succeeded; we overshot the runway in Beijing twice, and by the time we landed I had driven Zillah away. That was how I existed then: push, shut, close, seal, deny, forget. Forget. My heart was a palace of sealed rooms and my mind was a wasteland of facts. I walked off the plane, shaken and limp, and entered a cold gray building dimly lit by unshaded bulbs. Men in green uniforms stood by the walls and stared.

I stared back. I had a phrasebook with me, full of sentences meant to be used in places like this, but when I looked at the words they seemed hopelessly strange. I turned toward my husband, Walter Hoffmeier, hoping that he'd take care of things. But Walter wasn't there.

In the absence of someone to greet us Walter had taken charge of our group, lining us up, finding our baggage, assembling documents and patiently explaining who we were and what we were doing there. "International Conference on the Effects of Acid Rain," he repeated, enunciating clearly. The puzzled customs officials shook their heads. Fifty Western biologists, experts on the effects of acid rain, come to meet with a hundred Chinese biologists in a country with the worst acid-rain problem in the world. Walter had visions of international cooperation, economic reform, restored ecological balances; and behind him, like an army, stood synecologists studying woodland microclimates, ichthyologists studying trout, geologists mapping the bedrock's differential weathering, and botanists analyzing ancient pollen, not to mention the limnologists, the entomologists, the invertebrate zoologists, and all those whom the Chinese politely referred to as "accompanying persons," but who were, with two exceptions, wives. Tired wives, our voices shrill with jet lag and the rocky flight.

Our dresses were rumpled, our hair was mussed. Eyes kept sliding toward us. I felt like a cross between a goddess and a whale—a goddess for my long, straight, pale-blond hair, which was streaming down my back in wild disorder, and a whale for my astonishing size. I'd gained thirty pounds in the past nine months and hadn't been so heavy since I was sixteen. My arms quivered when I moved, and in that room full of short, slight men I felt as conspicuous as if I'd sprouted another head.

"Any radios?" the officials asked. "Any cameras, watches, calculators? All must come out which goes in."

We listed our goods and promised not to sell them and cleared the last booth, and when we did we saw a small man waving a cardboard sign embossed with the name of our conference. We'd missed him; to our stupid eyes he'd looked like everyone else. He'd been waiting for us all along.

"Liu Shangshu," the man said, pointing to himself and then pumping Walter's arm. "You call me Lou, okay? I am assigned to you, from Chinese Association for Science and Technology. Your host unit. Anything you want, you ask me."

And with that he herded us into a tiny bus and we headed for the Xiangshan Hotel in the Fragrant Hills. The hotel was half an hour northwest of Beijing, and I peered through the narrow bus windows as we rode into the city and out the other side, past block after block of concrete apartment buildings. Most of the roads had no streetlights and the city stretched dark and secret around us. The road narrowed to two lanes as we turned north, and the driver dodged platoons of bicycles that rose from the darkness like ghosts.

"Five million bicycles here," Lou said, answering someone's startled question. "Maybe six. Is crowded city."

It was. We flew ignorant and air-conditioned through a dense mist of life, our headlights shining on horse-drawn wagons piled with hay and sometimes crowned with a tired person or two, small carts pulled by tricycles, rivers of people walking quietly toward unknown destinations. A man dangled a white goose from a basket on his handlebars. In the open back of an old truck, two camels stood placidly. The fields beyond the road were flat and planted with something tall, which might have been corn. Camels belonged in the desert, I thought. Corn belonged at home. I had no idea what belonged in China.

Farther out, the road was under construction, and men stripped to the waist stood shoulder-high in ditches lit by gas flares. Digging, lifting out stones, laying in drainage pipe—it was almost midnight, and when our bus passed by, the workers pointed and smiled and spoke to us. I pulled down my window to listen to them, but Lou reached over and pulled it back up.

"Please," he said reproachfully. "Will be more comfortable with windows *closed,* air-cooling *on.*"

I got a whiff of the countryside and then it was gone. The road narrowed further and the traffic thinned as we entered the silent hills and finally came upon our hotel, which was white and set in a pool of light behind a tall metal fence. We'd been traveling for thirty-six hours and were frightened and weary and hungry and sore, and the sight of the glassed-in central atrium and jutting wings seemed pleasing at first, walling us off from everything. The night clerk was asleep when we entered, and the porters snoozed on straight-backed chairs. Lou moved like a sheepdog, herding us toward the desk.

My first week in China I saw almost nothing and misread everything I saw. I'd come reluctantly, although this trip had once been a dream of mine—events at home had left me sick and depressed and unreceptive, and it wasn't until I first saw Beijing that something opened in me. Then I grew anxious to look, and then frustrated when I couldn't; I couldn't escape the hotel except in the company of Lou and the other wives. Around me were wind and dust and constant construction; pleated slipcovers that rendered the furniture female and squat; warm beer and flat orange soda and the thick smell of Chinese cigarettes; plants I couldn't name and food I couldn't recognize. Modern office buildings went up inside shells of hand-tied bamboo scaffolding: a picture any tourist might have taken; while inside a life I couldn't imagine and yet yearned to enter went on without me.

Walter and his colleagues met with the Chinese scientists all day, every day, in a huge auditorium hung with banners and studded with microphones. He talked and arranged informal classes and paired his Western colleagues with Chinese scientists who had similar interests. He never left the hotel and I almost never saw him. I was packed in a minibus each morning with the other wives and taken on whirlwind tours of the Great Wall, the Ming Tombs, the Mao Zedong Mausoleum; I never took pictures because the images were frozen on postcards everywhere. We spent an hour or two at each sight before Lou herded us into the nearby Friendship Store, where goods the Chinese wanted but couldn't have were exchanged for our precious foreign currency. Outside each Friendship Store, men with hooded eyes slunk past us. "Change money," they whispered. "Change money?" Our pockets were stuffed with the crisp colored bills called FEC—Foreign Exchange Currency, not really money but tokens that allowed us to shop in the special stores and stay in our special hotels. Real money was forbidden to us; Lou chased the black marketeers away.

My thrifty companions bought jade and ivory and lacquer boxes as though there were no tomorrow, but the constant pressure to shop made us all short-tempered. Swiss, German, English, Canadian, American, Italian, French—the foul, polluted air of the city wore us down, and we wheezed and coughed and sneezed in grumpy concert. By the third day, I had a cold that quickly deepened to bronchitis, and something—maybe my rising fever—made me frantic with longing, tense with a desire I didn't understand. Nine million people around me living wholly different lives, and each time I tried to talk to one of them, Lou hauled me away. He rolled up windows, shut doors, hustled me across roads. He interposed himself between the people and me, and when I complained to Walter, Walter shrugged my words aside.

"Grace," he said impatiently, "this isn't Massachusetts. You go out on your own and you'll get lost or hurt or in trouble or something . . ." He winced when he saw my face and then he spoke again quickly, hoping to distract me from what we both knew he'd meant: the incident in the swamp back home. My proven inability to take care of myself.

"It's tough out there," he said. "That's all I meant. You don't understand the language, and it's a different world—at least it's comfortable in here."

But I was tired of comfort. We had comfort at home, comfort in spades, our lives as safe as soap, and I couldn't shake the feeling that somewhere in this swirling, gorgeous land lay the life I'd been looking for. I saw it in the children I glimpsed from the windows of our bus, who were so beautiful it pained me to look at them. I saw it in the old men airing their caged birds in the parks, in the girls holding hands on the street, in the students who crowded around Walter. I heard it in the Mandarin that I couldn't understand, the calls and shouts and trills and whispers, the rising inflections that weren't questions, the staccato barks that weren't commands. I felt it in Zillah's brief reappearance; she'd been missing for twenty-one years.

On our sixth night locked away in the Fragrant Hills, I made a break for it. After dinner, when all the scientists filed into the meeting room for another presentation and all the wives returned to their rooms, I walked out the front door of the hotel and into the surrounding park. Expecting an adventure—a chance meeting with anyone, an overheard conversation, a glimpse through the windows of one of the buildings that lined the bordering road. But the park was closed, the lights were out, and the only sound was the hollow beat of a horse's hoofs on the packed dirt road. I crept through the shrubs near the locked gate, and I caught a whiff of damp straw, green bamboo, horse manure. When I heard voices, I called "*Ni hau*" into the darkness—hello. Hello, China, I thought. Hello, anyone.

Two men leapt up, terrified, from the pillars they'd been leaning against. They were eighteen or so, boys in uniform, and their English was no better than my Mandarin. They looked at my hair; they looked at each other; they whispered furiously.

"Where . . . *from!*" one of them finally said.

I searched my mind for the words for our hotel and came out with *Xiangshan fandian*. The men whispered to each other.

"Is un-allowed," the short one said, and then they politely, firmly, escorted me back. We had a small scene in the hotel lobby, where an embarrassed Lou vouched for me, and then I slunk off to bed in a storm of frustration.

Walter was furious. "I can't *believe* you went out there alone," he said. "Are you *trying* to get hurt?"

"I'm sorry," I said, but I wasn't and he knew it. I thought I remembered a time when he might have made the same journey himself. He probably thought he remembered a time when I would have clung closer to him. We lay in our separate beds, the sheets drawn tight as skin, and when I said into the dark silence, "You hate me because I'm fat," he sniffed and said, "I dislike the way you act." Which may have been true—we hadn't made love in months, not since my last day tracking birds in the swamp back home, and in the absence of that connection we'd grown as strange to each other as a raven and a cat.

Our windows opened out to a dark garden arranged in stylized shapes: Pavilion Amidst Spring Greenery, Hibiscus on a Misty Hill, Azure Cloudless Sky. Somewhere a fountain murmured. The smells of trees and bark and wet stones drifted into our room, and in the silence I unwrapped a Hershey bar and fed my heart. By morning we'd decided we weren't speaking to each other, and we passed burnt toast across the table without a word.

The next night, we marched in silence through the halls of a university on the outskirts of the city, past guards who checked our invitations and into a large, worn lecture room which the science students had hastily decorated. The room had the feel of a high-school gym set up for a senior prom: folding chairs set in uneven rows around the edges, banners draped over tables, streamers and posters tacked to the walls, a piano and some sturdier chairs and a few microphones at the front. We were part of a small parade—Walter and me first, ignoring each other, and the others coupled behind us as if heading for an ark. Distinguished scientist, decorative wife, pair after pair; a few unmarried women linked for safety; one anomalous distinguished wife on the arm of her toymaker husband. Almost immediately Walter, guest of honor, was swept toward the front of the improvised banquet hall to be introduced to the Chinese scientists. I was funneled off with the rest of the parade. Chairs had been set for us amidst the sea of our Chinese hosts, all of whom seemed to be talking at once. A forest full of tree frogs, a classroom packed with cats; I couldn't make out anything and the hot smoky air set me coughing again.

"*Ni hau, ni hau!*" said the people as we passed. Hello, hello. I *ni-haued* back as I had all week and managed a *dui bu qi* when I stepped on someone's foot—excuse me. From the man's startled expression I knew I'd mangled his language again.

Half of Beijing seemed crowded into that room, all of us ricocheting off each other. Feet trod feet, elbows bumped elbows, shoulders and hips and thighs mashed together, glasses crushed noses, jewelry caught sleeves. My sleeves, especially—I was wearing blue, a soft, heavy-weave cotton shift with dolman sleeves and a slit neck that set off my blue eyes and pale hair but could not conceal my size. I was the biggest woman there, and my vast, rippling bulk formed a dam in the river of guests. Chinese men bumped against me like reeds, stood puzzled in the eddy behind my mass, murmured apologies, moved away. I willed myself to stop streaming sweat and found a seat near the edge of our foreigners' island.

There were three rows of people behind me and one in front. To my left, thirty or forty Chinese scientists whispered together. To my right, Walter sat on a raised seat, his shoulders high above a sea of dark heads. The scientists with whom we traveled were well-enough known, but Walter was the acknowledged leader of the acid-rain world and so the Chinese, sensitive to status, shunned everyone else in his favor. Walter was who they crowded around during coffee breaks; Walter who they introduced to their students and families. On the first day of the meeting they'd fallen silent when Walter stood at the podium in the lecture hall and explained, in his soft voice, how the sulfur dioxide from the coal-burning power plants was killing their lakes.

The Chinese scientists had murmured among themselves then as if Walter were prophesying. I knew how they felt—we'd been married for six years and I'd felt that power before. When Walter explained how the acid rain altered the lakes' pH, killing first the snails, then the tadpoles, then the bacteria, then the fish, hands shot up and questions flew in frantic, fractured English. Something in Walter's presentations had always made the possible probable, the probable certain, the future cataclysmic, and I could understand his listeners' concerns. Walter's predictions were often right.

Walter stroked his nose as a small man with an overbite introduced him in Mandarin. I heard the name of the university where we were; I heard *Hoff-er-meierr;* I heard some astonishing polysyllabic that may have been the Chinese rendering of Quabbin Reservoir, where Walter had done his first, best work. That was all I could catch—despite my best efforts with my great-uncle Owen's old language books and the new ones I'd bought, I'd learned hardly any Mandarin. All week long, listening to the crowds, I'd heard only a rising, falling, yowling sound, like a river tumbling over broken glass. When I'd struggled to respond with a few words, everyone had laughed.

As the small man rattled on I scanned the room. Food, great lovely heaps of it; I'd been starving all week. The table to my left was crowded with bottles of sweet pink wine, which women in homemade jumpers were pouring into glasses for a toast. The table to my right was dotted with large green bottles of beer and smaller ones of orange soda. The table directly in front of me was spread with food, dish after dish, and behind a whole fish drenched in brown sauce I saw a chocolate layer cake on which my name was written in icing. How had they known? I looked again—the icing said "Greetings," not "Grace." Across the room, the small man sat down and a pretty young woman moved to the microphone and clapped her hands twice. The shrieking and laughing and chattering stopped as if she'd thrown a switch.

"I would like to make a toast, please," said the woman in her careful English. She rolled her *R*s with a Beijing buzz, almost a Scottish burr. "To our var-ry distinguished guest of honor, var-ry far-murz Doctor Professor Wal-ter Hoff-er-meierr."

Everyone stood and clapped and cheered. Walter bowed and gave a speech, while I sat on my folding chair and felt my thighs overrunning the seat like a river. The head of the university spoke, some government official spoke, a visitor from the Chinese Association for Science and Technology spoke—all spoke and offered toasts, while I kept my eye on the chocolate cake. Someone kept filling my glass with sweet pink wine, and I didn't notice until the third or fourth toast that I was the only one draining my glass each time. I think I already had the fever then.

"Doctor Professor Hoff-er-meierr has agreed to allow pictures," the young woman said. A tidal wave of students and scientists flowed around and between the tables, leaving me more or less to myself. The German couple behind me mumbled; the Belgians talked to the Swiss. A young man with a bushy gold moustache was nattering on about some limnological problem. Katherine Olmand, a British ichthyologist I'd come to dislike for her prim aloofness, spoke to one of the waitresses in Mandarin and watched to make sure the rest of us had noticed. One Chinese woman sat alone, a few feet to my left; she exchanged a few phrases with Katherine and then with another woman scientist, but didn't seem able to strike up a lasting conversation with either of them. When she saw me watching her, she slid across the folding chairs and smiled nervously.

"Good evening," she said, with a heavy accent. "I may practice my English with you?"

"Of course," I said, wondering if this was how she'd approached the other women. I was lonely enough to want a conversation with anyone, and I was also flattered. At the meeting, the Chinese usually shunned me in favor of Walter.

"Dr. Yu Xiaomin," she said, tapping her chest. She had a small, sweet, delicate face, finely creased about the eyes. Her blouse was dove-colored silk, figured with small birds; her skirt was tan and apparently homemade. Her stockings were flesh colored and almost opaque and her shoes, black and clunky, might have come from my grandmother Mumu's closet. But she wasn't old—she was forty, maybe forty-five, no older than Walter.

"I am a lake ecologist, like your husband," Dr. Yu said. A worried look crossed her face. "Walter Hoffmeier is your husband?"

"He is," I agreed.

"Mrs. Walter Hoffmeier, then," she said. Her temples were damp, and I suddenly realized she was too shy to fight the crowd surrounding Walter and so had settled for the two women near me, and finally for me instead. I felt mildly insulted to be her last choice, but my curiosity was stronger than my hurt pride and I had no one else to talk to.

"Grace Hoffmeier," I said. "I used to be a lake ecologist too. Sort of."

"Yes?" Dr. Yu said. Her face relaxed. "What does that mean, 'sort of'?"

"I worked as my husband's assistant," I told her. "Years ago. Helped with his projects, gathered data, drafted papers . . ."

"Yes, yes, yes," Dr. Yu said, nodding energetically. "That is nice for a wife. You have children?"

I fell into a fit of coughing and then said, "No." How had we gotten so personal, so fast? I didn't think I'd ever see her again, and there seemed to be no point in telling her the whole history of our not having children, no point in going into who was to blame and why.

Dr. Yu's face fell and I softened my answer. "Not yet," I said.

"No?" she said. "You're so young, you could have many . . ."

"Not so young," I told her. "Thirty. How about you? Do you have children?"

"Three," she said proudly. "Two boys and a girl—was before the rule of one child only. Do you know this rule? My father had ten children, but now . . ."

"Sure I know it," I said. "It's hard to miss." All over Beijing, I'd seen posters exhorting couples to sign the one-child pledge. "One Couple, One Child," the most striking poster had said. "Eugenical and Well-Bred."

"Hard to miss?" said Dr. Yu.

"That's an idiom," I said, already tiring of this conversation. I looked over at Walter and saw him lean toward a group of Chinese students whose faces were upturned toward his like hatchlings waiting for their pellets. Loving every minute, as he used to love it when I'd listened to him, when he couldn't teach me fast enough and couldn't believe how fast I learned. If I'd wanted to catch him I couldn't have planned a better way. As I watched he raised his right hand and, with a gesture that still wrenched my heart, smoothed and smoothed again the thinning hair at the back of his head. His fingers were as gentle as if a child lay under them; as if, by his own touch, he could bring himself to life again. I could still hear his voice, teaching me in the old days: *There are two laws of ecology,* he'd said. *The first is that everything is related to everything else. The second is that these relationships are complicated as hell.*

Dr. Yu cleared her throat and I finished what I'd been saying. "Short for 'hard to miss seeing,' I think—you use the phrase for something very obvious, right there in front of your eyes."

Dr. Yu nodded sharply. "Yes, yes," she said. Her large earlobes were threaded with small pearls. "That's a good phrase. I will use in a sentence: 'Hard to miss that you are younger than your husband.' Is that right?"

"It is," I agreed; this woman didn't seem to miss much.

Walter, lean and balding and lined, looked ten years older than his forty-two.

Someone gave a signal for the toasts to end and the eating to begin. "Come," Dr. Yu said, plucking the sleeve of my dress. And although it had been wildly expensive, and was one of the few things I looked even passable in, for an instant I hoped she'd rip it. It was a wife-dress, a suburban dress. Something I never would have worn in the days before Walter, when my taste had run to black jeans and my brother's torn shirts.

"We should get some food," Dr. Yu said. She'd apparently decided to adopt me for the evening. "Maybe you would introduce me to your husband?"

I nodded and followed her, steering my way around the Chinese string quartet who were clustered at the microphone and mangling some Mozart. Walter nodded coolly to me and then turned away. Dr. Yu said, "Here, try some of this. And this, this is good, and this, and oh, you must have some of this, and this is delicacy, sea-cucumber, you have had?"

My stomach rumbled and Dr. Yu smiled. What she heaped on my plate could have fed six people if those people hadn't been me. Pork skin roasted in sugar and soy, chicken in white pepper and ginger, puffballs with bok choy, shrimp dumplings, deep-fried grass carp boned and cut to resemble chrysanthemums, marinated gizzards sliced fine, sea-cucumber with vegetables, roast duck. "This is good," Dr. Yu said of each dish. Although she couldn't have weighed ninety pounds, half of me, she heaped her own plate too and then turned to look wistfully at Walter as we left the table. With a full mouth and waving chopsticks, Walter was holding court.

"Maybe I could introduce you later," I said, following her eyes. "When he's not so busy?"

"Later," Dr. Yu agreed. "You wish to sit with him?"

"Are you kidding?" I said, and then we had to pick that phrase apart. She made me feel useful, in an odd way—every bit of idiomatic speech I offered delighted her. She asked more questions and I explained what I could, until the music silenced us both. The string quartet played more Mozart, a girl sang some Mendelssohn, a man in a tuxedo sang arias from a revolutionary opera.

While the musicians performed, I watched Walter and considered how I'd ended up with him. I could hardly remember—something was thumping at me just then, something that made me want to plant a bomb in the midst of that civilized scene. I wanted to tip the tables over, light a bonfire in the corner, burst out of the room and into the life that was streaming through the streets outside. I wanted to dance on the tables, screaming my lungs out all the while. Instead, I applauded loudly whenever Dr. Yu did. Her plate was already empty, I noticed. I hadn't seen her take a bite.

Smiling, she picked up a conversational thread I thought we'd snapped, and she said, "So, why have you no children? Who will carry on your name?"

I shrugged and said, "I don't know." The burr-voiced woman appeared at the microphone again, laughing this time. "Now," she said, "now, we have sung and made music for our var-ry distinguished for-eign friends. Now, we ask they sing for us! Everyone, sing your own country's songs!"

The Chinese clapped; the rest of us laughed until we realized she was serious. Finally two good-natured Americans, surely small-town boys, made their way to the front of the room and sang a bawdy Irish tune off-key. Walter frowned, offended. Dr. Yu said, "This is a typical American song?"

"No," I told her, laughing. "It's a very bad song."

Dr. Yu agreed. A troll-like man got up to sing a Hungarian song I almost recognized, and a Swede sang a song I was sure Mumu had once sung to me. Everyone danced and the tuxedoed man sang a Viennese waltz that sent people whirling around the room. A band—electric piano, two guitars, violin, drum—assembled near the microphone and tried with mixed success to accompany the singers. A Japanese limnologist sang a festival song that seemed to have something to do with a shovel. Three German algologists sang a lullaby; two Israeli invertebrate zoologists sang a folk song. More beer, more sweet pink wine. My dress was sticking to me and my armpits were damp. Dr. Yu, who seemed to think we knew each other much better than we did, said, "You tell me if I am impolite to ask—how did you meet your husband?"

No point in going into that—I couldn't explain it even to myself. I gave her the simple answer, meaning to be polite. "I was his student," I said, remembering how he used to read to me for hours, so caught up in his work that he'd hardly pause to catch his breath.

"Ah," Dr. Yu said with a smile. "Very good student?"

"Very good," I agreed. "Too good. Brownnose."

"Brown-nose? What does that mean?"

"Someone who is too nice to teacher, tries too hard, always sucking up . . ."

"Suck-up?"

"Never mind that one. Maybe you work with someone like this, someone who's always trying to be the boss's favorite—we call 'brownnose' from, you know—his face stuck to the boss's . . . behind? Rear end?"

Dr. Yu smiled, took a pen from her pocket, and quickly sketched two Chinese characters on her palm. She flashed them at me, rubbed them out quickly, and said, "We have a word, which translates in English as 'ass-face'—is that close?"

"Very."

"But you are not an ass-face."

"Sometimes I am," I said. "Sometimes I've been an enormous ass-face. You wouldn't believe."

Behind me, two Chinese scientists seemed to be discussing my new friend. I heard the word *yu* again and again, and I interrupted Dr. Yu's protestations to ask her what they were talking about.

"Same old thing," she said wryly. "Work. All so very ambitious here. This is the new way, new reward-for-responsibility system made by Old Deng—you know?"

"I thought I heard your name."

Dr. Yu laughed. "They are talking about what your husband does. They say *yú* with a rising tone—means fish, and *yǔ* with a falling-rising tone—means rain." She wrote the words on her palm in pinyin and added their tone marks. "Say after me," she commanded.

I did, amazed at her singing language. Until she coached me, all my tones had sounded exactly the same. Fish, rain, the effects of rain on fish, a rain of fish, a fishy rain—in my mouth there had been no difference. Dr. Yu kept drilling me, passing the syllables back and forth, and I didn't care that people stared at us. I was slowly beginning to get the idea and as I did I began to understand the men behind us, as if static had suddenly cleared from my ears. There were four tones, said the books I had studied. Flat, rising, falling-rising, falling—four. The books had been clear. But without someone to talk with, the tones had never made it from the page to my ears. "*Yǔ*," said one of the men behind me, perfectly clearly. Rain. At the reservoir, Walter and I had worked even when it rained, even when the sky was so cold, so gray, so bleak, that there seemed to be no boundary between the lake and the air, between night and day, between work and the rest of life.

As if we had conjured it up, rain began to fall outside. Dr. Yu fetched some more beer and then, while people around us danced and sang and told each other stories, we began trading words in earnest, correcting each other's pronunciation, building sentences, muttering tones. I drew words on my palm, matching the characters she drew on hers and warming, finally, to her charm and persistence. She told me how she'd been sent off to raise pigs in Shanxi province during the Cultural Revolution—"the blood years," she said—and I told her how Mumu, my fat Swedish grandmother from whom I'd inherited my weight and my hair, had taught me to catch shad and bake them for hours until the bones dissolved. How I'd loved to fish but had never meant to study the creatures until Walter came along.

"What is he like?" Dr. Yu said. "I mean, in his privacy?"

What was the harm in telling her? I thought about the way he wouldn't eat unless the food sat correctly on his plate—peas here, potatoes there; no drips, no drops, no smears. How he couldn't sleep without the top sheet tucked in all around him; how he liked his women as neat as his mother. Smooth, groomed, no visible pores or swellings, no fat—my God, my fat! How he dressed after the fashion of Einstein, in black socks, gray pants, shirts that varied slightly but were always subdued, jackets that were almost identical. And how uncomfortable he was here in China, how much he disliked the steamy, crowded buses, the old clothes, the crowded sidewalks, the open-air markets with their unrefrigerated offerings, the smells, the dirt, the noise, and the absence of wildlife, which implied to him that everything had been eaten. I thought about that astigmatism of his, that twist which made him see the worst in anything, and about his ability to make others see the same way, as if he'd etched their corneas with acid rain.

But I didn't say any of this. "He likes a clean house," I said instead. "He likes things neat."

"You live in a nice house?" Dr. Yu asked, and I said yes but then, pressed to describe it, found myself describing another house instead. Not our spacious, clean colonial so near the university, but the cramped bungalow where I'd grown up with my mother and father and brother and Mumu, who was stuck in a wheelchair and slept in the den. As I spoke I sketched the house's outline in the air, and I could see that it seemed luxurious to Dr. Yu.

"Six rooms," she marveled. "We have three, very large apartment for just three people, now that our daughter and youngest son are away. Kitchen, sitting room, sleeping room separate. Plus a bath with running water. Plus central heat. You could come visit us, and see."

I nodded. "Someday," I said. I thought this was only one of those conversations I'd had at a hundred cocktail parties. Vague promises, vague suggestions, all forgotten the next day and never followed up.

Dr. Yu finished her beer and looked at me. "So, what do you do now?" she asked. "For work, I mean."

I was embarrassed to tell her about my recent idleness and so I stretched the truth instead, casting back to the houses I'd bought and redone with my great-uncle's money. "I'm a renovator," I told her. "A rehabber."

"What is that?"

"I buy old, ruined houses and fix them up again. I make them look nice, and then I sell them."

Dr. Yu stared at me, apparently fascinated. "This is a *job?*" she said. "People pay you for your . . . your . . ."

"Taste," I said firmly. "People pay me for my taste."

"Really?" She seemed puzzled. "They can't fix these old houses themselves?"

"Well, they could," I said. "But they don't have the time, or they don't understand how to do it . . ."

"I see," Dr. Yu said. "That's very interesting. Perhaps you could explain . . ."

But suddenly the burr-voiced woman stepped to the microphone again, waved the musicians silent, clapped twice, and said, "Thank you for attending this our reception-party. Good night."

Instantly the room began to empty. I looked at Dr. Yu; Dr. Yu smiled and said, "The party is over. Time to go." She gathered her umbrella, her bag, and her books and moved into the stream of people headed for the door. Her bag had a damp stain on the bottom that was spreading up the side, and suddenly I knew where that plateful of food had ended up. "Our daughter and youngest son are away," she'd said, presumably meaning that her eldest son still lived at home. My father, heavier even than me, used to bring food home from the cafeteria where he worked, stuffed peppers and casseroles that he stowed in bags and then shared with me after my slim mother slept.

"Wait," I said to her. I felt I owed her something, and Walter was headed our way. "Would you like to meet my husband?" I had forgotten that Walter and I weren't speaking.

Dr. Yu nodded and blushed, and then Walter stood before us looking pained. "Walter," I said. "I'd like to introduce a colleague of yours. Dr. Yu Xiaomin."

Walter nodded, his dismissing, you-barely-exist-for-me nod, as easy to read in China as at home. He was tired, I knew, and depressed by the visit he'd made that afternoon to the university's science facilities. I'd overheard him talking to Paul LeClerc on the way to the banquet, and there had been no mistaking his distress. He'd described the classrooms, bare and scarred, and the absence of equipment that would have been basic at home. "No autoclaves," he'd said. "No coldrooms. No electron microscope. The library doesn't have any good journals. Thirty students share one dissection specimen. How are we supposed to help them?" They hadn't asked him for help, I knew; they had only asked to share their work with him and have him share his in return. But Walter had a missionary streak to him as wide as any river—he was apt to see lives different from his as something broken he was meant to fix. "We have to triage this," he'd said to Paul, quite seriously. "Separate the ones we can't help from the ones we can." I knew he saw Dr. Yu as someone past helping.

Dr. Yu's blush deepened as Walter tugged me aside and said, "Let's go, I need to get out of here. The others are all on the hotel bus already. And I promised I'd talk to Fred Dobzhinski, and I've got things to do . . ."

I could have wrapped my hand around his heathery tie and pulled until his head parted from his neck. I turned and saw Dr. Yu, already separated from me by a stream of people, fussing with the buttons of her blouse. She looked at me for a second and then looked away, and I looked at Walter again and saw a six-foot-tall carp standing on his tail. I pulled away from him, made my way to Dr. Yu, and said, "I'm sorry, he's such a prick sometimes . . ."

"Prick?" asked Dr. Yu.

"Schmuck," I said helplessly, knowing my meaning was still lost. "Asshole!" I said much too loudly, sure Dr. Yu would get this phrase despite my confusion of body parts and metaphors. "Not ass-face, ass*hole*."

Dr. Yu smiled. "Ah," she said. "Yes." She scribbled another character on her palm and flashed it at me. "Hard to miss," she said.

"Hard to miss," I agreed.

"You will come to have dinner at my home tomorrow night?" she asked. "We would be most happy—you can meet my husband and my son. My husband is a doctor and maybe he can fix your cough."

I hesitated; the idea was impossible. We had some presentation scheduled for the next night, some show or dinner or entertainment, as we did every night. All we were ever going to see of China was the thin, thin skin, creamed and powdered and rouged and depilated.

"Please," she said, watching me think. "It would be a great honor for us."

I looked back for Walter but he was gone, vanished the way all of this, the singing and dancing and drinking and talking, the eating and proud hospitality, would vanish if he had his way. Already a dark yellow, sulfurous cloud hung over the city and made my lungs sting, as if I were manufacturing acid rain inside my chest. I coughed, then coughed again. I looked out the window and saw Walter near the bus, clicking his index finger against his teeth and sheltering his head with a newspaper. He stood all alone.

"I'd be delighted to come," I told Dr. Yu, making my mind up that instant. I liked her face, and her curiosity. And even if she'd approached me only because of my connection to Walter, it was me she'd asked to visit. "Can I come alone?"

"Of course," she said. "That's what I meant." Quickly, while the waiters turned the lights off and the other guests left, she gave me directions. "Come to the Temple of Heaven," she said. "At five. Take a cab. I will meet you there at the Triple Sounds Stone and take you home—otherwise you will never find it. Is that all right?"

"That's wonderful," I said. She ducked into the courtyard and vanished, and I crept through the warm rain to our packed, polyglot bus. The lights inside the bus were on and the tired white faces of my companions shone starkly through the windows, mouths open in gaping yawns and eyes closed in irritation at the thought of the half-hour journey to the isolated splendor of our hotel in the Fragrant Hills.

The Forbidden City

> Having made mistakes you may feel that, come what may, you are saddled with them and so become dispirited; if you have not made mistakes, you may feel that you are free from error and so become conceited. . . . All such things may become encumbrances or baggage if there is no critical awareness.
>
> —Mao

The next day, I retraced some of my great-uncle Owen's footsteps. He had visited China several times in the 1930s, traveling all around the country before the Japanese occupation; he'd returned twice in the late 1940s, after the end of the war. The place he'd visited most often was Beijing, where he'd stayed for months at a time in a house he rented from a friend of his, a British journalist who periodically toured the southern cities, gathering information on the student movements and the rumblings of rebellion. In her absence, Uncle Owen had cared for her house and had tried to recreate a way of life that was already obsolete.

Uncle Owen had entertained me with his China tales since I'd been old enough to listen, and after he died his companion had sent me his Beijing diaries when I'd learned that I was to make this trip. From these, I'd formed a hazy picture of this city Uncle Owen had loved. The house he'd rented had belonged to a palace eunuch before it passed to the Englishwoman, and was very old-fashioned: no plumbing, no electricity, no central heat. He read by kerosene lamps, and at night he slept on a *kang*—a raised brick platform heated from within by a small stove. His rooms were heated by pot-bellied stoves in which he burned balls of coal dust mixed with clay. From the peddlers who came to his door, he'd bought iced bitter prune soup and steamed stuffed dumplings, and he'd struggled, as I had, with the melodic tones of spoken Mandarin.

In winter winds so cold that he'd worn two padded jackets beneath his robe, he'd strolled through the gardens of Beihai and sipped tea by the shores of the lake. He'd befriended the servants who cared for the house, and he'd thrown parties in the courtyard, under a mat roof raised on bamboo poles. Beijing was crumbling then, its palaces and fine homes being broken up, and he'd haunted the local curio shops, training his eye and buying fabrics and brass, copper and pewter, ivory and rugs and scrolls and lacquer and small exotic carvings. When he left Beijing for the last time, just after he'd seen the new government parade past the Gate of Heavenly Peace in 1949, he said the destruction and chaos had broken his heart.

Despite that, he'd managed to profit from the confusion. "Upper-class people sold Ming furniture by weight," he'd told me. "Porcelains and paintings and bronzes went by the crate—everyone wanted to get rid of the things that betrayed their class status." He'd packed up his treasures and sent them home to Massachusetts, where they'd kept his business going for the rest of his life and had sustained me as well. Still, he swore his treasures were nothing compared to what had lain within the gated walls of the Forbidden City. He'd spent days in those dusty palaces, and had described them to me so many times that I'd dreamed of them. He'd once said something that made me sure the Temple of Heaven lay within the Forbidden City, so when I broke away from Walter and hired a cab to bring me to Dr. Yu, I didn't even check my guidebook.

At Tiananmen, I dismissed my cab like a fool. The great gate guarding the grounds was still intact, as were the watchtowers guarding the corners, and after I paid my ten *fen* I stood inside the gate, right where Uncle Owen had been a score of times. I had a picture of him standing here, dressed in scholar's robes and holding a sprig of flowering plum, and I had forty-five minutes in which to see some of what he'd loved.

Only when I entered the first building did I remember the rest of Uncle Owen's tale: the palaces had been looted twice, once by the Japanese and then again by the Kuomintang. Nothing was the way I'd pictured it. In the Three Great Halls, the surviving Ming and Qing relics were jumbled with treasures brought from all over China to fill the gaps. Song and Yuan paintings, water clocks, jade seals, cooking vessels, archeological finds; none of the rooms were intact, and they had the feel of a junk shop or of a museum exhibit hastily arranged by an amateur. The things were only things, dusty and out of place, and I couldn't recapture Uncle Owen's rapt appreciation.

As I wandered past the Dragon Throne and the great bronze turtle whose mouth had once billowed smoke, I tried to feel the ghosts of the emperors and empresses, the eunuchs and the concubines, but the rooms were dead for me. I put my lack of interest down to tiredness and overexposure: I had seen too much in the past week, too much, too fast, too false. I turned away from the turtle and then I heard Zillah's voice again: *Of course you don't like it,* she said. *The whole place is a lie.*

Seven days since I'd last heard her; her reappearance frightened me. I knew my bronchitis was getting worse and that the waves of heat and cold flooding me weren't a good sign, but I wanted so much to see Dr. Yu that I willed my hands to stop trembling and refused to acknowledge what I'd just heard. So I'd heard a voice; it was only a voice. Maybe I was starved for English words.

"Where's the Triple Sounds Stone?" I asked out loud, as if someone might answer me. "It's almost five."

A group of women stared at me warily.

"*Ni jiang Yingyu ma?*" I asked. "Do you speak English?"

The women shook their heads and moved away.

"Triple Sounds Stone?" I said to everyone who passed. No one knew what I meant. I walked from hall to hall, up steps, down ramps, past carved pillars and painted dragons and another large bronze turtle, and still I couldn't find the stone or Dr. Yu. Five o'clock came and went, and then quarter past. I was trembling and weak and beginning to get concerned.

A man with a black and red eye and a strangely twisted mouth approached me near the Dragon Throne, after I'd circled past for the third time. "You are lost?" he said in English. "I may be of help?"

I was so glad to hear his voice that I reached out and shook his hand. "I'm supposed to meet a friend," I said. "At the Triple Sounds Stone."

"You have no guide?" he said. "You come here alone?"

I nodded. I couldn't help looking at his mouth, and he caught me. "My mouth twist from sleeping near open window," he said. "A draft. Please excuse this way I look. My eye—I have acupuncture for curing this mouth, and instead comes this coloring. You are American?"

"Yes," I said.

"Your friend you meet is Chinese?"

I nodded. "And I'm late. Already. And actually, I haven't been feeling so well."

He looked at me gravely. "This is visible," he said. "You appear to have a deficiency of *yin*—your nose and throat feel dry?"

"All the time," I said.

He shook his head. "Many fluids," he said. "Increase secretions. Also certain herbs are very helpful. Come—this stone is perhaps near south of compound."

We rushed through the halls at great speed, and only after a hot and sweaty thirty minutes did I think to mention to him that the Triple Sounds Stone was part of the Temple of Heaven. "I know it's here," I said. "I just don't know where. The stone is somewhere in the temple."

He groaned and pressed his small hands together. "Temple of *Heaven?*" he said, his voice rising in real anguish. "Not Triple *Sounds* Stone—you are looking for Triple *Echo* Stones, in temple—is not *here,* is across city, twenty minutes at least by car, and how you will get a cab . . ." With that he rushed me back to the main gate. There were taxis parked there, but all of them were spoken for, and after a long argument with two lounging drivers he dashed into the streaming traffic of Changan Avenue and tried his hardest to flag down one of the passing cabs. Finally he went to the white-coated policeman who stood on an island above the traffic, and by the time he'd finished shouting and throwing his arms about he'd convinced the policeman to step into the traffic himself and commandeer a cab. The driver resisted, pointing to me and then shaking his head, but he gave in when the policeman bundled me into the back seat.

"Temple of Heaven?" my rescuer said. "You are sure?"

I nodded and he gave directions to the driver. "How can I thank you?" I asked.

"You will get there," he called, as the car eased into the traffic. "No thanks are needed. But you must be more *care*ful."

Careful wasn't high on my list just then. If I'd been careful I would have spent the day in bed, tending to my bronchitis; I wouldn't have left the hotel, unarmed with guides or books, in search of Dr. Yu. All week I'd been listening to the humming voice of caution: *Don't drink the tap water; don't even brush your teeth with it. Don't eat any fruit or any street food. Don't lose sight of the tour bus. Don't go out without your passport. Don't buy jade without an expert's advice*. That voice didn't belong to Lou, our guide—it was the voice of breakfast, all the scientists and their spouses gathered at the long tables in the hotel dining room, exchanging warnings before they split up for the day. *Don't, don't, don't*—the list was endless and expanded each hour, and it brought out the worst in me. It made me want to stick my head under the faucet and gulp the water down, to sink my face into one of the smoked ducks that hung by their twisted necks in the smeared shop windows. Our hotel room—large, clean, privileged—had come to seem like a cage, and even when I ventured outside I carried it on my back like a turtle's shell.

I wanted to leap from the cab and find my own way across the city, but instead I sat and watched the back of the sullen driver's head. I was late, I reminded myself; I was an hour late already. I let the driver drop me off near the Triple Echo Stones, and I tried not to notice how he hovered until he saw Dr. Yu reach out for me. She moved through a rushing stream of people, and she laughed when I apologized for being late and told her what had happened.

"You must have been meant to go there," she said. "The places are separate, but also connected. In the old days, the Emperor marched out of the Forbidden City each October with his elephant carts and lancers and musicians and high nobles, and all of them headed here. The Emperor meditated in the Imperial Vault of Heaven, stayed all night in the Hall of Prayer for Good Harvests, and made a ceremony next day at the Round Altar, which decided the future. People hid behind their shutters and prayed again and again for everything to go well. It is an ill omen if anything goes wrong here."

"Have we done anything wrong yet?" I asked.

"No," she said. "Why?"

I closed my eyes and clicked my heels together three times, a gesture left over from a time when I thought ruby slippers and a good witch could fix my life. My future, the one I'd been waiting for, seemed to lie just around the corner, and what I wished for was that it would hurry up.

Dr. Yu smiled at my antics. "Is your husband still angry?" she asked.

I leaned against a pillar and coughed. "Still," I said. Walter's behavior at the banquet last night had broken down some of the barriers between Dr. Yu and me, and I felt I could tell her the truth. She'd already seen him at his worst. "Madder, now, since I told him I was coming to meet you. He went with all the others to the Exhibition Hall, to see some singers and acrobats and stuff."

Dr. Yu made a face. "That's so boring," she said. "It is only for tourists. Why does he stay mad so long? Is this typical of those from North Dakota?"

I laughed. "Maybe," I said. "How did you know where he's from?"

"I read it somewhere," she said. "I remembered it because my own father was trained near there—he got his Ph.D. in Minnesota before the Anti-Japanese War. Physicist. After Liberation, he returned here to aid his country."

"Really?" I said. "Where is he now?"

"Dead," she said simply. "They put a high dunce cap on his head and paraded him through the streets of Shanghai during the early part of the Cultural Revolution. They called him an American spy, a counterrevolutionary, a capitalist roader. His hat said, 'Cow's ghost and snake's spirit'—do you know this saying?"

"I'm not sure," I said. "My great-uncle used to tell me stories he learned here when he visited, about plants and rocks and snakes who could turn themselves into people and do remarkable things and then turn back to their original shapes."

"Different story," she said. "Cow's ghost and snake's spirit are demons who can assume human forms for the making of mischief. Mao said intellectuals resembled these—that they pretend to support the Party, like humans, but they revert to demons when criticized. They were called 'cows' for short; they were locked up in places called 'cowsheds.' My father was put in a cowshed at his institute. He died of fright, or shame, or anger—who knows? He had a bad heart."

"I'm sorry," I said; I didn't know what else to say. I'd hardly stopped to consider what her life had been like during those years, any more than I'd considered what she might want from me.

She smiled quietly. "It is in the past," she said. "I only remember my father said people from cold places have cold hearts. Your uncle visited with us?"

"My great-uncle," I said. "He visited many times before Liberation—it must have been around the same time your father was in the States."

"Such coincidence," she said, and then she waved her hand at the buildings behind us. "Do you like the temple?"

"It's lovely," I said. She showed me the sacred altar and the enormous vault and the main hall's painted, swirling ceiling, and then we stood on the Triple Echo Stones and clapped our hands together, listening for the sound to return—another thing, I knew, that Uncle Owen had done. We were interrupted by a group of Japanese tourists, led by a woman with a bullhorn and an umbrella crowned with a yellow streamer. Video cameras sprouted like snouts from the faces of the men. Dr. Yu and I moved away and examined an ancient tree and a garden of roses, all the time talking easily. I forgot about her family, waiting at home, and I remembered only when Dr. Yu looked at her watch and said, apologetically, "It's almost seven now—perhaps we should go?"

"Of course."

"We'll take the local bus to my home. It's very crowded, but not very far. You have ridden on one?"

"Not yet," I said. The bus was one of the things we'd been forbidden.

"You hang on then," she said. "Press when I say."

The bus that pulled up to the corner was full, overfull, bulging; it was absolutely impossible that anyone else should squeeze on. "PRESS!" Dr. Yu said as we reached the door, and then she shoved me into the tangled crowd. Her hands pushed my shoulders; her knees nudged mine; somehow we were on the bus and rattling down the street. People drew away from me, staring frankly at my eyes and breasts. I coughed loudly and they watched and coughed back. My chest was killing me. A baby three feet away turned and saw my face and burst into frightened cries, and Dr. Yu apologized to his mother. We rode toward the setting sun, and at a street corner indistinguishable from the others Dr. Yu wedged herself behind me and popped me through the open door. I tripped on the step.

"We'll walk now," she said. "Home is only three blocks away."

In the dusk the streets were lined with people. Old women crouched over charcoal braziers or bubbling woks, cooking their families' meals. Clumps of children darted by, falling silent at the sight of me. A man in a blue jacket pedaled past, pulling a load of kindling on a cart, and a woman who hardly came up to my waist tottered by on miniature, once-bound feet. Above me I heard birdsong, and when I looked up a man tending bamboo cages on a balcony spat at my feet and then grinned, exposing three teeth. An outdoor market covered much of the sidewalk.

Dr. Yu inspected everything as we made our way between the stalls, naming what she touched for me. *Zhusun*, bamboo shoots; *qiezi*, eggplant; *doufu*, beancurd. The steamed buns were *baozi* and the duck, *ya*. I drew the words in happily but knew I'd lose most of them. Dr. Yu explored four of the chickens, her hands pressing the breasts and thighs and checking the beaks and combs before she chose the fattest one. She paid with a handful of bills a third the size of my solemn Foreign Exchange Currency—tiny green notes printed with ships, even smaller mustard ones depicting trucks loaded with grain, misty mint ones bearing giant bridges. "*Renmibi*," she explained—the money Lou had forbidden us to have.

"Peoples' Money." She stuffed the newspaper-wrapped chicken under her arm.

"We are here," she said, pointing at a cluster of six pale green, ten-story, cement-block buildings. She showed me the cluster's coal-burning heating plant and its mountain of coal, as well as the primary school and the series of low bicycle sheds packed with identical bikes. But because she explained none of it, doing me the honor of acting as though I could understand what I saw, my head filled with questions as we climbed the unlit stairwell to her sixth-floor flat.

Dr. Yu's husband was waiting for us inside the living room, hunched on a narrow couch and watching TV while his oldest son read. Both of them stood when Dr. Yu brought me in. She said something quick in Mandarin and then she turned to me and said, "I present my husband, Dr. Zhang Meng. Also my oldest son, Zhang Zaofan. Zaofan in your language means 'Rebel.' " I smiled and she turned to her family. "Meet Grace Hoffmeier," she said. "Wife of famous lake ecologist Doctor Professor Walter Hoffmeier."

I nodded, although I didn't like being introduced as Walter's wife. The elder Zhang bowed. "So pleased," he said dryly. "Your husband's work is well known to my wife." Before I could respond, he gestured at the battered wardrobe, the sagging couch, the scarred table holding up the small black-and-white TV. "You will excuse our furnishings," he said. "All things of worth were taken from us. My father's books, his scrolls . . ." He shrugged. "It's an old story," he said. "Same old story you hear from everyone."

He wore his gray pants belted high over a small round stomach, which seemed to stem more from his horrible posture than from any excess weight. His worn white shirt had a frayed collar, and his shoes were laced so tightly that I wondered if they weren't a size too big. His eyes were deep-set, sunk in a nest of wrinkles, and they kept sliding to my hair. When I coughed, they shifted to my chest.

"Bronchitis," I explained.

"At least," he said. "At least. You should go to the doctor tomorrow if you're not better—you know where Clinic for Foreign Visitors is?"

I shook my head and coughed again.

"You go," he said, scribbling the address on a scrap of paper. "Call me if you have any trouble. I work in the hospital wing next door."

"You're a medical doctor?" I asked, and then I remembered Dr. Yu had told me this at the party and that in fact she'd offered to have her husband fix my cough. "I'm sorry," I said, embarrassed. "I knew that. It's just this fever, I've been confused . . ."

"Thoracic surgeon," Dr. Zhang said shortly. "This year, at least." He pursed his lips and, in a mincing voice said, "Is new Central Committee policy now: 'Intellectuals are to be esteemed and treated as valuable.' " He sounded as if he were quoting someone he didn't much like.

I stammered something clumsy and then turned toward the younger Zhang, who'd been waiting silently while his father spoke. Zaofan made me forget my cough and my discomfort with his father—in that tiny, shabby room, he stood out like a rhododendron. He was as beautiful as Randy, my first husband; as beautiful as Walter's student who'd caused me all that trouble back home. He was as beautiful as any man I'd ever seen, and when he smiled I forgot my bronchitis, my weight, and my foreign face and I felt beautiful too. Voluptuous, not fat; smooth and expansive and well-tended and creamy-skinned. I forgot how I was supposed to act. I was middle-aged, I reminded myself. I'd been married for six years. The back of my neck began to sweat.

Zaofan's hair was long, held back by dark glasses, and he was dressed in jeans and a tight blue T-shirt emblazoned with the slogan "Chongqing Construction Company—More, Better, Faster." A huge digital watch adorned his wrist. In Massachusetts, he would have looked hoody, but here I knew his appearance meant only that he was young, that he leaned toward Western ideas; that he was, or had been, a student. I'd seen thousands of young men dressed like him on the streets and the campuses. None of them had had Zaofan's startling eyes or elegant bones, but many had shared his aura of eagerness.

He held out his hand and said, "Call me Rocky—my American name." His voice was surprisingly deep.

I said hello and touched his hand, and when I did my palm sprouted sweat like a sponge. His hand was square, broad-palmed, strongly lined, with large, curved nails; despite the film of sweat between us he held me firmly.

Dr. Zhang cleared his throat and frowned. "Zaofan is waiting-for-employment," he said. "That's what we call it here, when students leave school and then wait and wait to be assigned to a job that never appears. He has made a small business selling jeans, radios, cigarettes on the street; he makes more money than we, his parents. All illegal. His friends, those *liumang*—they are profiteers. Petty thieves."

"What should I do?" Rocky said. "What else is there for me?" He squeezed my hand before he let it go, and in an echo of his father's mocking voice he said, "Some must get rich first. That's the new party line."

"That's the current wind," his father said bitterly. "You should be less like tree, more like bamboo. The wind now is just like it was in the early sixties—free markets, individual contracts, go-it-alone. But a new wind can come, as winds did then. Even a new Gang of Four . . . you wait, Old Deng is so old his brain has turned to stone."

Rocky shrugged as if he'd heard all this before, and Dr. Yu smiled nervously. They might have been any family back home, the anxious parents of one of the boys I'd hung out with when I was fat and dressed in black and was everybody's bad girl. Rocky shot me a small, conspiratorial smile, which I tried not to return but did. "*Liumang*," he said to me. "Means hoodlum. You like what my father calls me?"

Dr. Yu, who'd been watching all this, tugged me into the kitchen. No bigger than a closet, it had gray, unpainted concrete floors and blue-painted concrete walls. A small wooden refrigerator was jammed next to the sink, beneath a pair of rude cupboards. She unwrapped the chicken she'd bought and placed it, head and beak and all, in a covered wok. Then she opened a bottle of beer and poured it into two heavy glasses. "Do not mind Zaofan," she said, gulping at her beer. "He is—what do you say?—in a *stage* right now."

"I don't mind him at all," I said. My left hand found its way to my right arm, which felt hot. I stroked the skin above my elbow as if I could stroke my fever down, and Zillah with it. "He's charming," I said to Dr. Yu. "Your son, I mean. He seems very bright."

She made a wry face. "He likes all things American," she said. "Music, dance, sunglasses, art. All he knows of politics is the Cultural Revolution—bad times, bad food, no school, struggle sessions. Political education meetings every day. Everything is bad for him because of us. He got in some trouble selling dried sweet-potato slices he appropriated, perhaps without full permission. Also a few things later on. Now the art school refuses him because of his record, and so he has to work at this odd job. He makes his father unhappy."

"His father seems unhappy," I said, thinking how much the set of Dr. Zhang's mouth resembled Walter's.

"Always," Dr. Yu said, making another face.

Those were the last words Dr. Yu and I exchanged alone that night. The four of us sat stiffly in straight chairs, eating dumplings and pressed *doufu* and the chicken Dr. Yu had steamed with soy and ginger, and we talked as if we'd been elected by church committees to demonstrate cultural exchange. Science and daycare and education, all dry as dirt; the weather. The state of the world. My fever seemed to come and go, heat rushing from my feet to my face like a wave and then subsiding, leaving me cold and dry. "Women hold up half the world," Dr. Yu said. "That is our slogan. We work the same jobs as men, receive the same money, have the same responsibilities. But somehow all the household chores are also still ours. Is this true for you?"

I rolled my eyes and Dr. Zhang sniffed. "I have marketed," he said. "Many times."

Dr. Yu looked at him skeptically and changed the subject to my rehabbing career, not understanding that I'd put it behind me. "Re-habbing?" Dr. Zhang said. "As in re-habilitation?"

I nodded.

"We know about rehabilitation," he said bitterly. "We have been rehabilitated ourselves."

"Here?" I said, misunderstanding him completely.

"Not *here*," he said. "*Us*. Ourselves. What could you do with this place? What could anyone do? And this is an excellent apartment for Beijing, we waited six years for my *danwei* to assign it to us. Excellent, of course, unless you're a high Party cadre. You could work for *them*, perhaps . . ."

"What is *danwei?*" I asked.

Dr. Zhang scowled. "You don't know *danwei?*" I didn't; there had been no such thing in Uncle Owen's time. "*Danwei* is work unit," Dr. Zhang continued. "In the city, *danwei* is everything. Not just the working place but more like a village, or a tribe—our food coupons come from our *danwei*. Our apartment belongs to mine. Our children's school, permission to marry or move—all is *danwei*. *Danwei* is god."

Rocky interrupted him and said eagerly, "You have redone houses? You know about architecture? And art?" I nodded—at least part of that statement was true—but his father cut us off again.

"Art?" Dr. Zhang said. "We have had no good art for forty years—not since my grandfather's time." He sighed and adjusted his belt. "My family were scholars," he said. "Always. Scholars, teachers, doctors, all in Suzhou. We suffered during the Japanese occupation, and also after Liberation because of our bad class origins, but we struggled hard and I passed the exam to come here to Beijing for medical training."

He gestured toward his wife. "Her family were teachers also. But they supported the Party—her father even came back here from America. And she passed the university exams with high marks, and they took her here also, at Qinghua. We married in 1961, during the famine, after I had already started work as a surgeon and when she graduated and started teaching. But then 1966 came and they decided we were bad—bad families, bad education, bad attitude not with mass line. In 1969 they sent us to Shanxi province for *laogai*—labor reform. You know about this?"

I nodded. I had heard.

"We lived in huts. She helped the workers raise pigs. I worked in the brigade clinic, training barefoot doctors. The nurses there, who knew little, made me do cleaning and low work to improve my attitude. No paper, no books, no supplies. No school for our children. Zaofan was six already when we were sent down; Zihong was a baby and Weidong was born there. 'Eliminate the four olds,' they said—old ideas, old habits, old customs, old culture. Ha! Almost, they eliminated us. I spent all that time, six years almost, building a memory palace and filling it with all I ever learned. Later, we were rehabilitated—'Sorry,' they said. 'We made a mistake. Here is your old life back.' As if it could ever be the same."

His voice was as dry and cold as if these events had happened to someone else. Rocky had dropped his sunglasses over his eyes as his father spoke, so that no one could read his expression. Dr. Yu stared at her hands, which lay quietly in her lap. "Noodles," she said in a faraway voice. "Millet. The Shanxi vinegar was as thick as oil, and it smelled like mold." She shuddered and helped herself to more beer and chicken.

I tried to make myself as small as possible, hiding the folds of flesh I'd built with chocolate bars, mashed potatoes, steak, oysters, cake. Dr. Zhang, as if reading my shame, pushed the platter of dumplings toward me and raised an eyebrow when I shook my head no. "Is this enough for you?" he asked, his eyes roaming over my bulk. "*Meiguo ren*—Americans—you are used to different food."

I changed the subject. "What is this memory palace?" I asked.

Dr. Zhang seemed surprised. "You've never heard of this?"

I shook my head. Dr. Zhang looked at his wife and said, "You explain it best."

Dr. Yu sighed delicately, the same sort of ladylike puff I often found myself making at home when Walter tried to draw me out during one of our endless faculty dinners. "It's an old idea," she said. "It was brought to China by a missionary named Li Ma-tou, and passed down and down for the use of students taking examinations. You make a mental picture for each thing you wish to remember, then put each picture in a corner of a room of the building—the palace—you have in your mind. My own mother learned this, in her Catholic school."

Dr. Zhang interrupted his wife and turned to me. "You wish to learn?" he said, with the first spark of interest he'd shown all night. "It's a good way to remember Chinese characters."

"Sure," I said. Rocky frowned and left the room.

"Pick a place you know well," Dr. Zhang said. "Anyplace—only make sure you can see all the rooms and details clear in your mind."

I closed my eyes and recalled the house I'd grown up in, the one I'd described to Dr. Yu. I saw each door and window, each corner and crevice, each cupboard and table and chair.

"Now," Dr. Zhang said, "you stick pictures of things you want to remember in those places, where your mind can always find them." He picked up a book and said, "The character for your word *book* is *shu*—sounds like English 'shoe.' You have a bookshelf in your palace?"

I nodded. In the den where Mumu used to sleep was a small wooden bookcase crammed with her Swedish books.

"Imagine a shoe, then—a particular shoe, one you like very much. Place this on the bookcase, which is in a particular room. Now, whenever you want to remember the word for 'book,' you will go to that bookcase in your mind and always you will see the *shu*."

I wasn't sure about this, but I smiled as if I understood. I didn't want to tell him that a good memory wasn't something I desired. I'd spent years trying to forget all sorts of things.

"You see the idea," Dr. Zhang said. "It's a way of holding concepts in your head by making abstractions concrete and arranging them in order."

"What did you use for your palace?" I asked him.

"My parents' house," he said. "They had an old, courtyard-style house, with many rooms and central gardens. You have seen these?"

"Sort of," I said, and Dr. Yu smiled at the phrase. "Out near the Fragrant Hills Park. There are some like that, but they've all been converted to apartments."

"When we were young," Dr. Yu said softly, "where we grow up in Suzhou, we have these houses in our families for generations . . ."

Dr. Zhang made a small, courtly bow toward his wife and smiled his first smile of the evening. "Suzhou is famous for its beautiful gardens and beautiful, melodious women," he said. "Even Marco Polo said so. The house I lived in when I was young had many rooms, many secret places, and I used all of them. In Shanxi, I filled those rooms with every fact I ever learned in school, French and English and anatomy and chemistry and all the knowledge of Chinese traditional medicine I learned from my father—everything. I tried to store whatever I knew, so that someday I could teach my children and others. And now Zaofan sells radios he gets from nowhere . . ."

I let this all sink in, and then I turned to Dr. Yu and said, "Did you do this too?"

She smiled and nibbled at a dumpling. "I forgot what I'd learned," she said. "Forgot on purpose. I tried instead to dream of life to come."

"That's important," I said, and we looked at each other for a long minute. *Life to come*, I thought. Sometimes that was all that had kept me going.

"You should use this system," Dr. Zhang said. "Try it. It works."

"I will," I said. I couldn't see that I'd ever want it, but I knew enough to thank him for the gift.

Getting me home proved harder than any of us might have guessed. The streets outside were empty, of people as well as cars, and the four of us walked six blocks to a small guesthouse before we could find a working phone. When the cab Dr. Zhang called finally drove up, the driver, who spoke no English, took one look at me and shook his head. Two firm movements, the same movements the driver in front of the Forbidden City had made. In the dim light of the doorway I looked down at my white skirt and saw how inappropriately I was dressed. How inappropriate I was—my hair hanging down in a pale sheet, the gold watch on my wrist, the silk scarf draped across the front of my blouse. Everything about me proclaimed my separateness. There were buses leading back to the Fragrant Hills, but I couldn't be put on them. This guesthouse where I stood was forbidden to me. I was very thirsty, but the water dripping from the outside tap might as well have been salt. Like some pale, consumptive child, I needed bottled water and special food and private transportation. Of course the driver didn't want to take me—who would want the responsibility?

Dr. Zhang placed his hand on the driver's elbow and spoke softly but firmly to him. "He doesn't know the hotel," Dr. Zhang said a minute later. "But he knows the Fragrant Hills—can you find the hotel once you're in the park?"

My room, calling me again; my room, which was almost as big as their apartment. "I think so," I said. I smiled at the driver, trying to look competent and undemanding. Trying not to show my discomfort—it was past midnight already and I knew that the Exhibition Hall had long since closed, that Walter and Katherine Olmand and the other scientists who'd gone in a group to watch dancers in fake folk costumes and acrobats with flaming hoops must be back at the hotel already, sound asleep. Except that Walter wouldn't be asleep, because of me. Walter would be pacing the carpeted floor and tapping his index finger against the crystal of his watch. I looked at Dr. Yu and Dr. Yu looked at me. "I kept you too late," she murmured.

Rocky stepped forward. He'd said little all evening, but now he looked at his mother and announced his plan. "I'll go with her," he said. "It isn't safe otherwise."

The family held a whispered conversation I couldn't understand, and Rocky shifted a flat cardboard package under one arm. He'd picked this up as we'd left his parents' apartment, and I had seen his mother give him a puzzled glance. "*Wo qu,*" Rocky said, and then he repeated himself in English. "I'll go."

There was more conversation I didn't understand, and then Dr. Zhang, glaring at Rocky, said, "I accept. You take the bus back."

I slipped Dr. Yu my phone number at the hotel and she promised to call me. Then Rocky and I settled into the cab's back seat, which was slipcovered in brown fabric and dotted with crocheted antimacassars. *Lucky you,* Zillah said. *This boy . . .* I jumped and Rocky's knee touched my thigh.

"Go to the clinic tomorrow!" Dr. Zhang shouted as we drove away. "To clinic!"

As soon as we left them we were lost, but Rocky and I were so caught up with each other that we didn't notice at first. "So," he said to me. "Did you have a nice evening?" And then he laughed as if he'd said the funniest thing in the world. "Be more like bamboo, less like tree," he added in his father's voice. "Unbelievable. Did he drive you crazy?"

"Not at all," I said. "He made me sad. All the things that have happened to him . . ."

Rocky smiled and touched my hand. "You're so nice," he said. "So beautiful." He had less of a Beijing accent than either of his parents, but he had something else I didn't recognize at first. I had to fight off an urge to seize his fingers before he moved his hand away.

I laughed nervously. "I'm glad you think so," I said. "Mostly everyone thinks I'm too fat. Especially my husband."

"You are kidding," Rocky said. "You look like a Rubens. Or a Rembrandt."

He edged closer to me on the seat and I edged away. My palms were drenched again. "How do you know so much about Western art?" I asked.

"That is my dream," he said. "I have loved it since I was little. In the country, where we were sent, was a farmer from Manitoba who came here to help the peasants farm better. He made friends with me when I was small—he was who taught me English."

His voice, now that I listened again, had a faint Canadian ring to it.

"Wilkins," Rocky said dreamily. "That was his name. He was an amateur painter, and he used to put his easel in the fields and paint when he wasn't working. He taught me drawing, and also let me look at his books from home. All kinds of art books, that I could look at as long as I wanted. I thought I could be like him when I grew up. I knew nothing about politics then—nothing. If anyone had ever told me that I'd be selling clothes on the street, and that there would be no good job for me ever . . ."

He reached into his cardboard package, which he'd laid on the seat between us, and he drew out a Rapidograph and a magnifying glass. "He gave me these," Rocky said. "My two best things in the world."

"They're lovely," I said. "Where do you get the ink?"

"I have to grind it myself," he said sadly. "It's never as good as the ink Wilkins had—I use the ink cake we have here, for calligraphy, and I mix a special formula. But sometimes it clogs my pen."

I looked out the window and couldn't recognize anything, despite all the times I'd been driven between the Fragrant Hills and the city. The driver, who'd been silent so far, caught my eye in the mirror and quickly looked away.

"Where are we?" I asked Rocky.

He looked around. "No idea," he said. He leaned forward and spoke quietly to the driver and then leaned back against the seat, close to me. "The driver says we are west of the airport, and east of Qinghua. He thinks. But do not worry."

"I'm glad you came along," I said. "I'd be nervous by now if you weren't here. I hate that I can't get around by myself."

"Please," he said. "I will take care of you." And I felt that he would, somehow; that he had a store of resourcefulness and intelligence that would keep me safe. "Why does your husband let you out alone like this at night?" he asked. "He must be blind."

I turned my face away. "It's hard to explain," I muttered, staring out the window at the low, blank buildings. "Our marriages are different than yours."

"Not so different," Rocky said blandly. "I have two

friends who work at the Great Wall Hotel—have you been there?"

"No," I said.

"You ought to see it," he said. "It's very elegant—chrome columns, deep carpet, health club, glass elevators. Hot water at all hours. I have not been inside, but my friends say it is much nicer than this place where you're staying. Yours is owned by the government."

"Excuse me?" I said. My attention had drifted; I was trying to imagine a place more luxurious, more cut off, than mine.

"State-run," Rocky said patiently. "The Great Wall Hotel is a joint Chinese-American project. My friends who work there, they are paid very well and have excellent uniforms, and they learn proper business attitudes from American bosses. It's a very good opportunity for them—they meet many people. One of my friends is trying to get me a job there, so I can make some contacts. The benefits are very good—my friends pick up many things the foreigners throw away. Pens, paper, cosmetics half-used, clothes with one small spot or rip, plastic bags; also books. I read the American novels they give me—you have divorce, adultery, many problems with couples. Us too. It is harder for us to get divorced, but the situations are the same."

I sighed. "We're not getting divorced," I said. "It's not like that."

"No?" he said. "What's it like?"

He was six years younger than me, hardly more than a boy, and yet somehow I wanted to tell him everything. His was the face I'd been looking for in the crowds I'd seen through the minibus windows. His was the sympathetic ear. I imagined my story unrolling before him, stunted and stilted and common and sad; insignificant compared to his father's; the same old story. Except that he wouldn't have heard it before. I raised my hand and then let it fall onto his cardboard folder. Rocky looked down.

"You want to see these?" he said.

"See what?"

"My drawings."

He lifted a flap and pulled out a sheaf of papers, which he held up before me. The inside of the cab was so dark that I couldn't make out anything. "Wait," he said. From his shirt pocket he pulled a pair of Bic lighters and lit one with each hand. His face lit up, the dark hollows below his cheekbones echoing his dark eyes, dark hair. His hands looked almost transparent. In the yellow glow his drawings sprang to life. Birds, bees, fish, plants, grain, farm implements. A moth's antennae grown huge, the mouth parts of a bee; the convolutions of a hummingbird's tongue. No people, not a single portrait. No landscapes. Meticulous renderings of tiny things, beautiful as well as accurate and displaying a naturalist's fascination with detail and form. I pointed to the most mysterious one, of a jar filled with bubbling liquid and shreds. "What's that?" I asked.

"Something my mother discovered," he said. "She found this new strain of yeast that digests ground-up cornstalks and straw and sorghum stems so the pigs can eat it—she said it is like giving the pigs a rumen, as with cows or goats or sheep. I call it rumen-in-a-jar. It saved the production team lots of grain, but she got no credit for it."

He sighed. "I want to be a scientific illustrator," he said. "Do you think I have a chance?"

He drew like Darwin; he might have done the Galápagos finches justice. "You're very good," I said. "I used to do some work like this for my husband, but you're much better. These are as good as any illustrations I've ever seen."

He sighed and let his lighters go out. "I knew it," he said. "Last year, in the spring, I took the examinations for industrial art college. My modeling, painting, and drawing were better than anyone's and still they wouldn't let me in. Still, I am selling radios, and saving money that does me no good. Even if I could arrange to go abroad, my money would be worth nothing outside."

He pressed three of his drawings into my left hand. "Would you give these to your husband?" he said. "Maybe he can hire me for work where you live."

I took the drawings and tucked them into my purse, not wanting to tell him how unlikely that was. We were out in the country by then, long past the city limits but not in any place I'd ever seen. I reminded myself that it was dark and that I didn't know the landscape well, but still I was almost sure this wasn't the way to the Fragrant Hills. As if to confirm my fears, the driver pulled over and held a whispered consultation with a lone bicycle rider on the side of the road.

"What's going on?" I asked Rocky.

He shook his head and smiled. "Lost," he said. "I should have known." He got out of the car and joined the conversation. When he got back in, the driver turned the car around and headed off in a new direction.

"How bad?" I asked.

"Hard to say," he said. "I haven't been here before—we are far north of the city." He picked up his cardboard folder and set it on the floor, then moved over until his thigh brushed mine. "Tell me about your life," he said. "Your life at home. You have shopping malls? Art supplies? Unrationed pork?"

We drove deeper into the night, and as we did I tried

to paint for him a picture of life in a college town. He listened happily, asking me questions now and then and trying to square my words with his own imaginings. A sharp noise punctured the night and then the car tilted left and stopped.

"Flat tire," Rocky said. "What luck."

He got out to help the driver, but the spare in the trunk was flat as well. The two men argued for a bit, and then Rocky turned to me and said, "He will go for help. I will stay here and guard you."

The driver left, rolling the spare before him and leaving me and Rocky alone in the warm, yeasty-smelling night. Rocky got back in the car and locked the doors.

"This is our luck," he said softly. "I wanted so much to be alone with you."

"The driver will be back any minute," I said.

"No," he said serenely. "He has to walk all the way to Yiheyuan Road for help. It's at least one hour." And then he turned to me and touched my jaw with one warm finger. That was all I needed; I bent and kissed him. And when, after the first moment's hesitation, he kissed me back, I closed my eyes and let what I'd wanted to happen happen. His slim strong legs, the delicate skin of his forearms, his mouth moving from my ear to my throat, his hand slipping up my thigh. It was a dream, that unreal—this man I didn't know, this country I didn't understand, the corn hissing softly in the sweet breeze, the utter darkness, the occasional bat. Hands as gentle as birds alighting on the peaks and valleys of me. *Lucky you,* Zillah said again.

"You're like a temple," Rocky said. He was a ghost, a spirit, an angel. He weighed nothing at all. "You are beautiful." The willow trees lining the road moaned, announcing a gust of wind. "You are my luck," he said, when we were done. "My luck." I heard Zillah laugh.

A sudden band of fire ringed my chest and set my heart stuttering. My breath came fast and shallow, each breath a stab, and the sweat that had filmed my palms now bloomed from all of me. I felt a sharp pain lower down on my side, separate from the pain in my chest and as precise as if a needle had pierced me. A click and a drop, like a quarter falling into a slot machine; *mittelschmerz*, middle pain, another egg dropping wasted from my ovary. Outside, a bird called mournfully.

"You are sick!" Rocky said. He touched his palm to my forehead and pulled away as if he'd been burned. "You have *fever*," he said.

"I do," I whispered, and then I curled against the cool window and passed out.

The Clinic for Foreign Visitors

> New things always have to experience difficulties and setbacks as they grow.
>
> —Mao

I was worse when I woke the next morning. The night had passed in a black swirling dream, leaving me with no memory of how Rocky had finally found the hotel or what Walter had said when he'd seen us; no idea how Rocky had returned to his home. And by the time I woke I was too sick to worry about anything more than what was happening inside my chest. The pain was astonishing.

"Jesus," Walter said. He sat across the room from me, his face so drawn and tired that I suspected he'd been watching me for hours. "Why did you go out last night if you felt this bad? You know we're traveling tomorrow."

"I thought I was all right," I said. "Then on the way home I got so much worse so quickly . . ." I paused, struck by a sudden vision of me and Rocky in the back seat of a cab. Had that really happened? Our limbs sprawled in strange directions, our feet against the windows, my skirt rucked up and my pantyhose torn in the rush? I lifted the sheet and found I was wearing a sweat-soaked pink nightgown, which might have meant that Walter had undressed me. On the floor near my bed I saw my clothes piled untidily and knew he hadn't; he would have folded everything. Casually, trying to look innocent, I leaned over and snagged my pantyhose from the pile. There was a fist-sized hole near the top of one thigh.

I buried the pantyhose under the pile and looked at the rest of the room, but I wasn't reassured by what I saw. The walls were vibrating in the sun and the pink peonies and golden birds in the prints had turned mean. The curtains framing the glass doors moved as if they were breathing. I closed my eyes and felt the pulse pounding at my temples and the base of my neck, and when I sat up the room began to waltz. Slowly, carefully, I said, "Did you meet Dr. Yu's son? Zaofan? She sent him along with me because she was afraid the driver might get lost."

"I met him," Walter said shortly. "So did everyone who was still in the lobby. He and the driver carried you up the steps. How could you let everyone see you like that?"

"It's not like I had a choice," I said.

He shook his head and tore a tissue into long, thin shreds, every line in his face declaring his anger. *Alien germs are nature's secret agents,* he'd told me a few days earlier, when I had tried to eat a pomegranate. *They're like kudzu in a temperate climate. You don't have any resistance to the organisms here.* I knew he was going to blame me for what I'd caught.

He waved a strip of tissue at me. "I suppose I should be grateful," he said. "I was. I am. They got you back here in one piece, and that boy—what's his name?—speaks decent English. Enough to get me down to the lobby, at least. Enough to tell me you'd passed out in the cab. But how you could agree to ride with him in the middle of the night, with a driver who can't speak English and doesn't know his way here . . ."

"You don't understand," I said. "It's not like there were cabs hanging around everywhere. This was all Dr. Yu and her husband could find."

"You're right," he said wearily. "I don't understand."

He was tense beneath his coldness and I knew why: we were supposed to leave Beijing the next day so he could lecture in Xian and Shanghai and Chongqing and Guangzhou. He'd made the plans months before—he and Katherine Olmand and another scientist I didn't know were to give lectures in the major eastern cities. He'd looked forward to this as much as he had to the conference itself, and here I lay in bed, grunting with each painful breath and not even packed. My clothes were strewn all over the room—dresses, skirts with elastic waists, billowy blouses, queen-sized bras. I had brought entirely too many things, liking myself in none of them. Six pairs of shoes because I had nice feet; a dozen scarves to draw attention away from my body and toward my face and neck. For years, I'd rested my hopes on good shoe leather and interesting neckline treatments.

Walter sat in one of the gray chairs near the lemon-colored table, sipping green tea and regarding me in my sweat-soaked bed as if I were a plague sent to ruin his life. He didn't touch me, didn't rest his palm on my brow, didn't hold a glass of cool water to my dry lips. I could hardly blame him—I'd been impossible for months.

I made myself as small and helpless as I could. "Dr. Yu's husband gave me the address of a clinic," I said. "He told me to go there if I wasn't better today, and I'm not. Will you take me?"

Walter sighed and folded his arms around his narrow legs. "If you'd just stayed in last night," he said. "If you'd just been more careful . . ." He sighed again. "Get dressed. I'll call a cab."

We hardly spoke during the long ride into the city. "I'm sorry," I said once or twice. "It's all right," he said, and he patted my hand, but I knew he'd added another entry to that long ledger of wrongs he carried in his mind. I added an entry to my own ledger; he was acting like a prick. I was streaming sweat, delirious, my head swarming with words and visions not mine. I saw an old man, Dr. Yu's father, staggering inside a circle of vengeful children. Books burning, manuscripts torn, paintings slashed; a sea of schoolboys waving their little red books and quoting Chairman Mao. I had read that book before we left home; anyone could buy a copy in the university bookstore. And I had browsed through my great-uncle Owen's maps and letters and dictionaries and books, as well as a few more recent accounts that detailed the glory of the socialist transformation.

I had a phrasebook I took with me everywhere and studied each night, and all that half-knowledge was rattling around inside my head, bumping up against Dr. Yu's stories and her husband's mad strategy. I saw the house Dr. Zhang had grown up in, and then the cramped version of it he'd fixed in his imagination, the corridors littered with bones and joints and muscles and nerves, the walls dotted with chemical elements, the rooms crammed with French and English verbs. As if a mind could stand to remember all it ever learned, as if the art of forgetting weren't just as important as the art of memory. I knew that, if anyone did. I was a master of forgetting.

Walter said something to me, but I couldn't hear him. I drifted away again and imagined myself foot-bound, willowy, with lacquered hair, swaying above a stream like an apple blossom. My fingernails four inches long, my robe brocaded and stiff, alone in an ornate room like the Dowager Empress Cixi. We had something in common, Cixi and I—she had stolen the money meant to rebuild China's navy and had used it to redecorate the Summer Palace and to restore a marble boat. I had done something almost as strange with my great-uncle Owen's legacy.

Why did you do that? someone said. Zillah? Maybe not. When I opened my eyes I was out of the cab and Walter was leading me down Dongdan Street in search of the clinic. Whoever had spoken wouldn't acknowledge it. I peered into the faces I passed, looking for my interrogator, but the people cut their eyes away and then slid them back and looked furtively at my sweat-drenched clothes and the hair knotted down my back in a ratty tangle. *Why do you live this way?* I heard. I spun around, wrenching myself from Walter's grasp, but behind us was only a mass of black-haired people, eyes cast down.

I'd given Walter the scrap of paper Dr. Zhang had given me, on which he'd written the clinic address in both English and Chinese characters. Walter kept stopping people and waving this paper under their eyes, and those who had any English told us to go down the road and then take a right. We walked to the intersection and turned right: no clinic. Walter showed the address to another man, who told us to go back where we'd come from and turn left. We found nothing but a bookstore, a small restaurant with a window full of roasted ducks, and a shop selling radios. By then Walter was half carrying and half dragging me. Each face I passed seemed to speak to me and I wanted to stop, to ask what they meant. Why were they looking at me? They got up in the morning, dressed, ate, worked, shopped, talked, came home to their families or to bare walls, narrow beds, nights that stretched on forever and a world full of things they couldn't have, that we were all reaching for: light, beauty, connection, hope. And still they got up, dressed, ate, worked. As if they knew why.

I could tell you, I heard; Zillah. It had to be. I coughed so hard my ribs ached. More people, more directions: turn right, turn left, turn right. The bells of the bicycles rang and rang, chiming off-key. At last we ran into an old man who sent us back down the road to the *hutong* we'd disregarded. The *hutong*: the alley. Beijing alleys run like veins, piercing the blocks of tall new buildings lining the avenues and leading to the blocks' secret cores, the remains of the old city. This alley was dark and narrow and cobblestoned, lined with crumbling old houses and littered with paper and broken boxes and leaves and bones. But at its end was a courtyard surrounded by stately brick buildings—the hospital, at last. One wing bore a small sign in English, announcing the foreigners' clinic.

The door to the clinic was open, but we saw no one inside at first. A high white ceiling, glossy yellow walls, a splintered wooden floor. The rooms off the corridor were empty, inhabited only by metal cots and wooden desks and chairs, everything scrubbed and worn. At the end of the hall, at the reception desk, two women sat cackling and sipping tea from a battered metal thermos. Their broad faces shone beneath white paper caps.

Walter was trembling with the anxiety that always overcame him in strange places. "Doctor," he said, his voice cracking. "My wife needs a doctor."

The two women looked at each other. *"Meiguo ren,"* said the shorter one. She reached behind her and brought up a tattered, paperbound book, which she held in front of me. I looked at it dully, not knowing how often I was to see it. *A Dialogue in the Hospitals,* I read, beneath a set of Chinese characters. *English-Chinese.* The woman opened the book to the third page and pointed out an English phrase. *Do you want to see a doctor?*

"Yes," I said, and looked at her closely. She had a mole below her mouth and three creases on her neck.

She blinked at me. "Hello?" I said.

She smiled but didn't say anything. I pointed to the next line in the dialogue, the line assigned to "Patient." *Yes, where shall I register?*

She nodded approvingly and pointed to the next line, marked "Nurse." *Have you been here before?*

I shook my head no and she pulled out a stack of forms. My ears were ringing and several conversations seemed to be going on inside my head at once. "I can't do this," I told Walter. "Can you?"

"I'll try," he said. I collapsed in one of the slipcovered armchairs stretched down the hall in neat rows, each one dotted dead center with a crisp white doily. Behind me, I heard the two women and Walter struggling to make sense of each other and the forms. The women spoke no English and Walter didn't know a word of Mandarin. The women flipped through the book, pointing out sentences for each other and speaking louder and louder. Walter raised his voice, enunciated more and more clearly, separated his syllables more distinctly. "They don't understand loud English either," I told him. Walter shot me a dirty look and struggled on, repeating my name, my birthdate, our hotel address, the reason we were here—why were we here?—and our host organization. The women nodded and smiled, nodded and smiled, understanding nothing. Walter stopped talking and filled in the forms. One of the women took them with her into another room, while I sat and sniffed at the sweet, warm smell in the hall. Soap and herbs and starch and fabric dried in the sun; nothing like an American hospital. Walter threw himself into the armchair beside me, mumbling something I didn't catch, and then the two women reappeared and led us into the doctor's office.

The doctor was young and spoke very little English, relying on a bilingual dictionary and the same book the women at the front desk had used. Her office was almost bare: a desk, three wooden chairs, a glass jar full of warped tongue depressors, an ancient stethoscope and an even older blood-pressure cuff. I could feel Walter shuddering at the germs, at the microscopic cracks in the wood. The doctor waved us into the chairs.

"Wo jiang de hua ni ting de dong ting bu dong?" she said, slowly and precisely. All I could catch from that was *de dong*—understand. I suspected she was asking me if I could understand her.

"Wo bu dong," I said faintly, the first phrase I'd learned. *"Bu dong."* I don't understand.

She smiled and bent over her books. Walter, waving me silent, took my phrasebook from my purse and began flipping through it. "Let me deal with this," he said. "How do I tell her I'm a scientist?"

"Look up 'occupations,' " I whispered.

"Doctor, lawyer, teacher, farmer," he muttered. "Closest is doctor, I guess. What is 'American'?"

"Meiguo ren," I told him.

The doctor, puzzled, was turning her head between us as if we were playing table tennis. Walter straightened himself and mangled the words he thought meant "American scientist." *"Wo shi Meiguo ren yisheng,"* he said.

The doctor's face crinkled in a smile. "Dr. Amurr-ika?" she said.

I closed my eyes. Dr. America—not far from Walter's vision of who he was.

"Bronchitis," Walter said loudly. "Bronchitis. *Bronchitis!"*

The doctor shook her head and thumbed through her book, opening it to the entry for "Cold." She held the book so I could see it, and she read the English version of the first line haltingly. "What seems to be the problem?"

I read the second line back to her, pointing at the Chinese version as I did. *I think I have a cold,* I read, but I shook my head at the same time. "No. No cold."

She took my temperature and laid her stethoscope over my chest and back, tapping me lightly with her fingers while indicating that I should breathe. Then she flipped to the next entry in her book and showed it to me.

"Pneumonia," I read. I shook my head again.

"Pneu-*monia,"* she said loudly. "Yes." She pointed out the appropriate lines. *Do you cough up any phlegm?*

I nodded reluctantly.

She pointed to the next line. *What color is it?*

"Yellow," I said.

"Yen-no?"

I pointed at the word in the book; she nodded and pointed again. *Do you have fever?*

I nodded again. She knew that; she had taken my temperature. Maybe she wanted to know how long I'd had it.

"Bronchitis!" Walter said. "Tell her you have bronchitis!"

I heaved myself over and grabbed her dictionary and her handbook. Her handbook had entries for "Cold" and "Pneumonia" but nothing for "Bronchitis." I found the word "bronchus" in her dictionary and showed her the Chinese definition, tapping frantically at my chest and coughing, coughing. "Bronchitis," I repeated.

"No," she said, and tapped her own chest in return. "Lungs full." She took back her handbook and pointed out a section to me. "Need draw blood. Chest X-films."

From a drawer she pulled a needle and a syringe that looked as old as her stethoscope; I didn't want to imagine the age of her X-ray machine. Likely it dated, as did everything here, from the early 1950s. One shot from that and I'd glow for years.

"No," I told her. "No blood. No films." She frowned and I tugged at Walter's sleeve.

"What do you want me to do?" he whispered. "Should we leave?"

"The paper I gave you," I said. "There's a phone number on it. Dr. Yu's husband works here in the hospital somewhere, and he promised he'd help if we had problems. Call him—his name is Dr. Zhang Meng."

"What good will that do? Maybe we can get this woman to give you some pills." He turned to the doctor. "Medicine?" he said. "Erythromycin?"

"Bed," she said firmly, studying her book. "Here, hospital." She checked something in her dictionary. "Ox-y-gen," she said. "Peni-cillin, by needle. Not go home."

Walter rolled his eyes at me. "I'll call," he said, and he stepped into the hall. I drew my knees to my chest, trying to splint my racking cough. Trying to figure out what was happening to me. The doctor came over, syringe in hand. "Blood?" she wheedled.

I pressed my arms to my chest and covered my elbows

with my hands, promising myself I'd run before I'd let her stick me.

"No," I said firmly, and then I faded away again, caught up in a vision of the children at the model nursery school we'd visited earlier in the week. Row after row of obedient faces, singing a welcome in unison. On the playground they'd moved in neat groups like flocks of birds. "Chinese children very well-behaved," our guide, Lou, had told us, as our group of Western wives and mothers gaped in astonishment. "We give discipline early," one of the teachers said. "Discourage bad behavior." There were no children crying, beating up on each other, tearing the wings off of flies; no solitary ones hiding in bushes or dreaming alone at the top of a ladder. The scene had charmed us all but left us all uneasy, as uneasy as I was making this doctor now. I knew she was wondering how I'd been brought up, why I was so resistant to her well-meaning help. I retreated into unconsciousness, the melody the children had sung repeating in my ears, and when I came to myself Dr. Zhang was there, arguing furiously with Walter in front of the silent young doctor.

"She is correct," Dr. Zhang said. "Wife has pneumonia, absolutely. We will admit her here. This is the best hospital in our country."

"No way," Walter said, so angry he was shaking. "No way. We have to leave tomorrow for my lecture tour."

"Yes?" Dr. Zhang said. "You wish her sick in Xian, where there is no good hospital? You wish to cause extraordinary incident?"

Walter glared at him coldly. "Bronchitis," he said. "She's had it before. All she needs is some erythromycin." He was eight inches taller than Dr. Zhang, but Dr. Zhang stood firm.

"It started as viral bronchitis," Dr. Zhang said patiently.

"But it's pneumonia now, most probably pneumococcal. Bronchitis interferes with the clearing of bacteria from the lungs. She has consolidation now in right and left lower lobes—she should not be moved."

"Walter," I said feebly, "I think he's right. I've never felt this way before."

His face fell and he stared at me miserably. "Really?" he said. "Really? Jesus, Grace, I don't know what to do. All the lectures are set up and they're expecting me, and Katherine and I have been working on this joint presentation . . ."

"Katherine?" I said.

"Katherine Olmand," Walter said. His cheeks reddened. "The ichthyologist? You sat next to her at the banquet? We've been working on this thing, a comparison of British and American lakes . . ." His voice trailed off. "But if you're sick," he said. "If you're really this sick—I thought this morning maybe you were just giving me a hard time."

I thought for a minute and then looked over at Dr. Zhang. "You go," I told Walter. "I'll stay here. Come back and get me when you're done."

Dr. Zhang, kind man, picked up his cue. "Yes," he said. "Absolutely. You stay. My wife and I will look after you here, and make sure all medical care goes well."

Walter's relief was written on his face. "She'll be fine here," Dr. Zhang said, as if reading Walter's mind. "Tell the people at your hotel what has happened, and have them send her papers here. I'll speak to the hospital director and to the CAST liaison. You give your lectures, and return here when you are done. How long will you be?"

"Eight days," Walter said slowly. He turned and touched my face, and I watched him struggling not to smile. I couldn't blame him—hell for Walter would be eight days in a Chinese hospital nursing a sick wife. Eight days watching me when he could have been listening to applause. I wondered what he was working on with Katherine Olmand, and why he'd spoken of her. He'd dropped her name several times; he'd been dropping it all week. But Katherine was dry and wry and at least as smart as Walter, and I'd never known him to find that attractive in a woman.

"You'll be all right here?" Walter said.

"Fine," I told him. I had never felt worse in my life, but I knew having Walter around wasn't going to fix me.

"I'll admit you as my patient," Dr. Zhang said. "It's irregular, but we'll make up some reason for why you need a thoracic surgeon. Then I can watch you legally."

"Fine," I whispered. "Thank you." Walter and Dr. Zhang huddled together and I passed out again.

When I woke, Walter was gone and I was upstairs in an open ward, tucked into a narrow bed at the far end of a long row. There was a bandage on my left elbow where someone had stuck me after all, and a sore spot higher up on my arm where someone—Dr. Zhang, I hoped—had apparently given me a shot. In my other arm an I.V. dripped clear liquid. The sheets were crisp and cool except directly beneath me, where I'd soaked them with sweat. They smelled of nutmeg, like the rooms downstairs.

Walter was gone—that sunk in slowly. Walter was gone and I hadn't even had a chance to say good-bye. For company, I had nine other patients lying hot and wasted in their beds. I wondered if Walter had seen this room or if Dr. Zhang had spared him. The floors in the ward were dark wood, the walls and ceilings tan, and there wasn't a scrap of aluminum or plastic in sight, no disposable anything anywhere. No monitors, no televisions, no beeps or flashing lights, no call buttons, no drapes, no rails on the beds. On the table next to me was another copy of the English-Chinese hospital dialogue, thoughtfully placed within my reach. An orange paper slip marked the pages someone must have thought I'd need.

"Admission and Discharge," I read aloud, and then I scanned the next few pages. There were lines for all the things I might need: food, help, the bathroom, a haircut, an enema, the telephone. All the ways I might feel—hungry, thirsty, listless, constipated, insomniac, allergic to certain foods—and what I might prefer to eat: clear soup or cream, milk or tea, cake or soda crackers. There were complaints and wishes: too hot, too cold, too noisy; open the window, close it, please; turn the heat on or off; my wound is hurting; I need a pill. And one sad little line: I am so scared. I have never been in a hospital before.

The nurse's and patient's lines alternated in both languages, like lines in a play, and although they were soothing I didn't know what I'd do if I wanted something that wasn't included in the script. I flipped through the pages and found a dialogue in case I broke my leg, one for a pebble in my eye, another for cramps and bad periods and another for epilepsy. More and more, cancer and TB and chicken pox, hernias and ulcers and gas, even a small psychiatry section in case I went suddenly mad.

All this—but no doctors, no nurses in sight. We were alone in the dusky ward, and when I realized that I started to panic despite my reassuring book. But just then Dr. Zhang appeared, with two X-ray films under his arm. Behind him came Dr. Yu, bearing a big wicker basket. I opened my mouth, wanting to say how happy I was to see them, but I'd lost my voice.

"Do not attempt to talk," said Dr. Zhang. "I need only to inform you of your status. Your blood culture was positive for pneumococci, your sputum showed polymorphonuclear leukocytes and cocci, your X-rays showed homogeneous density in the right lower lobe and some parts of the left. No doubt whatsoever you have pneumococcal pneumonia."

I opened my mouth again but closed it quickly.

"So," Dr. Zhang said. "You stay here for six or eight days—likely your fever will fall in about four days and you'll begin to feel better. No talking. No walking. Penicillin twice each day, plenty of fluids. And sleep. Sleep all you can."

"Waa . . . ," I croaked.

Dr. Yu stepped forward and sat down on the empty bed next to me. "Walter leaves for Xian tomorrow," she said. "With Dr. Katherine Olmand and another scientist. Very early—too early for him to come here first. But we have made all arrangements with him. He says he will call my husband each day to check on you, and he asked me to convey to you his love."

I couldn't help it, I started to cry. I knew she'd added that last part herself.

"It's all right," she said softly. "Everything will be fine. I will sleep here in the bed beside you each night, and I will take care of all your food. See?"

She opened her wicker basket and took out a huge thermos, some delicate cups, two pairs of chopsticks, a rice bowl, a porcelain spoon, and several lidded tins. "Hospital food is very expensive," she said. "Also very bad. No one eats it unless they are alone in the world. All these people here"—she gestured around the room—"all these people, their families care for them, bring their meals each day, leave someone sleeping by the sick person each night. Is this like you do at home?"

I shook my head no, unable to explain that this was better.

She tapped the book on my bedside table. "Point out

the line for 'no food' when the nurse asks," she said. "We will take care of you. We are your family this week—me, Meng, Zaofan. Also, Zaofan sends his regards to you."

Rocky, I thought, and I felt my face grow hot. For an instant I saw him, felt him, smelled him. His hair had smelled slightly musty, slightly damp. Dr. Yu laid her cool hand on my head.

"Such fever you have," she said. "I brought you weak tea for tonight, and soup with special Chinese herbs. Please—you drink what you can." She took off her black shoes, stretched out on the empty bed near me, and opened the book she'd brought with her. "You let me know when you want liquids," she said. "I am right here."

"I will leave, then," said Dr. Zhang, who'd been watching us silently. "I will return in the morning. The nurse will check you in the night."

Zillah's voice moved in for good that night, burrowing through my head and rendering me deaf and helpless. No one had been on the street that morning, asking me why I lived as I did and offering to explain the world—that voice had been Zillah's and now it settled in, strong and persuasive but blended somehow with Dr. Yu's gentle accents. Or maybe Dr. Yu spoke to me as well.

"My youngest sister worked at the Ministry of Culture," Dr. Yu said—that first night? Another? The room expanded, the walls drifted away, the other patients vanished; my body lay still and hot and heavy, just beyond my reach. On the table a red flower appeared and disappeared.

"The Ministry of Culture," Dr. Yu said with a gentle laugh. "Mao named it Ministry of Ghosts. My sister, before she was sent away, called it Ministry of Truth, after your writer Orwell. You remember this? In each office is a slot called the memory hole, where all old things no longer wanted are made to vanish. My sister made people vanish from photographs."

Did she tell me that? Did she tell me the stories I thought I heard, while the white curtains lifted and swelled and fell back again, moving like sails in the night? "My grandmother had hair like swan's down," she said. The black rubber stopper fell out of the I.V. bottle hanging above my bed. "The lines," she said. "Those lines—I rose at three to wait to buy some fish, and when I got to market I found a row of tiles and stones and chairs, marking the places of those who'd come earlier." Someone turned my pillow for me, over and over again, and in the background, fading in and out, Dr. Yu spoke of her childhood and the lives of her parents and the fates of her sisters and brothers. I tried to listen to her, but more often I heard Zillah.

Shy Zillah, strange Zillah. What was she doing here? Hanging behind my right temple, just above my ear, her voice came bearing everything I preferred to forget. *Watch this,* her voice said, and behind my closed eyes I saw a picture of my thyroid, nested under the skin of my throat like a small warm bird. My thyroid was a place like Mumu's bookcase and the image Zillah sent to sit there was a *shu*. A shoe. A white sneaker, I saw, with a rubber-tipped toe and green stains. Along with that picture came everything I remembered of Zillah and hadn't thought about in years. Her thin, spiky hair, hacked off in the pixie cut her mother preferred; her pale-blue glasses with the upswept corners; her broken front tooth. At the base of the gravel pit we'd huddled together, glad to be out of our strange homes and caught completely by the games we played.

We had pranced like horses through the dry gray pebbles, whinnying through our teeth and holding imaginary reins. We had named the rocks, befriended the trees, woven tales in which our families were transformed into goblins and came to the ends we believed they deserved. We had made villages out of leaves and twigs and had always known that we were different, that when we grew up we'd be nothing like the adults surrounding us. We had a wild hunger in us, to merge, blend, connect, and although we couldn't have put it into words we knew what we felt. We glued the feathers we found on the ground to our arms and meant to live like birds, and the broken arm I suffered the day we jumped from the crumbling cliff, our hands spread and holding our shirts like wings, did nothing to dissuade us. Later we fastened cotton wings to our clothes, as if our bones would hollow out in sympathy.

Zillah hadn't grown up at all. I had grown into something I despised. The darkness came and went, a cool sponge passed over my arms and legs, a trickle of warm, aromatic soup flowed down my throat. "At the university," Dr. Yu said, "they pulled the foreign-language books from the shelves and burnt them in the courtyard."

I tried to listen, but Zillah's voice took over. She walked me through my body and gave me a guided tour of my life—the skin stripped off, the deep and superficial fascia pushed aside, the muscles reflected gently until the cavities lay open. Then the brain wrapped in its meninges; lungs and bronchi tucked in the pleura; trachea, esophagus, and heart confined in the mediastinum. Below the diaphragm, the abdominal organs hid modestly behind the fatty omentum. I found that I knew my way around, that it was no great leap from the animals I'd once studied to me.

Pay attention, Zillah said. *These are the rest of your places.*

"The place where they sent us was like another country," Dr. Yu said.

My organs lit up one by one, as they had in the film strip I'd seen in college before our first dissection. *Stomach, esophagus, small intestine*: smooth, pink, slick. *Spleen, gallbladder, liver*: softer, darker. *Uterus, ovaries, fallopian tubes*: tangled, twisted; *kidneys and bladder* firm like fists; *lungs and trachea* hollow.

"The pigs had parasites," Dr. Yu said. "We had no grain to feed them."

Can you see the places? Zillah asked.

I could. I could see my body as if it lay below a hanging cold light, each organ well lit and clearly defined.

You are a palace, Zillah said. Rocky had called me a temple.

"These people here," said Dr. Yu, "the ones here side by side with my husband, they are the same who stood against us in struggle sessions. The same who broke our things, destroyed our papers, labeled us bad elements. When we were rehabilitated we returned to them, to our *danwei*, and now we all must act as though the lost years never happened."

These organs are your places, Zillah said, overriding Dr. Yu. *These pictures are the ones you need to find your memories.* In the beds across from me, rows of bodies tossed and turned and sought some bit of comfort, some form of peace. I plucked at the damp sheet between my legs and struggled to hang onto Dr. Yu's voice, to hear what she was giving me. Zillah's voice drove out everything else, recounting my past deeds and telling me truly the whole week long the history of my heart.

▪ III ▪

Lost Lives

1974–1986

Patient's husband: *Doctor, I am sure my wife has become mad. Half an hour ago, I went home with my son. As soon as we walked into the yard, then I saw a woman standing under the big tree. Oh! What a dreadful sight! A rope was hanging on that tree. The very woman preparing to hang herself was my wife, so immediately we brought her here. We trust you, Doctor, you can save her.*

Doctor: (turning to patient) *What's the matter?*

Patient: *I am tired of life. I cannot sleep. Everything irritates me. I feel that everything in the world and even my life is senseless to me. I am not only useless but also a burden on other human beings. I think that killing myself will benefit other human beings. I wish to die.*

Doctor: *Everyone has something bothering him, but they don't always look at the world through dark-colored glasses; they can correctly deal with such things. I am sure we can cure you, if you co-operate. From now on, you don't have to be upset about such trifles.*

—*adapted from* A Dialogue in the Hospitals

A Green Painting Marked with Blue

Chief among the things I had wished to forget was my brief marriage to Randy Martone.

We'd met in 1974 at an art class at the University of Massachusetts, when I was a freshman and he was a junior and only a little crazy, just crazy enough to be irresistible to me. He showed up in my dorm room after our second class together, armed with a sketchpad and a box of charcoal, and when I opened the door he said, "Let me draw you. You're beautiful."

I weighed a hundred and forty-five pounds then, after six months of crash-dieting to celebrate my escape from home and my entry into college. Forty pounds less than I'd weighed during much of high school—not slim, not by anyone's standards, but not bad for me. My breasts and hips had emerged like lost islands from my adolescent sea of flesh, and I had a shape, a very ripe shape. I had a navel unencumbered by a roll of fat, wrists and cheekbones and a notion of a waist, long blond hair and pretty shoulders. I looked better than I had since I'd been four, but no one ever called me beautiful. In our figure-drawing class, I sketched nudes like everyone else and had plenty of time to draw the body I wished I had.

"I have to see your legs," Randy said. "Why are you being so shy? This is all part of learning to be an artist."

I wanted to believe him. I could believe his interest in my body was artistic—we were art majors, both of us, full of grand plans—but I hadn't willingly let anyone see my thighs in years and it took weeks for Randy to talk me out of my clothes. I embarked on the world's longest striptease—my arms one week, and then my arms and shoulders; my feet and then my calves and then my knees. Working always toward the center, draped demurely in a sheet; the sheet eventually dropped to expose the tops of my breasts and then, a week later, my whole chest. Randy went into raptures and I almost believed him—my breasts, overblown as they were, were the only parts of my body I'd ever liked.

A week later the sheet dropped entirely and Randy set aside his drawing pad and led me to bed, what he'd wanted all along. What I'd wanted too, although I couldn't admit it—Randy was beautiful, black-pelted and swarthy and strongly muscled, and when I curled my arm around his waist his strength and solid roundness amazed me. He felt like a tree: that rooted, that alive. I felt like a thief. I couldn't believe I could get away with touching him. I couldn't believe he wanted me. He praised every part of me, the soft flesh swelling my inner thighs, the endless reaches of my hips, and in his drawings I looked voluptuous and rich. Under his hands and eyes my flaws seemed to melt away, so that on certain mornings I'd cross the room in front of him without clutching a towel to my waist. Sheer miracle, I thought, and I dove in fast.

Randy was a skilled draftsman, with a line as pure as Picasso's, but he gave up on that while we were still in school and turned to painting instead. Color, vibrancy, thick blobs of paint; paint thrown and dropped and swirled. His paintings were startling and full of bite, and meanwhile I drew plants with a pen and finished them with quiet watercolor washes. I hated oils and acrylics and froze when I had to work with them. Randy made fun of my timidity, but he did so gently and when, after two years, he said, "Let's get married," I said yes, not caring that I'd have to drop out of school or that neither of us had any money or any prospects. Randy loved my ass and that was all I needed.

"Let's go to Philadelphia," he said, his square-palmed hands on my knees.

He figured New York was too expensive but that Philadelphia was close enough. He had a cache of paintings and ideas for more and was sure that he could sell them, and I had faith in him. I'd waitress, I thought. Or drive a cab. Something romantic and bohemian. And at night I'd work on my own drawings, under Randy's guiding eye. Randy had visions of us in a loft somewhere near South Street, celebrating the sales of his huge paintings and smiling under the flattery of gallery owners.

But nothing worked out the way he wanted. No one wanted Randy's paintings, which bore a disconcerting resemblance to the work filling the gallery windows. And we couldn't afford to rent a place even remotely close to downtown. We ended up banished to the blue-collar northeast, where rows of three-story houses stood welded together at the sides. Rank after rank, stone and brick alternating with asphalt shingles: they were dark and airless, with windows only front and back, and the top floor we rented in one proved to be noisy as well. Our landlords argued downstairs, their voices rising and falling with the passage of the commuter train that ran behind our block. Our neighbors drove buses, worked in factories, built buildings and roads, typed and filed, ran day-care centers in their living rooms. Everyone struggled simply to get by. Women walked back from the grocery store with single bags of food, which they pulled behind them in metal carts. The dogs were thin. The cats were wild and dirty. The children had scabs on their lips.

I thought I was prepared for that life. I thought I wanted it. During my first two years of high school, before my grandmother Mumu died and I got fat and strange, two boys—Mark Berman, Chuck Saylor—had been my best friends. Most of our classmates had referred to us as the Nerd Patrol, and it's true that we were an odd trio. Me chunky, in chinos and my father's cast-off shirts, no make-up, no blow-dried hair, no anything my mother liked; Chuck with his almost albino curls and pale freckled skin and watery eyes behind black-framed glasses; Mark gangly and goofy-faced and floppy-jointed. Chuck had five brothers and sisters and lived in a rambling, broken-down house that smelled of kielbasa and sauerkraut and had dim halls leading to rooms that went up two steps, down three. Mark had no father and lived with his mother in public housing down by the river, down where Zillah used to live. All three of us were embarrassed by the ways we lived, and we tried never to bring each other home. Whenever we could, until it grew so cold we couldn't bear it, we hung out behind the Star Market or beneath the railroad bridge or in the woods, and we yearned to be old enough to have a car. Not that any of us could have bought one—but we didn't think about that. We thought about rolled windows, a heater that worked, privacy.

"Marx was poor," Chuck used to say, when we paced the woods in our old coats. "No food, no money, never a decent place to live."

"Lenin was poor," Mark said. "Dostoevsky. Van Gogh. We're *supposed* to be poor. Everyone interesting was poor when they were young. I think it's a rule."

"Some rule," I said. Oh, we were pathetic, always sitting together in class, ignoring the teachers, ignoring the other students while we buried ourselves in books we hardly understood, books we carried around so that people could marvel at their strangeness. We read dark things, foreign things, things beloved of troubled teenagers. Kafka, Baudelaire, Henry Miller. Dostoevsky (never Tolstoy), Celine, Camus, Marx. Nietzsche. Schopenhauer. Always in cheap paperbacks that we bought secondhand, the thin, tightly printed pages heavily marked by strangers' notes. We read to escape, to make sense of a world in which we had no place. We read because we were so impossible socially that we could do nothing else. We read to kill time, to obliterate the awful years until we could emerge as adults.

Chuck and Mark played chess and wrote. I drew and played the guitar. We agreed that our families were unbearable, pawns of a capitalist system, and we knew that we'd be different when we grew up. Mark was going to be a writer, Chuck a socialist. I was going to be some sort of artist. We worked after school at the Star Market, Chuck and Mark stocking shelves while I fried doughnuts in the bakery, and while our plans were vague they always included a moment when we emerged full-grown from our disfiguring skins and startled everyone: larvae into luna moths.

Chuck and Mark had vanished from my life when Mumu died and I dove into my motorcycle stage, but I thought my time with them had set me up for life with

Randy. I told myself that the kind of poor we were living wasn't the poor of my childhood but the *right* poor, the interesting poor, the kind of poor Chuck and Mark and I had dreamed about. Virtue. Solidarity. We were having an adventure. We set aside one of our three rooms for Randy's studio, so he could paint the pictures that would make him famous and change our lives, but he couldn't work.

"Too ugly," he said disdainfully. "Look at those people. Look at those *streets*."

Our neighborhood wasn't so bad—it looked like Westfield, where I'd grown up, or like Holyoke, where Randy had. Maybe a little worse. "The light's bad," Randy complained. "There's no one to talk to. No stimulation. The streets look like shit. What do you want me to do?"

Get a job, was what I was thinking by the time we were six months into our marriage. I wasn't finding our poverty so interesting after all. *Teach,* I thought. *Do something.* But he wouldn't consider working, not even part time; he said work interfered with the flow of his energy, and that I'd have to support us for a while.

I got a job out of self-defense, typing income-tax forms for three Swedenborgian accountants. Randy resented this wildly, especially during the late-spring crunch. "How can you work for these people?" he said, although he was glad enough to have money for beer and paint and pot. "They wear suits. They drive station wagons. They think they have a pipeline to God."

"You have a better idea?" I asked. I would have taken that pipeline myself if I could have found it; it was months since I'd touched a pencil or a pen, months since I'd done anything.

"You have to have faith," Randy said. "In me. If you had more faith in me, I'd be doing fine. It's *because* you took this stupid job that I can't get a break. You jinxed me." He rambled on and on, and I couldn't believe what I was hearing. As spring passed into summer and fall, winter again, spring again, he developed a new theory—that if we let ourselves go completely, gave ourselves over to the flow of luck and life, we'd be rescued by good spirits before we hit rock bottom.

Some theory. He stopped making love to me except on weekends, when my skin no longer carried the film he said fell over me at work. I started eating doughnuts, cannolis, cream puffs, cookies from the Italian bakeries nearby; I gained twenty pounds, thinking that was why, and Randy stopped sleeping, stopped eating, stopped going outside except to buy beer or score some pot. He decided he could live on air and sunshine, like a plant. He lay on the balcony all day, convinced he was photosynthesizing, and at night he paced and painted and drank beer. "For the minerals," he said. "Like fertilizer for a plant." I wasn't scared of him—I didn't think he'd hurt me—but I was scared *for* him, scared for us. And by then that "us" included more than just him and me.

Just after our second anniversary, I learned that I was pregnant. For a few days I held the secret to myself—the pregnancy was an accident, the timing was all wrong, and I was terrified at first. But then, to my own surprise, I found myself wildly happy, and it was in that mood that I told Randy the news.

We were eating dinner when I told him, or rather I was eating and Randy was pushing his noodles around on his plate and carving holes in the table with the bread knife. He looked at me as if I'd grown a second nose before his eyes. "We can't afford it," he said. "We can't have a baby *now*."

"You could get a job," I said—something I hadn't mentioned in a long time. "Even part time. Or you could stay home with the baby, and I'll keep working afterwards."

He pricked his knife into the table again and chipped out another hole to add to the halo around his placemat. "*I* am at a turning point in my career," he said. By then he'd lost as much weight as I'd gained, and his paintings, when he painted at all, swirled out of control. "I can feel it," he said. "Everything's changing for me. You understand?"

"But we're having a *baby*."

"*You're* having a baby. You want a baby, you're on your own."

We argued and argued about it, all the rest of that week, but in the end he won and I went to a clinic where they vacuumed me out. I got an infection that kept me in bed for six weeks and distracted me from the real pain of what I'd done, and afterward I felt as though all the nerve and courage had been sucked out of me, along with the soft bits of tissue and blood.

Things turned bitter for us after that. One night, the following spring, I came home from the accountants' office and found that Randy had set up his easel in the living room. He'd spread newspapers around and laid out tins of paint in shades of blue and green. A platoon of brushes marched across the floor, and a Joan Jett album was blasting from the stereo. Randy was prancing around in time to it, as naked as a stone.

"Painting time!" he called when I came in the door. "Time for Grace to paint."

He had a glitter to his eyes that made me nervous. "Randy," I said quietly, "I don't like to paint. And I don't have time to draw these days. As soon as things straighten out for us I'll go back to school. I promise."

"Who needs school?" he said. "Grace has Randy. Grace has me."

He started undressing me and I was happy for a minute; I thought he wanted to make love or even, possibly, start another baby. But when he'd stripped off all my clothes he put a long-handled brush in my hand and then, with a pencil, drew a faint line diagonally across the huge canvas he'd stretched.

"Paint," he ordered. "You take the top half. I'll do the bottom."

"I don't know how," I said.

"Come on, Grace. You used to be creative. Remember? Back when you believed in me and I believed in you . . ."

He was chanting his words, almost singing, and as he did he danced around the canvas, dipping his brushes in blue and green paint and flicking them at the taut surface. Green and blue fire, green plants in a blue sea, green teeth in a deep blue mouth.

"Paint," he commanded.

I laid down a base of light green and started a pattern of blue boxes over it, precise and geometric and repetitive, pretty in the worst sense. The pattern resembled expensive drapery material; it was horrible, but I couldn't help it. I tried to paint with my ass canted away from Randy, so he couldn't see where those doughnuts had landed. I tried to keep one arm across my stomach. I needn't have bothered; Randy wasn't looking at me. For every stroke of green paint he laid on the canvas he laid one on his body, so that he was green almost everywhere when we were done. His half of the canvas radiated weirdness, green and blue and blue and green and blue, and he looked like the stem of some strange flower. I feared that he might hack off an ear at any moment.

But he was strangely calm. "There," he said, pointing at the finished painting with a brush. His face was green; green paint matted his chest hairs and pooled in his navel. "Look at that." The painting was wildly schizophrenic, my obsessive, overlapping boxes crowning his flares. "That's us, Grace," he said. "You and me. How did we get this way?"

I stood staring at him, open-mouthed, and he leaned forward and drew green circles around my breasts. "I used to want to draw you," he said bitterly.

One of the Swedenborgian accountants took me in. His wife made up a bed for me in their spare room; his children, blond as dolls, were unfailingly kind. I stayed with them for four weeks, while I got myself a lawyer and started divorce proceedings and decided what I wanted to do, which was to go back to Massachusetts and finish school. I called the university admissions office and wheedled my way back in; I filled out forms and applied for loans. I worked overtime at the accountants' and tried to save some cash, and I didn't go back to my apartment until the day I was ready to leave the city for good.

I went in the heat of the day, hoping Randy might be asleep, but he was wide awake. The apartment was littered with paintings and he was working on a new one, the stereo still blaring and him still not wearing any clothes. He was drunk that morning, not because he'd started drinking early but because for him it was still night. How long had he been awake? A week? A month? How long since he had eaten anything? All the paintings were blue and green.

"You're back," he said, when I walked in. "I knew you'd come back."

"I'm leaving," I said. "Going back home. I just came to pick up some things."

"Coward," he said, jabbing his brush at the canvas. "Drone."

He kept painting as I carried armfuls of clothes and books down the stairs. When he saw that I was almost done, he wrapped a towel around his waist and followed me to the sidewalk, lugging the painting we'd made together.

"Take it," he said, ignoring the fat women in house-dresses who pushed their chairs forward on their porches for a better look at us. "You ruined it. I don't want to see it."

"You take it," I said. "It was your idea."

He tried to shove the painting into the front seat. The frame on which he'd stretched the canvas was bigger than the tiny car door; anyone could have seen that the painting would never fit. I got into the driver's seat and started the engine, but Randy kept pushing at the painting.

"Take it!" he screamed.

He drew back and aimed a kick at the bottom, shattering the stretcher frame. I pushed the broken painting out of the car, pulled the door shut, and drove away.

A White Picket Fence

When I came back to Massachusetts in the early summer of 1979—hurt, discouraged, looking only for a haven—what I noticed first was the white picket fence framing the green yard that sloped around the nicest house on the village square of Sunderland.

The fence had a sign on it that said "Room for Rent," and a room was what I needed. A place to lick my wounds, look over what had happened. Figure out what I'd done wrong. Outside the fence was the town's main street and a leafy square marked by a pink gazebo and a granite statue of a soldier; inside was that white house shaded by old trees, stately and calm. I looked at that house and thought it was just what I wanted, just where I needed to live. Square. Solid. Respectable. I lifted my eyes to the second floor, admiring the shutters, and a woman threw open a window just then and started shouting and tossing things into the air.

Red, green, black, pink, lilac, aqua, lemon. Soft bits of

fabric—stockings, leotards, skirts, and scarves—spun and drifted and fell silently to the ground. Soft-colored dancing shoes with elastic straps across the insteps. "You *shit!*" the woman screamed. For a second I thought she was screaming at me. "Stand there like that—why don't you *say* something?" She threw more shoes, more delicate clothes. They rained down on the man below her, who was standing so still that I'd almost missed him.

"Eileen," the man said quietly. "Do you have to make a scene?"

I stood just outside the fence, leaning on the black Volkswagen in which I'd fled Philadelphia. As I watched, the woman tossed out a white fur jacket, a long red dress, an emerald hat with a wide brim. A flashy dresser; perhaps a dancer from the look of all those slippers. She postured at the window as if aware I was watching her.

"Asshole!" she shouted at the man below her, who had his back to me. "Prick! Stupid, self-absorbed piece of *stone!*" She threw out an armful of silky underclothes and slammed the window shut.

I was close enough to hear the man sigh. He was very tall, thin but slack around the middle, and he stood in the drift of bright discarded clothes like a tree by the riverside. He was close enough for me to see the pale skin of his back where his shirt had untucked itself. I walked a few steps closer to him and rapped my knuckles on the fence.

"Excuse me," I said, as softly as I could.

He whirled to face me. "Who are you?" he said. His high forehead was creased with unhappiness. "What are you doing here?"

I knew it was a bad time, but I couldn't afford to wait. "Your sign?" I said. "You have a room for rent?"

He straightened himself and walked over to me, an aqua slipper in his hand. I rested my hands on one of the fence posts. He held onto two of the slats. Him inside, me outside, the fence between us; the sun burning on our shoulders. The day was very warm. "Who are you?" he said.

"Grace Martone," I told him, sticking my hand over the fence. Quickly I corrected myself. "Grace Doerring."

He ignored my hand. "Which is it?"

"Doerring. Grace Doerring. I just got divorced." Of course I wasn't, yet, but I'd filed the papers before I left Philadelphia and so that felt true enough.

He shook his head. "You're still so young. My wife . . ." He turned toward the house, but the woman at the window was gone.

"That was your wife?" I asked.

"That was," he said. "Is, was . . . hell." He stuck his hand over the fence toward me. "Walter Hoffmeier," he announced. "I suppose you want to look at the room?"

I wasn't so sure anymore; I didn't think I wanted to share a house with this man's wife. "I'll come back," I said. "Maybe in an hour or two, when things have calmed down—I'm sorry, I wouldn't ask at all, but I really have to find a place to live today."

He shook his head, his eyes fixed on the statue in the square. "It's all right," he said. His voice was quiet, abstracted or resigned, I couldn't tell which. He unlocked the gate and held it open for me, his manners as formal as a butler's.

I stood outside. "Really," I said. "I'll come back." The scene reminded me all too much of how I'd left Randy—dramatically, publicly, all the neighbors watching. I didn't want to get caught in this.

"Please," he said. "Come in. It's so strange, you'd think she'd toss *my* things—she could have just packed up her own. Why do you think she did that?"

"I don't know," I said.

"So come in," he repeated. "Look at the room. She won't act so crazy if there's someone else around."

I stepped inside the fence. The flagstone path was cool, shaded by a pair of tupelos. The front door was old and made of oak; it was also locked. Walter stood with his hand on the brass knob, turning it again and again. "Really," he muttered. "Really." He turned to look at me. "Come around to the garage," he said. "I'm sure the kitchen door's open."

Eileen had either forgotten the kitchen door or had failed to reach it yet. I heard her upstairs, slamming doors and drawers.

"We usually rent the extra room to a student," Walter said, as he led me through the kitchen and the living room. The walls were tan, the upholstery beige, the curtains cream; suburban good taste overlaid with filth, which somehow, even then, I suspected had come from Eileen. I couldn't believe Walter was showing me this.

"I *am* a student," I said, trying to fix on what was important. "Or I will be this fall. I did my first two years a while ago and now I'm going back."

"Oh?" Walter said. He stood at the foot of the stairs, perhaps afraid to go up. On each step was a pile of magazines: first *Scientific American*, then *Science*, then *Nature*, then more I couldn't see. And yet he struck me as a man who, in better times, would have filed them in matching binders.

"That's right," I said, with more firmness than I felt. "My student loan came through, and they're giving me credit for all the courses I completed. All I have to do is find a summer job and some part-time work for the fall. And a cheap place to live."

"You don't have a job?" he said.

"Not yet."

He picked at the chipped stair railing and listened to the noises above us: crash, bang, rustle. He shook his head. "That woman," he said. "Can you cook?"

"Of course," I said, caught by surprise. "I was married for almost three years."

"Do you like being outside?"

I didn't know what he was getting at. "How do you mean?" I asked.

"Out*side*," he said impatiently. "Plants, animals, rivers, fish—you know. The woods. Camping. Have you ever slept outside?"

"Once or twice," I told him, stretching the truth.

"Maybe we can work something out," he said. And with that he turned and started up the stairs, leaving me to follow. The master bedroom was at the top of the stairs, with Eileen inside, wild-eyed and furious and muttering to herself. She wasn't crazy—I knew how crazy looked—but she was pissed. Her drawers were open and her closets were empty, stripped of the things she'd thrown from the window. Eileen was pacing back and forth and trying at the same time to fix her hair and do her face. She had a tube of lipstick in one hand and a hairbrush in the other. I was standing in the hall behind Walter, and so she didn't see me at first.

". . . and I mean it this time," she was saying, either to Walter or to herself. "This is it, this isn't like the other times, I'm not coming back this time. I'm going to Boston. I have a lawyer. I have a life. I'm not putting up with this shit anymore and there's nothing you can do . . ."

She broke off and looked over Walter's shoulder and then pointed her lipstick accusingly at me. "Who are *you?*" she asked.

I wanted to see how Walter would manage this. Quietly, he said, "She's a student at the university. She's come to look at the room."

Eileen pushed him aside to get a better look at me. "*Your* student?" she asked, eyeing me up and down. I let my stomach out and dropped my chin so that a fold of flesh appeared below my jaw, knowing I wasn't a threat to any decent-looking woman. Eileen's face relaxed.

"No," Walter answered. "She's just an undergraduate. She's majoring in—what did you say you were taking?"

"Early childhood education," I said vaguely. "Or maybe art education, or maybe art . . . that's what I used to do. Art. I thought maybe I'd try teaching art to kids . . ."

I was nervous, I was rambling. Walter cut me off. "Whatever," he said firmly, and then he turned to Eileen. "You're really leaving?" he said. "Again?"

"For good," she said, pacing the room as she drew on a pair of angry red lips. "Absolutely permanently for good."

"Fine," Walter said, with the first trace of anger I'd seen him show. "Fuck yourself. Go. You're crazy if you think you can jerk me around like this again—I've had it."

"I've had it," Eileen said, mimicking Walter's tight, trembling voice.

Walter clamped his teeth together and turned and headed down the hall without another word. I stared at his back—was that it? Surely he meant to do something else. Randy—even Randy—had painted my breasts green, and although that hadn't been an attempt to keep me at least it had been a response. Eileen looked up and caught me watching Walter. Her hair was cut in a shag and she was dressed like a student, but I saw in her face that she wasn't so young. Thirty, thirty-five—she had a fan of fine wrinkles around her eyes and her neck was gaunt. She picked up a purple satin pillow and clutched it to her chest. "Trot after Walter, fat girl," she said, waving me away.

I blushed and did as she said. Walter stood at the end of the hall, waiting patiently at a door set perpendicular to the others. When I reached him, he opened it.

"The room's above the garage," he explained. "So it's a little cool in the winter, but I'll give you a space heater and an electric blanket. The other students have liked it fine."

I shuffled past him and looked in. My room—a narrow bed covered with a rose-print quilt, a desk, a chair, a reading lamp, a closet, and a small counter with a hot-plate and a sink. Cream-colored walls that sloped toward the roof and a worn hooked rug worked in faded pinks and greens. My room.

"There's a bathroom next door," Walter said. "We don't use it. The hot plate is only for boiling water, but you may use the kitchen downstairs, within certain guide-lines. We—I—travel a lot, and you'd be expected to look after the house when I'm away. That's why we rent this."

I was faint with hope, giddy with desire. I wanted this room more than I'd wanted anything in years.

Walter ticked off the rules on his fingers. "No loud music," he said. "No male visitors. No visitors at all when I'm away. No smoking. No drugs."

"No problem," I said. "All I want is a quiet place to work and sleep." I took a breath and asked the big ques-tion. "How much?"

"Depends," he said.

"On what?"

He looked down the hall. Eileen had finished stomping around and was headed for the stairs, her purse and her purple silk pillow under her arm. "She's leaving," I pointed out, thinking, *Go. Go after her. Do something.*

"I know," he said. He crossed his arms over his stom-ach, holding his elbows in his hands, and when I looked at him quizzically he shook his head. "What am I supposed to do?" he said. "She's crazy. She hates men. This is the fourth time she's taken off, and I hope to hell she stays away this time. You can't imagine what it's been like, living with a loony-tune who blames you for every goddamn thing in her life. That women's group of hers, they've got her so twisted around she thinks I'm the anti-Christ."

He sighed and ran his hand over the back of his head, where the hair was just beginning to thin. We stood there in the silence, looking away from each other and listening to the house empty itself. We heard the front door slam, the click of heels down the flagstone walk, the soft rustle of clothes being gathered into bags. The fence gate creaked, opening and closing. Walter parted the white curtains and stared out the window until the car below started and drove away.

"She did it," he said, his voice full of disgust. "She's gone. Good riddance."

"I have to go too," I said nervously. "I'll call you later, maybe, and we can talk some more about this . . ."

He sighed again and squared his shoulders, and after a minute more he turned to face me. I couldn't tell if the lines in his face were from pain or age. "I'm going to need some help here," he said. "Cleaning, laundry, perhaps some shopping and cooking. Would you be interested in doing that in exchange for rent?"

It was too strange to be true. I knew I shouldn't have seen any of this, shouldn't be in this house, but I had hardly any money and no other place to live. I leapt on his offer before he could change his mind, before I could think what I was getting into.

"I'd love to," I said. "I'll keep to my room, you'll hardly know I'm here, and whatever I find for a summer job won't get in the way of the housework."

"Fine," he said. "Move in whenever you want." He reached down and straightened the rose-print quilt on the bed, which was already perfectly taut.

A Curtain Lined with Bats

I spent most of that first summer at Walter's house alone.

Walter and his herd of graduate students stayed at his research station at the Quabbin Reservoir, collecting numbers: how many yellow perch lived in a certain part of the reservoir? How many trout? How many bass? How many square feet of algae, how deep the mud, how warm the water, how high the levels of pesticides, organophosphates, dissolved oxygen and nitrogen; along the shores and in the surrounding woods, how many rabbits, voles, moles, shrews, hawks? Each member of Walter's team was tracking something, and all of them generated numbers. Walter brought the numbers to me.

I was working for him—my title was "Laboratory Assistant" and he'd arranged to pay me for the summer from his research grant. Once or twice a week, he drove the twenty miles back from the reservoir to pick up some clean clothes and drop off his raw data. I didn't understand his work, that first summer, and I blinked vaguely when he explained how he hoped to feed all his data into the university computer and build a simulation model of the reservoir's ecosystem. But I didn't have to understand. All I had to do was to transcribe the data he brought me each week onto index cards and careful graphs. Walter praised my neatness and accuracy and I *was* neat—I had my Rapidograph and some lettering templates, and the graphs I made were better than he'd ever had.

When fall came and I started school, Walter encouraged

me to study biology rather than art. "You already *know* how to draw," he said. "Why don't you learn something new? You have a real flair for biology." I was so lonely then, so eager for praise from anyone, that I took his advice. I took general zoology, introductory chemistry, and botany my first semester; when spring came I took genetics and physics and math. The work came easily to me, more easily than I expected, and by my second summer I was beginning to understand what Walter did. My hard work was repaid, then—Walter asked me if I'd like to join the summer team at the reservoir. This was an honor, he let me know; I'd be the only undergraduate there. And because the two of us had shared a house all year as innocently as siblings, sticking to our separate rooms even though I cooked, cleaned, did laundry like a wife, I didn't think to question Walter's motives.

"I could use another pair of hands," he said. "You could stay in the trailer with me and help out with the perch study."

I was glad to be asked. I was glad, at first, to stay in the trailer and not in one of the shabby tents. The trailer, ugly and green, was parked on a grassy slope fifty yards back from the reservoir. When the wind blew, the undersides of the maple and basswood leaves near us shone soft and silvery, and at dusk swarms of swallows darted low over the water. The canvas tents where the students slept were surrounded by scrub and had no view at all. The students made fires down there in circles of blackened stones, and they played their radios and danced on the silty shore. Sometimes they pulled their sleeping bags out and slept under the stars. At night their voices would drift up to me, along with the sweet smell of marijuana and occasional shrieks of laughter, and sometimes I wished that I could join them.

The trailer had two bedrooms—one for me and one for Walter—along with a combination living room and kitchen and an attached laboratory that ran the trailer's whole length and held the deep freezers, the scales, the dissecting equipment, the microscopes and buckets and nets and poles. Walter's students had parceled out the birds and mammals and amphibians among themselves. Walter and I were working on the fish. Each day we rose at dawn to row across the reservoir and haul the nets we'd set the night before. The water was so cold that it numbed my hands, and often I wouldn't feel my stabs and scratches until later, back at the dock, where we hunched together over the net and disentangled the fish from the meshes. Trout, yellow perch, sunfish, suckers, bass. Their scales, under the dissecting scope, showed rings like trees.

Walter, wild with enthusiasm, lectured to me all day. In the boat, on the dock, during the afternoons in the makeshift lab as we dissected hundreds of fish in the shimmering heat and weighed testes and ovaries, determining fertility indexes and rushing to get through the day's catch before the fish rotted in our hands. We froze the reproductive organs so we could test them for pesticides later. My hands always smelled of fish. I never felt clean. At night I dreamed of legions of perch standing up on their tails and chasing me, and during the day I listened in a trance as Walter colonized my brain, transplanting huge wads of knowledge from his head to mine. When I sat at my lab bench he stood over me, wrapped his long arms around me, used his fingers to guide the scalpel in my hands. He leaned his thighs, cool on the hottest days, against my back. He told me I had a wonderful mind and lovely hair, and he made me first author on the paper we wrote together. He fed our data into the university computer, cross-matching it with his students' data on insecticide use, acid rainfall, wind patterns, temperature change, and one night he said he couldn't imagine how he'd lived without me.

That was the night of July Fourth, and so everyone everywhere was celebrating. In the small towns surrounding us, people marched in parades and waved flags and roasted themselves at cookouts. Aging men injured themselves at softball games. We worked, a day like any other, and when the fireworks splattered the sky that night, Walter looked up from his papers and cupped his ears and identified the displays by sound. "Ware," he said. "Barre. Athol." He might have been a bat. He listened rather than looked because we weren't outside, standing in the water with his students and waving sparklers and catching the occasional high explosion over the trees. We were inside the trailer. I was lying on the floor, my legs up on the arm of the couch where Walter sat, reading his manuscript to me. It was sixty-three pages long and had to do with the effects of changing water pH on the reproductive success of various fish. The effects of acid rain.

He read to me for three and a half hours, pausing only to sip at a lukewarm glass of water. I listened. I listened hard, trying not to be distracted by the pop and thump of the fireworks, by the celebrating students, whose laughter occasionally rose and broke, by the low bass notes that emerged from someone's tape player and moved through the ground and up the hill to me until I felt them in my back. I listened, knowing I'd have to ask intelligent questions when he was done. Wanting to ask those questions—the work was good, it was interesting, part of it was mine. All of it was what I thought I wanted to do.

Walter finished reading just before midnight. "Well?" he said. His face was tired and drawn, but he looked happy.

"It's wonderful," I said, and it was. It was original and interesting and well-written. It wasn't hard to praise.

"Really?" he said. "Really?" He slid down the couch to the end where I'd draped my legs, and he touched me shyly on the shin. I raised myself up on my elbows and looked at him.

"Really," I said. "This is wonderful stuff."

He reached for my leg just as the students galloped up the hill and pounded on the door. Each night after supper, they all came to the trailer for a general meeting, to discuss the plans for the following day. But they had never burst in like this before. Walter glared at the door, his fingers an inch from my leg. I scrabbled to my feet and went to intercept the students. There they were, the six of them, and in the front stood the dark-haired one named Tony, whom I had sometimes stared at. I was twenty-four then, no older than most of them; Walter was thirty-six and old for his age.

"You *guys,*" Tony said, peering through the door at Walter surrounded by his papers. "I can't believe you're still *working.*"

"We've been going over the new manuscript," Walter said stiffly.

"Come on," Tony said. "It's a holiday. We've got some beer down there, and some barbecued chicken, and some tunes . . ."

"I can't," Walter said. "But thanks for asking. You enjoy yourselves."

My hand was resting against the doorframe and Tony covered it with his. "What about you?" he asked, so softly that Walter might not have heard him. "You don't have to stay—just come down for a while, get high, relax a little . . ."

I turned my head over my shoulder and saw Walter, watching me intently. I turned my head back to Tony, who was smiling. Whose hand still covered mine. "I don't know," I said, more drawn than I wanted to admit. "Maybe . . ."

"Yeah?" he said. "Great."

But when I turned my head again I saw that Walter's face was stricken. We hadn't finished talking about his paper; we'd only barely begun. He'd read to me for all those hours and I'd hardly given him anything back. "Um, actually," I said to Tony, "maybe not. Or at least not till later."

Tony laughed and made a curious face, almost a smirk, almost a leer. One of the students behind him whispered something to another and then both of them giggled. I realized, for the first time, that they all assumed Walter and I were sleeping together.

I shut the door. I sent them away. For an hour I told Walter, in great detail, how good his paper was, and then we went to our separate beds and Walter had one of his frequent nightmares, which he never discussed but which I knew about because he sometimes called out in his sleep. That night, while I lay awake listening to Tony and the others party on the stretch of sand below us, I heard Walter make his broken cry; he sounded so unhappy that I crept across the corridor to his room and woke him up. I led him gently to the living room and made some coffee, watching as the still invisible sun began to lighten the sky. Walter sat heavily in his striped pajamas, his face droopy and fogged.

"I dreamed I lost my research grant," he said. "That I had to go back and work for my old advisor. As a *technician*. Jesus."

The window in the living room was half-hidden by a pair of ugly fiberglass curtains framing it on either side. We kept it open for the breeze, even though the screen had long since rotted away. Walter had talked about fixing it for weeks, but the plague of bugs we'd dreaded had never materialized, and so he kept putting it off. Because the window faced the woods, I had never drawn those curtains closed. I had never touched them until that morning, when I tugged at the drawcord and tried to open them wider, so the dawn could lighten Walter's clouded face.

The curtains hardly moved at all. When I pulled the cord again, we heard a noise. "What's that?" Walter asked. I heard a tiny scritching sound, like toenails on glass.

"I don't know," I said. I moved to the center of the window and grasped a fold of curtain in my hand, peeling it away so I could examine the rod. Rusted hooks, maybe. I rolled the fabric over and then froze, staring at what I held in my hand. The curtain was lined with tiny brown bats, a solid mat from edge to edge and floor to ceiling, like a moth-eaten moleskin coat. The bats hung upside down by their claws with their wings wrapped around them like shawls and their small faces, cross with interrupted sleep, peering out at me. I screamed when two of them moved, and Walter rushed to my side.

"Jesus!" he said. "This is *fantastic!* A whole colony, probably sleeping here every day after they finish feeding for the night . . ." He turned back the other curtain, which was similarly lined, and at that second touch the bats stirred themselves, the whole mass shifting and unwrapping their wings. When I started crying, they poured out the window in three streams that looked like smoke.

Walter put his arm around me, genuinely puzzled. "What are you afraid of?" he asked softly.

What makes you cry in your dreams? I wanted to ask him that, ask him why he'd kept me up in this trailer, listening to him, while everyone else played below; why he'd let me live in his house for a year when he didn't travel all that much and had no plants to water, no pets to feed.

"They won't hurt you," he said, his hands stroking my hair. "There's nothing scary about them. They're like spiders—very friendly and smart. Useful. They eat bugs—that's probably why we've been so comfortable here without the screen."

Stroke, stroke; very calm and rational, as if he were afraid of nothing in the night. I hated spiders almost as much as I hated bats, and I wasn't comforted. The bats had been there all summer, roosting secretly after their nighttime expeditions, and I had never noticed them. They could have nested in my hair. I couldn't stop crying.

Walter stroked the back of my neck and then my back and then my hips. I'd lost thirty pounds since I'd started school and so I didn't feel I had to fling his hand away. Gently, he closed the curtains and led me to the couch, where the manuscript he'd read to me still lay in a yellow heap.

"Ssh," he said, laying me down among the papers. "Don't worry. I'll take care of you."

The bats made a whispering noise as the last of them left, and we made love surrounded by fish. People gave these to Walter, because of the work he did: fish pictures and fish statues and fish cups and vases and bowls; fish lapel pins and cuff links, fish ties, fish hats. Walter had arranged these along the shelves and walls, and all summer I'd smiled at this evidence of something warm and boyish in him. I thought any man who'd keep these things and display them so proudly must have a sweet inside. Walter was shy, I thought. The fish eyes glinted at me. Walter was reserved. But I knew him better than anyone, I could find what was hidden in him.

"You're so soft," he said to me later, and his clumsiness told me he meant it. "So smooth."

Walter screened the window for me and the bats never returned. In the weeks that followed, we worked at the lab or on the lake all day, and when dusk fell we showered and made dinner and met with the students and then read. Walter read old volumes of natural history, liking to know every creak and call and whistle and song in the woods, while I, years behind, always behind and ashamed of it now, read the journals Walter marked for me. Each night we read until eleven and then went to bed, and on the nights Walter decreed, when he wasn't too tired and we didn't have to get up too early the next morning, we made love.

A Family Photograph

Thanksgiving in Fargo, North Dakota, with Walter's family; Christmas in Westfield, Massachusetts, with mine. That was the deal we worked out the first year we were married and stuck to every year after that.

In 1980, those holidays were also our first meetings with each other's family, because our wedding had been private, secret, almost furtive. Walter had wanted it that way. Him in a blue suit, me in a simple dress; two of his students for witnesses; two plain rings and a civil ceremony. "It's a second wedding for both of us," Walter had said. "Why fuss?"

And that was fine with me. He had proposed to me over the kitchen table—upright, not on his knees—ticking off on his fingers the reasons we should join our lives, and I had liked that too. I liked that he was so sensible and sane. I liked that he had a plan for our lives. Budgets, goals, investments. Lists and planned recreations. On Sundays we were to sit by the fire or, if the weather was good, outside, and eat lunch from trays and read together happily. And in time, when we both felt ready, we were to start a family. Two children, we decided. A boy and a girl, two years apart. We'd start savings accounts for their college tuition as soon as they were born. Walter's calm predictions for our future thrilled me.

On our first Christmas we woke in Walter's house—our house—and had coffee in bed and exchanged presents and made love clumsily, buried beneath the blankets. Walter's fish watched over us, as they had since our return from the reservoir; he'd brought his collection back when I'd told him I liked them. And if our lovemaking no longer had the edge and fervor it had had in the trailer, still it was good enough. Our bodies fit well together, and Walter was patient and gentle. Sometimes Randy, so strange and wild, appeared when I closed my eyes, but when he did I chased him away and tried to focus on Walter instead. When I whispered that his hands were cold, he warmed them on his own thighs.

Two feet of snow buried everything that day. On the drive to Westfield I got carsick and threw up, but I couldn't convince Walter to turn around and take me back home. "It's Christmas," he said gently. "Don't you want to be with your family? Don't you want me to meet them?"

Yes and no, yes and no. Secretly, I'd feared Walter might bolt if he saw my family before we said our vows, and all fall I'd made up excuses for why we couldn't visit them. Now I was sick with all I'd hidden. Walter's parents, whom I'd met a month earlier, had been tidy and respectable. "They're a little . . . unusual," I said. "I'm afraid you won't like them."

"How bad can they be?" he said, but his smile faded when he first saw the house. The asphalt shingles were loose in several places; a squirrel had tumbled one of the garbage cans and tossed orange peels and paper across the snowy yard. Great-uncle Owen's BMW contrasted oddly with my father's old station wagon and my mother's tired Pontiac. The windows had been sealed with plastic for extra insulation, and a ragged corner on the hall dormer flapped in the wind. The front door was framed with strands of plastic holly and decorated with a cardboard Santa Claus.

My mother greeted us. She wore a red dress, red high heels, red lipstick; she'd dyed and teased and lacquered her hair into a coarse black helmet. When she opened the door she smiled as if she were glad to see us. "Merry Christmas, darlin'," she said, with a trace of the Virginia accent she'd somehow held onto for years.

"This is my mother," I murmured to Walter. "Roxanne Doerring."

"Call me Roxy," she said brightly to him. "Everyone does."

She led us inside, where nothing had changed since I was small. We'd had the green plastic tree since I was in elementary school, along with the white plastic candles and the dusty bulbs and the poinsettia-printed tablecloth. My mother laid her delicate hand on Walter's long arm. Always the smallest one in the room, always the most noticeable, she'd stayed tiny through an act of will, five feet of skin and bone and sinew.

"She works as a school librarian," I'd told Walter earlier. "She raises roses. She tapes books for the blind."

But I hadn't told him how she and I had been at war for as long as I could remember. She was from Virginia and I was not; I was half my father's child and his half was all that showed. I'd weighed ten pounds when I was born, and although my father called me healthy and his mother, my Mumu, called me pleasingly plump, my mother was appalled. She kept her own weight down by rigorous dieting, and by the time I was five she was already hiding food from me.

"You have your father's metabolism," she'd say, setting down my afternoon snack of carrots and celery sticks. "Look at him. Look at his family. You have to be careful."

Behind her back I'd eaten everything I could find. I cleaned out my friends' refrigerators, spent my allowance at the candy store, hid the chocolates Uncle Owen brought me from Boston and ate them at night. When I grew old enough to babysit, I swooned over my employers' cupboards and ate everything but the baby. Morning and night I sat down to my mother's skimpy, carefully balanced meals, and when she weighed me each Sunday she shrieked in horror as I tried to look bewildered.

"Are you doing this to *spite* me?" she'd ask.

Perhaps I was. My mother had had no outlet for her intelligence beyond raising me and Toby, changing the wallpaper every three years, nagging my father. She didn't go to work until Toby and I were grown, and so during my childhood she focused on me, trying to make me into what she'd wanted and missed. Harping on the things I wasn't to do: I was not to marry a man who'd meant to be a New York chef and had ended up as a cook in a Westfield school cafeteria. I was not to have children so young that they ruined my life; not to live with my Swedish mother-in-law; not to have to scrimp and scrounge over every penny. I was to hold myself dear, be somebody; beautiful and aloof and fastidious, well-dressed and socially adept. My mother wanted my next-door neighbor and enemy, Luellen Barnes, and what she got instead was me.

"It's lovely to meet you," Walter said, detaching his arm from my mother's grasp as he followed her over to my father's chair.

"My father," I said. "Edwin Doerring."

Dad rose slowly and swallowed Walter's hand in his, silent as always in my mother's presence. "He's a cook," I'd told Walter, but I hadn't explained where, nor had I told him how, when my father came home from his job in the cafeteria, he used to slip me the treats he'd hidden in his huge black coat. He never ate supper with us; he'd been working with food all day and he had no appetite. Instead, he'd take a long shower and then retreat to the room he'd made for himself in the attic. After supper, after we'd done our homework, Toby and I were sometimes allowed to go up to his room and play quietly while Dad worked on his stamp collection. He shuffled tiny, jewel-colored bits of paper from Cameroon and Mozambique, Belize and New Guinea and Chile, and because he liked me fat he sometimes met me in the kitchen late at night, after my mother and Toby had fallen asleep, for a shared, stolen snack.

I had never told Walter that either—not how my cheeks puffed, my thighs swelled. How my belly grew high and wide, an echo of my father's, or how my mother fumed when the salesgirl at Filene's steered me toward the chubby section, toward vertical stripes and concealing navy blue. I was big-boned, thick-waisted—chubby, but not much worse than that until my last two years of high school. Girl-chubby, genetically chubby; chubby because I was built that way and also because my father and Mumu and Uncle Owen liked it.

Walter thanked my father for inviting us and then moved toward my brother Toby, who rose from the floor where he was playing with Cindy and Samantha, his twins.

"Grace," Toby said dryly. "How nice of you to honor us."

He pushed his girls forward and then tugged his wife,

Linda, up from her seat on the hassock. My mother murmured introductions. Toby took after her—small, neat, precise. When I was two, he had tried to gouge out my right eye with one of his long, thin thumbs, and our relationship had never changed much after that. He had never gotten over the humiliation of me running around with his high-school friends.

Walter stood in the center of this crowd, uneasy, nervous, damp. "You're a marine biologist?" my mother said. "Is that what Grace told me?"

"Freshwater, actually," Walter said. "I'm a lake ecologist."

"Oh, isn't that interesting," Linda said.

"Grace was your student?" Toby said. He knew; although I hadn't brought Walter home before I'd spoken about him often enough when I'd called.

"One of the best students I've ever had," Walter said.

"Makes sense," Toby said. "She used to be a real teacher's pet."

Meanwhile Uncle Owen sat in the easy chair near the fireplace, in which a fake fire of electric logs glowed. Always, until Mumu died, he had sat in that chair on one side of the fire, while Mumu pulled her wheelchair across from him. My father's uncle, not mine; Mumu's brother. But where Mumu was crumpled and soft and pale, her legs useless from the nerve damage caused by her diabetes, he was broad and tanned and vigorous. And wealthy, too—he had a flourishing business in Boston, dealing in Oriental art and antiques, and his apartment in Cambridge had been my favorite place in the world. Silk hangings, a blue enamel bird in a cage, music boxes, black lacquer chairs, old rugs, plants in huge pots, and a succession of handsome young male companions who kept house for him and answered his phones and petted me when I visited. Uncle Owen had stayed with us often, all throughout my childhood, and he had rescued me from my mother many times in minor ways and once spectacularly.

Which was yet another thing I hadn't told Walter—how it was that I, from a family like this, in a town like this, had managed to go to college at all. No one knew about the deal Uncle Owen and I had made. When Mumu died, my sophomore year in high school, I had put on fifty pounds as an act of grief and sympathy, also as a blow against my mother and Grandpa Jack. I cracked a hundred and eighty pounds and discovered that fat girls came in two flavors: mousy, lank-haired, scholarly; everybody's maiden aunt. Or loose, sluttish, wisecracking. I shed Chuck and Mark, my bookish, freakish friends, and I chose the second way—danger. Boys. Dangerous boys. I let my grades slip and started hanging out with boys in Toby's class, boys who had motorcycles and leather jackets and slim pints of whiskey in paper bags. Boys who had parties in basements and didn't mind a fat girl if she was good-humored and easy. There was a tradition here, old and honorable; I discovered how easy it was for a fat girl to get laid. I loved the rumors that flew around, the prissy mouths the cheerleaders made when I flaunted a hickey in the showers after gym. I loved Toby's fury and my mother's shrill dismay. I let myself go for a year like that and might have gone on forever if Uncle Owen hadn't taken me aside and proposed his plan. The fall of my senior year he had said, "Where are you applying to college?"

"Nowhere," I told him. "What's the point?"

"You want to live in Westfield forever?" he asked. "You want to be like your mother? Like Toby?" Toby was working as a salesman for a lawn-care service then.

"Of course not," I said.

"So?"

"So what?"

"So I'll make a deal with you. You apply to school now. And if you lose forty pounds by June, I'll pay your tuition. You have to get out of Westfield, Grace. Introduce yourself to the world."

My grades had slipped so far by then that the best I could do was UMass, but I applied and got in and lost all forty pounds. By the time I entered college I was thin enough to pass for normal, thin enough for Randy.

I trusted Uncle Owen more than anyone else in the world, and I wanted very much to see how he'd respond to Walter. He sat and watched and listened without saying anything or rising from his chair, and when Walter stepped into the kitchen with Toby and the others moved into the dining room, I went over to him. He kissed my hand and then shook his head sadly and looked at me. "Grace," he said. "My dear. Two in a row?"

"He's not like Randy," I bristled. "You don't even know him."

"I know what I see," he said. "He's not like Randy. He's worse."

"You're not being fair," I said. I was furious; also scared. Uncle Owen was famous for his snap judgments, which were almost always right.

Uncle Owen shook his head again. "Well, it's done," he said. "We have to live with it. And the good news is that you look marvelous—do let me see your hair."

I turned sullenly so that he could examine my festive French braids. "Lovely," he said. "Very nice."

All that afternoon I stared at Walter, trying to determine what had set Uncle Owen off. Was it Walter's thinning hair, his stooped shoulders, the way he barked when the twins tied his shoes together? Perhaps it was his deference toward my mother or the way that, during dinner, he failed to remark on the plate my mother handed me, which bore only a thin slice of white meat, a mound of squash, and a dab of cranberry sauce. No stuffing, potatoes, gravy. No creamed onions.

"Your weight," my mother said brightly, as she passed the plate to me. "Can't be too careful."

Uncle Owen traded plates with me and then, without comment, sent his new plate back to be filled properly. So perhaps it was that, or perhaps it was the way Walter flushed angry red when Linda spilled wine on his coat. Or maybe it was what happened later, when Walter caught sight of the photograph hanging from the plastic Christmas tree.

This was a family photograph—blurred, black-and-white, framed in red and green construction paper and edged with a crumbling white doily. A loop of ribbon glued to the top suspended it from the tree. I had forgotten about it, and Walter might never have seen it if the twins hadn't pulled him down next to the tree to examine their loot. Cindy tossed her Nerf ball at him and his hand swung back to catch it, and as it did he caught the edge of the picture and pulled it down.

"What's this?" he asked. Oh, I couldn't believe he held it in his hand. Every year I had tried to steal it, burn it. Every year my mother had rescued it.

"Our family," Uncle Owen said sternly. "All of us."

Before I could snatch the picture from Walter, Toby moved into place. "All of us," he told Walter smoothly. "Have you ever seen what Grace used to look like?"

"Never," Walter said.

I sank down on the floor next to Uncle Owen's chair and buried my head in my arms. That picture had been taken when I was ten and Toby was twelve. My mother was thin, my father was fat, Toby was thin and sharp-featured, and I was at my worst stage, made worse by the way my mother had dressed me. My round face made rounder by the ribbon pushing back my hair, my round body emphasized by the tight white dress, my round arms sticking out from the sleeves like clubs. I was standing by Uncle Owen, whose arm cradled me protectively and did its best to conceal my deforming outfit.

I couldn't stand for Walter to see me like that. He knew I had to watch what I ate, that I had a small problem with my weight, but I didn't think he'd ever suspected my fat past. And there Toby was saying, "Why yes, of course that's Grace. She was such a little butterball." And my mother was adding, "If you knew what a struggle we had trying to get her to slim . . ." And the twins were puffing their cheeks out and giggling, and still the worst was yet to come. Because in the picture were two people absent from our gathering, the two people I had never meant Walter to know.

"Who's this?" Walter asked politely.

I knew he was pointing to Mumu, whose wheelchair was pulled up beside Uncle Owen and me in the picture. Mumu was sixty-two there—four years before she died. But she was sick already, already in her wheelchair and confined to the downstairs den that my mother had grudgingly made over into her room. She weighed two hundred and eighty pounds and wore black dresses and hairnets and thick elastic stockings and steel-rimmed glasses, and I suppose she looked awful to someone who didn't know her. But she had been my chief escape in the years between losing Zillah and finding Chuck and Mark. Between her and my mother was a dislike so strong that it could only be managed by good manners and endless small courtesies, and I had always known whose side I was on. Mumu had read to me in Swedish, translating and embroidering as she went, and she'd told me fairy tales with such authority that for years I believed they were true. She told the story of the Snow Queen as if she'd been the little girl whose childhood companion had had his heart pierced by the sliver of evil mirror, as if she'd ridden the back of the talking reindeer through the Scandanavian wastes herself and had carried the message written on a dried cod from the Lapland woman to the Finland woman who had sent her to the frozen palace. She told me about the summers when the sun never set, and about the ocean her mother had crossed as a young woman, frightened and alone. She told me about her husband, who had died before I was born, and about the bakery her parents had run, where she and my Uncle Owen had worked in clouds of flour like snow.

I raised my head and looked at Uncle Owen, who'd been watching us silently. "That was my grandmother," I told Walter. "We were very close." And then I drew a breath and answered the other question he was sure to ask. "The other man, the one in the tweed cap, was my Grandpa Jack. Mom's father."

"He died years ago," my mother said. "We were all very fond of him."

I blinked at her stupidly. Fond? Grandpa Jack was an old man smelling of chewing tobacco, who had lived in the small Virginia town where my mother was raised and who had visited us each Christmas. He came empty-handed, wearing that cap, and he slept in Toby's room but crept into mine each morning to wake me up.

I had always hated him; I had never mentioned him to Walter. I had never told him how, when I was in high school, an earnest English teacher with unshaven legs had spent a month trying to interest our class in old-fashioned poetic forms. Sonnets, sestinas, villanelles—we were sixteen and plagued by hormones and parents, and we had other things on our minds. My mind, particularly—Mumu had died that summer and I had shed my friends and my books and was busy laying on the lard that would recreate her.

"Write a villanelle," the teacher told us one week, and we laughed at her, but then, trapped in the stuffy room, set about to do as she'd asked. Something about the villanelle's shape, the obsessive repetition of lines, induced a kind of trance in me. I wrote as if a voice were dictating to me, and this is what slipped out:

Villanelle for a Grandfather

You touch me, and your skin is pale and cold—
You kiss me, and your kiss could kill the day.
Tonight, I notice you are old.

Your fingernails are iced with milky mold—
The cuticles an epileptic gray.
You touch me, and your skin is pale and cold.

You sit by me, and often try to hold
My hands, and other things, and then you pray
I will not notice you are old.

You twirl your cap and crease its faded fold—
You kiss me, and your lips are crumpled clay.
You touch me, and your skin is pale and cold.

And recently, you have become quite bold—
You touch, and do not ask me if you may.
Always, I have known that you were old.

These days your antics seem not quite so droll—
These days I hesitate to let you play.
Tonight, I noticed you were old.
You touched me, and your skin was pale and cold.

I didn't know where that had come from or why I let Mrs. Dorfman read it. After she read it she sent me to the school psychologist, who wanted to know what was going on with me at home.

"Nothing," I said. "I was kidding." Perhaps I thought I was. "I was just trying to yank Mrs. Dorfman's chain."

"Oh?" the counselor said. He made a note in his file. "You don't like her?"

"She's a jerk," I said. "She's always trying to get us to express our feelings. I just made that up because I knew it would upset her."

The doctor let me go. I went back to Mrs. Dorfman's class and never wrote anything like that again. But her response gave me an idea, and later that week, when I was doing my homework at the kitchen table, I let that poem fall out of my notebook and onto the floor, where my mother had to see it. When she read it she slapped me and demanded to know who I thought I was, making up such dreadful trash. But after that, until Grandpa Jack died, my mother made sure he slept downstairs on the couch, away from me.

I looked at my mother, daring her to say more. She blushed. "Actually," I told Walter. "I wasn't all that fond of him."

"Well," Walter said.

On our ride home from Westfield Walter was silent, and for several weeks after that he treated me with extra kindness. A few times he tried to ask me more about my family, but when I shrugged his questions aside he backed off.

"It's so hard to imagine," he said then. "So hard to imagine you growing up like that. I'm just trying to understand what it was like."

"It doesn't matter," I told him. "It's done."

And I believed it was. That year, as I had every year, I fled my old house in Westfield so fast that I left chunks of flesh behind. That house, that family, that sense of everyone holding me back, tripping me up—I cut that part of my life right out, the way I'd cut out Randy, and when my parents called I shut myself behind chatter about work or the weather. Walter said he understood and, although I knew he didn't, I liked it when he tried to shield me from them. I let him cast himself as a rescuing knight, swooping me up from the muck and the mire, and when he blamed my moodiness on what he could guess of my strange past I never once discouraged him. Sometimes I was tempted to tell him more, to tell him everything. But I held back. I had a sense, even then, that he could only deal with so much of me, and I woke some nights to find him staring at my face, as if he'd found himself in bed with a stranger and was trying to figure out who I was.

A Silver Plane

Each year, on the Wednesday before Thanksgiving, Walter and I stood in airports struggling with our baggage. Bulky clothes, food, gifts—we struggled with those, and we struggled for precious seats, and both of us struggled to calm me down. Our first Thanksgiving trip had been my first time on a plane, and although I'd looked forward to the journey my body rebelled, as if I'd been exposed to some exotic pollen. After that, I was allergic to flying. I broke out in hives, sweat, tears when I got near a plane. I took tranquilizers, sleeping pills, dry Martinis; I tried self-hypnosis and biofeedback. Nothing made a dent in the panic I felt when the plane first began its unholy levitation.

On our second trip to Fargo there were blizzards in Milwaukee and Cleveland, ice storms in Detroit and Buffalo, a cold wave seeping across the continent. I huddled in my seat from Hartford to Chicago, drugged to a near-coma, and I tried to persuade myself why planes should fly. "Airfoils," I whispered. "Lift. Drag. Aerodynamic force." My palms still sweated. My heart still raced. In Chicago, the stewardess had to help remove me from the plane, and when a bland voice announced that the next leg of our trip would be delayed because our plane needed extensive de-icing, I wept.

"Grace," Walter said. "Don't worry. Please."

He held me with one hand and thumbed through the new issue of *Science* with the other, looking for the article he and a student had published there. They'd mentioned me in the acknowledgments, but I didn't want to look; I leaned into his shoulder and sobbed. I liked his parents, and I looked forward to visiting them, but I had wanted to go by bus or train or car. The way we did all our other trips—when Walter had meetings in New York or Philadelphia or Baltimore or Charleston, we took a little extra time, and we drove. I packed picnic baskets full of delicacies, thermoses of hot coffee and cold drinks, books to keep us entertained. When Walter drove, I read to him and kept him supplied with food and drink. When I drove, he did the same for me. We had a good time, and I couldn't see why people raised their eyebrows at us. So we needed a few extra days. "It's a two-day drive to Fargo," I'd told Walter that second year. "Three at most . . ."

"Six extra days," he'd said. "For a three-day visit—Grace, we *have* to fly."

And so we'd flown. In Chicago we waited for two hours while our plane was de-iced, and then after we boarded we sat for so long that the wings iced up again. Men in padded suits rolled steel towers up to the wings and then stood high above the ground shooting jets of steaming liquid from thick hoses. I took another Valium and tried not to hear the passengers discussing the weather.

"Thirty below," I heard someone say.

"Minneapolis is closed," said another.

"I hear the air gets thinner when it's this cold," said a third. "So there's less left, which must make it harder for the plane to stay up . . ."

I plucked feebly at Walter's sleeve. "Please," I said. "Let's stay overnight here. We could find a hotel."

"They wouldn't let us fly if it wasn't safe," he said.

The rolling towers pulled away and the plane began to back up slowly; if I'd been the praying type I would have prayed. In the absence of that, I tried to distract myself by calling up a picture of the cat I'd been dissecting in my vertebrate anatomy class. My teacher was a plump man with a red toupee, whose idea of fun was to place loose bones in a silk bag and have us plunge our hands in, identifying tibias and fibulas by feel. He and Walter had been friends forever.

"Splenic flexure, cecum, bladder," I muttered, my eyes shut and my fingers clawing at the armrests. We took off; we flew. The ride was turbulent all the way to Fargo and the attendants couldn't serve drinks, and by the time we arrived I'd sweated through all my clothes. My mascara ran. My hair was plastered to my forehead. Walter's parents looked concerned when they first saw me.

"Have you been waiting long?" Walter asked them. He kissed his mother's cheek and shook his father's hand.

"Three hours," Ray said placidly. "Not so bad."

I could picture them sitting there, plump legs spread, hands folded in their ample laps. Ray, who taught agronomy at the state university, could talk for hours about the wiles of nitrogen-fixing bacteria. "I have a passion for legumes," he'd confided shyly on my first visit. Walter's mother, Lenore, had taken me on a tour of their Lutheran church, where she was head of the women's committee. She'd needlepointed seat cushions for the pews, embroidered banners for the walls, organized bake sales, knitted sweaters for raffles. Now she slipped her soft hand beneath my elbow. "Welcome back," she said. "I brought you some coffee—it's in the car. In a thermos. You're so pale."

"Bad flight," I said weakly.

Walter and his father, ahead of us, were already discussing work. They settled themselves in the Jeep's front seat, leaving Lenore and me in the back.

"Drink this," Lenore said. Black coffee, boiled with eggshells, the way Mumu used to make it. While I sipped at it, Lenore showed me the seat cover she'd been needlepointing in the airport. On a field of dark purple she'd worked a bible verse in violet and cream and pale pink. "See?" she said, and then she read the text to me in her thin girlish voice. "For nothing is secret that shall not be made manifest; neither anything hid that shall not be known and come abroad."

I shuddered and closed my eyes.

"That's good coffee," she said. "Isn't it? Strong." Then she stroked her seat cover again. "Luke," she said happily. "Eight-seventeen. It's part of a series I'm doing for the choir stalls—all from Luke. Twelve-two: 'For there is nothing covered that shall not be revealed; neither hid, that shall not be made known.' Twelve-three: 'Therefore whatsoever ye have spoken in darkness shall be heard in the light; and that which ye have spoken in the ear in closets shall be proclaimed upon the house tops.' Pastor Lundquist has been using the denunciation of the Pharisees and the discourse against hypocrisy as his texts all fall, and you wouldn't believe how interesting his sermons have been . . ."

"Mother," Ray said soothingly, "now don't you go bending her ear."

"I'm fine," I said faintly. Usually Lenore's bible chatter rolled right off me, but that evening I listened with sick fascination. Luke had been Mumu's favorite reading and I knew those verses from her, although I'd heard them first in Swedish. Hearing them in English, from Lenore's mouth, was like hearing the dead speak.

We drove through the snow over land as flat as the sea, and as we did Lenore stopped quoting Scripture and pointed out Walter's elementary school, Walter's high school, the fairground where Walter had won first prize with a calf. "Remember when you won the science fair?" she asked, leaning forward to touch Walter's shoulder. "Those rats you bred?"

"Genetics," Ray said happily. "Even then." We'd had the same conversation the year before, passing the same sights.

"And remember the flatworms?" Lenore asked. "And the project you did with the *Lycopodium?*"

It was dark by then, and I couldn't tell if Walter was blushing. I couldn't imagine growing up with such proud parents.

That was the way our visit went, the way it had gone the year before and the way it would always go. Peculiar, sometimes funny; and yet somehow also touching. In the Hoffmeiers' neat white house were the bookcases Walter had built; in the yard were the trees Walter had planted and the fence Walter had designed. Lenore fixed the same meals Walter had always eaten. Walter and Ray strode off in the afternoons, looking at land, talking science, discussing each other's work, and Lenore and I sat warm in the white house, watching TV and drinking coffee and cooking huge feasts. Part Swedish, part Finnish, part German, Lenore loved the idea of my Swedish grandmother and paid homage to our shared ancestry by digging out her old recipes. We made cardamom bread, krumcakes, Swedish meatballs scented with nutmeg. In between, while dough rose and sauces simmered, we leafed through books of old photographs and examined Walter at two, four, ten, twenty; every age and situation.

"This is Walter when he was four," Lenore said, showing me a picture of a small lean child making a terrible face. "He was so fussy about his food—I'd just given him a Saltine, and he was making a face because it was ugly. He couldn't stand the way some of the crackers had those little blisters."

Another picture, Walter at two in a high-chair, smiling. "Ray took this," she said. "We were so happy that day—every time we fed him, we'd wait to see if he'd look at his plate and start screaming. It took us the longest time to figure out what was upsetting him—the food was crooked on his plate. Ray took this picture the day we arranged the food symmetrically and Walter stopped crying. Such a relief—you have no idea."

"I have an idea," I murmured.

"He's still fussy?" she said.

"A little. About how his shirts are ironed, and where I get his jackets dry-cleaned, and how I clean house, and how I cook . . ."

Lenore smiled. "Hoffmeier men. That's the way they are—Ray's just the same, and so was his father. I remember cooking Thanksgiving dinner with Ray's mother, out at their place on County Line Road. The two of us scared half to death that the men would find something wrong with it—but then that's the fun, too. The pleasure of pleasing them. Praise from a Hoffmeier man *means* something. He takes good care of you?"

"The best," I said, and I meant it. He sheltered me the way Uncle Owen had, keeping my family at bay. "He's always helping me with school," I told her. "Always trying to improve me."

"And he's affectionate?"

"Pretty much," I said, knowing I couldn't tell her how our lovemaking had turned into a weekly event. Always Saturdays, always at night, always with the lights off. Always the same words, touches, moves. The science of love. We slept in Eileen's bed, on Eileen's sheets, with Walter's fish looking down on us and Randy and Eileen as present, sometimes, as if their bodies were there. Eileen, whatever her faults, had had a dancer's body, and I knew Walter still thought of her now and then. Sometimes his hand, running up my inner thigh, would stop and seem to stutter there, as if he found the excess flesh unfamiliar.

"So," Lenore said, leaning toward me. "So you'll have a child?"

I blushed. There seemed to be no harm in telling her, cementing our alliance. "We're trying already," I admitted. "I'm graduating in June, and we thought any time after that . . ."

She wrapped me in her yeasty-smelling arms. "I'm so glad," she said. "I always hated Eileen because she wouldn't. Such a selfish woman, so caught up in herself—all that dancing. Never taking care of Walter. But I knew you were different. And Walter will be such a good father."

I'd had sneaking doubts about that, now that I knew him better, but I'd put them aside since we'd started trying. We had a lovely home, he was up for tenure, I was almost educated. Our lives stretched before us, secure and changeless. Any child of ours would lack for nothing.

"A grandchild," Lenore said. Her face was radiant. "Oh, I can't wait."

When I looked at her, I couldn't wait either. "Maybe this time next year . . ." I said.

"Whenever," she said. "The Lord will provide." She ran her eyes approvingly over my broad figure. "You have a good pelvis," she said. "You'll have an easy time. But after, you'll have to—you know. Work together. Balance Walter a little—he and his father are firm men. They have firm ideas."

"They do," I said.

"So you'll soften that a little. Provide the comfort, the flexibility—you're a good girl. You can do that."

"I can try," I said.

"Of course you will. And as far as church goes—if you can find a pastor like our Sven Lundquist, you'll be ahead right there." She vanished into the bedroom and returned a minute later with a small book covered in blue watered silk. "Walter's baby book," she said. "Pastor headed all the sections with appropriate verses, and then Ray and I filled in the rest. First step, first tooth, first words . . . I'd like you to have it."

I thanked her, thinking how, when we were home, Walter mocked his mother's soft ways and simple piety. No child of Walter's would ever set foot inside a church.

"A girl," Lenore said. "You'll have a girl, with hair like yours."

"A girl," I echoed, and suddenly I yearned for one. Small, pink, sweet-smelling. Someone all my own.

The men came home then, from their Saturday afternoon in the fields. Walter showed me his high-school track trophies, as he had done the year before. He showed me his old bed, his old room, his old microscope; he grew wistful there in Fargo, something I'd never seen in him before. He handled his old rock collection as if the rocks were jewels, and when I showed him his baby book he turned the pages carefully. As he did, I made a connection I had failed to make earlier: Walter yearned for the past. He mourned for it, grieved for it, wept for a time when, in his eyes, the world was simpler, kinder, more at one with nature. He'd frowned on the drive from the airport, when his parents had pointed out a new apartment complex, but I hadn't thought of how, at home, he refused to go to shopping malls and averted his face from new houses. He gave money to save the whales, save the snow leopards, save the Amazon, the Arctic, the Serengeti, but he voted Republican and seemed not to want this messy, peopled world of ours at all. What he wanted was what he'd once had, what his grandparents had had on their outlying farms. Empty land. Land where the snow could start blowing and drift for twenty miles.

Down in the basement, Ray showed us his woodworking shop and pointed out the cherry chest of drawers he'd made.

"Next year," Lenore said, "maybe this time next year, you'll be making a crib."

"Yes?" Ray said. He looked from Walter to me and smiled broadly. "Yes? You're expecting?"

"Not yet," Walter said. "But we're hoping."

I slipped my arm through his. We might have a child, I thought there in that basement. Live in the dense network formed of our child's accomplishments. Buried in my mind was another, secret wish—if we had a child I might not have to go on to graduate school, might not have to work as Walter's helper for the rest of my life. Already, although I could hardly admit this to myself, I was losing interest in school. It seemed as if all I'd really wanted was to be able to walk through the woods and name every bird and tree, and somehow I hadn't understood that watching and naming was natural history, while picking and prying was real science. And I wasn't a scientist after all. Scientists trusted in planes—the curved shape of the airfoil, the stream of air bending over the top, rushing below, thrusting up. The air pushed; the plane flew; a cell revealed spindles and mitochondria and microtubules. Walter had showed me those things, but I had trouble believing in them.

And yet in that house, in that flat, plain land, everything felt simple and possible. We felt like a family there, and I could forget what our lives were like at home—Walter's driving ambitions and fussy ways, my secret discontents. I could even forget the dreams I sometimes had of Randy. I had chosen my life: adult, dignified, settled. And if I itched sometimes, if I ached from the confinement, I had Fargo and my dream of a family to anchor me.

A Black Harley Electra-Glide

When spring came, I still wasn't pregnant, and I began to worry.

"We've only been trying for eight months," Walter said. "That's nothing." He was calm about it, he was fine, but he began making love to me twice a week instead of once, and when his parents called he ducked their questions. "Don't worry," Lenore told me. "It'll happen when you least expect it. You have to relax." But then she'd follow up these soothing words with tales of women in her church who'd spent years and fortunes trying to conceive. Thermometers, ovulation charts, special douches and positions—all that lay ahead of us if my body failed, and then doctors, operations, eggs teased apart under a microscope and gently washed with sperm. "There's always a way," Lenore said as the months passed. "Always." She sent me bookmarks inscribed with prayers and words of comfort for the barren. *For God indeed punishes not nature, but sin,* read one. *And therefore, when He closes a womb, it is only that He may later open it more wondrously, and that all may know that what is born thereof is not the fruit of lust, but of the divine munificence.* The bookmarks made Walter fume.

"She's just trying to help," I told him.

"We don't need her help," said Walter. "We'll be fine. Once you graduate, you'll relax and it'll happen."

"You're right," I said. "That's probably it."

I had never told him about the abortion I'd had when I was married to Randy, or about the infection I'd had afterward; and although I dreamed about my lost child each night, more and more sorry for that life I'd rejected, by the time Walter and I were trying to make another life I couldn't confide in him. I'd lent my past actions so much weight by not disclosing them sooner that now, almost by accident, I had a big secret. Maybe a guilty secret—when I bent double once each month, stabbed by ovarian cramps, I refused to go to the doctor. "This is normal," I told Walter. "It's just the egg passing through." Meanwhile I was sure my insides had been scrambled and fused by my past mistakes, a nest of adhesions and scars and wounds, nothing left pink and shining.

As the spring wore on, I found myself making love by the calendar and not enjoying it at all, my pelvis propped up on pillows to help the sperm swim in. I worried about the thickness of my vaginal secretions and about the tilt of my uterus. I wondered about the patency of my fallopian tubes. All my attention was focused on my physiology, and I couldn't concentrate on school. My worst class was an upper-level population ecology course—half graduate students, half seniors like myself—which was taught by a pompous fool with whom Walter often collaborated. "I ought to drop the course," I'd told Walter. "It's making me tense." He'd pointed out that this was my last semester, that I needed the credits, and that my classmates would help me acclimate to graduate school. I'd applied, after all, under pressure from him—to his school, to his department. Of course I got in. I had good grades and great recommendations, and I didn't tell anyone I planned to drop out as soon as I got pregnant.

The only good thing about my bad course—the only good thing about spring—was Page. I met her the day the teacher lectured on cyclic population changes. "These are the snowshoe hares," he said, drawing a jagged graph on the board. "The population peaks every nine or ten years and then crashes." He drew another line that roughly followed the first. "These are the lynxes," he said. "Their population peaks about a year after the hares. Then it crashes, as they starve once the hares are gone."

The woman sitting next to me turned and whispered in my ear. "Excited?" she said. "This guy could make sex boring."

I had been lost in my own eggy thoughts, and when she spoke I was so startled I smiled. Page was a year or two younger than me, blond, sharp-featured, and bright, and when we had coffee together later she told me she was a first-year graduate student specializing in the lepidoptera.

"I'm only taking this course because it's required," she told me in the cafeteria. "That asshole, Tinbergen—he's never spent a day in the field in his life. Makes me sick, the way he goes on about lemmings and snowy owls like he ever actually *saw* any . . . God. This place. Where are you going when you graduate?"

"Here," I said. "I guess. Same department as you."

She groaned and then laughed. "Why would you want to come here?"

"I'm married to Walter Hoffmeier," I confessed.

Most of my classmates knew that; it was why they

avoided me. Page's eyebrows shot up. "Him?" she said. "No kidding. He's so much older . . ."

"It's not like he's ancient," I said. "You probably don't know him."

She laid a placating hand on my arm. "I don't, really," she said. "I'm sure he's nicer than he looks."

"He is," I said. "It's just that he's so private. He really only opens up to me—we pretty much keep to ourselves."

She made a wry face. "I bet. I was going to ask if you wanted to come to a party—a bunch of us first-year graduate students get together every Friday, and this week we're meeting at my place. But I guess you wouldn't want to come."

"I would," I said, surprising myself. "I'd like to."

"With Walter? That might not be so good."

"I'll leave him at home," I said. It was true that we kept pretty much to ourselves—Walter kept me so close to him that I'd had no chance to make friends my own age. But I yearned for some company just then, some entry into the graduate-school world I felt I was being forced into.

Page seemed ready to welcome me despite my connection to Walter, and all that week we sat together in class and mocked Professor Tinbergen's papery voice. "Animals associate in different ways," he said. He read directly from our textbook, his thin hand fussing with the buckle of his belt. "Varieties of association include mutualism, competition, commensalism, parasitism, and predation."

"Food and sex," Page whispered to me. "That's all he's saying—who they eat and who they fuck and how and when."

"Something you'd like to share with us?" Professor Tinbergen said.

"Not a thing," Page replied.

While he droned on, Page drew butterflies on a notebook page, fantastic creatures with humanoid eyes and legs and oversize antennae and ridiculous clothes, pompous creatures engaged in silly acts. One was a caricature of Tinbergen. One was the department chairman. One, inevitably, was Walter, a pair of wings drooping sadly from his thorax and scalpels bristling from his feet. I laughed at that, and then felt immediately guilty, but Page was so open and friendly at first that before I'd known her a week I'd told her entirely too much. When she asked me how I came to marry Walter I described our summer in the trailer at the reservoir, cutting up fish and weighing gonads. She contended that I'd been overwhelmed by all that biology, and I couldn't offer a better explanation.

Page told me tales about our classmates. "Stay away from Timmy," she said. "He gets weird when he drinks. John Webster sleeps in the woods for weeks at a time, watching hawks. Suzanne is married to Lon Brinkman, over in botany, but she's fooling around with Tony Baker. The one who works in Wasserman's lab?"

"I've seen him," I said; Tony was the student who'd worked with us at the reservoir and who had tried to invite me to the July Fourth celebration. My throat still got dry when I looked at him.

"They'll all be at the party," Page said. "You'll meet everyone."

It was easy enough to get Walter's permission to go—all I had to do was tell him it was a meeting of my fellow students. "So I'll know some people," I explained the evening of the party. "So I won't feel lost next fall."

"You know all the professors," he told me, straightening some piles of paper on his desk. "You've been having dinner with them for two years." Then he checked his calendar and looked at me sheepishly. "Tonight's one of our nights," he said, meaning I was mid-cycle. "Try not to be late?"

"I won't be," I said. "I just want to meet some of these people I'll be working with."

"Have a good time," he said.

I went off to Page's place alone. All the windows were open in her small apartment, letting in the warm April air. When I came up the stairs, I found only Page and a man in a black leather jacket, who had a beaked nose and a shock of dirty blond hair that fell in his eyes when he moved.

"Hey," this man said, fixing me with a hawk's predatory glare. "Fresh blood. Who's this?"

I blushed dark red. Before I could answer him, Page came out of the kitchen. Her hair was frizzed from the steam of the couscous she was cooking, and her breasts swung soft and loose under her Indian smock.

"Grace," she said. "Meet Jim. Jim, Grace." Jim was still staring at me and I was staring at him, my feet edging me closer and closer. I felt like I might kiss him any second, and that if I did it would only be an accident, something I couldn't help. Page smiled wickedly and ran her hand down Jim's back. "Jim's my little secret," she said. "He paints houses. He amuses me." She turned and headed for the kitchen again.

"Why don't you take her for a ride?" she called over her shoulder. "Keep her entertained until the others get here."

Jim laid his broad, warm hand on my shoulder. "Would you like that?" he said. "You want to be entertained?"

I nodded dumbly, trying not to shiver as he gathered up my long hair and twisted it into a rope.

"You're a pretty thing," he said. "Where'd Page find you?"

"In class," I said faintly.

"In class," he mocked, his voice as high and tremulous as mine. "Well, put your coat on, missy. We're going for a ride." He stomped down the stairs in his heavy black boots, leaving me to follow.

"Have a good time," Page called after me. "Don't do anything I wouldn't."

Her laugh followed me down the stairs. Outside, Jim was already sitting on a huge black Harley Electra-Glide with a headlight as big as a grapefruit and sleek, curved fenders.

"Hop on," he said, handing me a helmet. "Ever ride one of these?"

"Never," I lied, putting out of my mind the boys I had known in high school. I sat behind Jim and he pulled me close to his back.

"Settle in," he said. "Wrap your arms around me. All you have to do is remember to hold on tight and lean with me on the curves. Don't fight the machine. Don't fight me. It's like dancing. Like sex. You understand?"

I nodded and tucked my hair into the helmet. He jumped hard on the starter and then we were off. Through the back streets of Northampton, down by the railroad tracks and the warehouses; then up through the edge of the Smith College campus, startling pale, thoughtful girls; then into Florence, past the diner and around the square. Up Route 9, through the dark parking lot of a silent factory, down quiet residential streets. The engine roared. Fast, then faster, my chest mashed against his back, my hands clutched across his stomach, my hair tumbled from my helmet and whipping across my face; Jim shouting and laughing, taking corners hard, screaming at me to lean. Me leaning, finally screaming too, my mouth open wide and stretched as the night air roared past us and the buildings passed in a blur. When we screeched to a stop in front of Page's building I was trembling all over, and Jim bent with laughter when he pulled me off his machine.

"You liked that," he said. "You loved it." He pulled me roughly to him and I buried my face in his chest. He was very tall.

That was it. That was all that happened, but I felt as if I'd been in bed with him for a week. I walked up the stairs on shaky legs, acutely aware of Jim behind me, and when I entered the living room, now full of people and noise, I felt as exposed as if I'd shed my clothes on the ride. I met the rest of Page's friends but I hardly noticed them; I ate couscous and drank too much wine and tried to keep myself from creeping across the floor to Jim. All night long he watched me, smiling whenever he caught my eye, and when I finally got up to leave he smoothed my hair away from my cheek and ran his thumb along the curve of my ear before he turned away. For years after that I dreamed of his back: that back, that beautiful back. I went home to Walter that night, my knees rubbery with lust, and if ever I should have conceived a child it should have been then.

A Row of Glass Jars

That fall, I discovered that I couldn't share Walter's joys. I wanted to; I meant to. But once I entered graduate school, all I felt was duty, pressure, grinding work.

Biochemistry, embryology, research methods—everything suddenly seemed harder and much less fun than it had when I was an undergraduate. Hundreds of textbook pages blurred past me; grainy films flickered by; a fertilized egg cleaved into two, four, eight cells, formed the hollow ball known as the blastula, indented as if pressed by a thumb into the double-walled gastrula. Everything went by too fast. I grew weak and faint, stunned by all I didn't know, the mornings I sat in the lecture hall. When I went home to Walter at night, I lied through my teeth.

"It's fine," I told him. "The work's really interesting."

"Isn't it?" he'd say, his eyes sparkling. While I bent over my books he leaned over me, his chin in my hair and his hands warm in mine. "Isn't this *wonderful?*" he'd say. "I can still remember learning this for the first time. The archenteron, the blastopore, the growth of the neural plate . . ."

When I looked in his face I saw true joy, true excitement. Oh, he loved his work—and that was one of the things that had drawn me to him at first. Sometimes, when I wandered the halls of the zoology department, I'd stop outside his classroom and listen to his voice crackling with enthusiasm. But even with him to help me I fell behind. My teachers grew more and more distant, the students in my lab sections grew openly contemptuous, and Page and her friends, who had initially welcomed me, began to pull away.

My worst course was embryology, which confused me completely: an endless sequence of movements and changes to memorize. These cells move here, those move there, this turns into that and that into something else. An eye is derived from this structure, a finger from another. Black magic. When I said, "How? But *how* does this happen?" my teacher spread his hands in the air and said, "Answer that and you'd win a Nobel Prize. But you can't begin to ask *how* until you know the sequence of development as well as you know the alphabet. You're learning a *language* here. Vocabulary."

But I was stuck on grammar. He was trying to teach me "what" and I wanted "how" and "why," and our classroom became a battlefield. I grew to dread it, and as

I lost confidence there I dreaded, even more, the switch I had to make three times a week from student to student teacher.

Our department ran thirty sections of lab for Zoology 101; I had to teach three of these, as did all the graduate students. For weeks I'd stood in front of the blackboard, my hands shaking as I tried to discuss the basic properties of animal cells. I'd talked into my bosom, eyes lowered, head ducked, and I'd tried to make up for my lack of knowledge by covering the board with colored drawings. The students stared at me coldly in that huge dim room, squirming on the wooden stools that surrounded the lab benches, and when they grew bored they hung paper airplanes from the plastic human skeleton that guarded the door. They smirked and whispered among themselves when I put the wrong slides in the microscopes, the wrong transparencies in the overhead projectors, assigned the wrong workbooks. They yawned through the endless afternoons and galloped away when I ran out of breath hours before their labs were meant to end.

One November afternoon, after I'd stayed up for two nights studying for a huge embryology exam, I walked into the lab late and found all twenty students at the back of the room, clustered around the specimen jars arrayed on the windowsill. Pickled fetal pigs floated in cloudy liquid, next to pale corrugated brains and bifurcated sheep uteri, but the students weren't studying those. Instead, they were staring at the series of human embryos I'd always avoided. Brian Mankowski, a student from Boston whom I'd come to dislike for his slyness and stupidity, was perched on a stool and lecturing in my place.

"These are the results of abortions," he said. "Pure and simple. These are human children that someone killed and removed on purpose, and then pickled like cucumbers, and then sold to this department for money."

He looked up when I walked in, but he kept on talking. "This is an *out*rage," he said. "We should refuse to work in this room. The people who bought and sold these have no respect for human life, no respect for those of us who have accepted Christ and the holy scriptures. We should refuse to tolerate this."

One of the girls giggled nervously and a boy stabbed a pair of dissecting probes into the pockmarked black wax of a tray. "Brian," I said. "That's enough. We have work to do."

I knew I had never had any control over this group and that I was about to lose them for good. I tried to imagine how one of the other teaching assistants would handle the situation. They had tips and tricks and favorite students. They always seemed to know what to do.

"Tell me why we should put up with this," Brian said.

I searched my mind for what the department head had told us. "Because what you're saying isn't true," I said. "Those specimens are miscarriages—spontaneous abortions. They were already dead. They came from hospitals. It's perfectly legitimate."

I wasn't sure I believed this myself—the specimens disturbed me and I'd always avoided the back of the room where they stood. "They're the best way for you to understand the sequence of human development," I said. "They're meant to teach you respect for human life. Not to cheapen it—look at them. You can see how early they have a shape, hands, a heart. You can see what a miracle life is."

"They're pickled," Brian said. "Like meat. Where's the respect in that?"

On another day, I might have had an answer for him. But I was unfed, exhausted, wired from too much coffee, and when I looked at the jars again, at the gray, faded bodies with their folded knees, their shadowy faces, their eyes closed in endless sleep, I burst into tears. Brian was right; they were horrifying. Plastic models, pink and cheerful, would have served just as well.

The students moved silently toward their seats, leaving me alone with the jars. One of those embryos—fifty-six days, eight weeks—might have been the child I'd given up for Randy. A recognizable small person, with an enormous head, tiny arms and feet, a ghost of an ear, an eye. I had gone to the clinic alone, more frightened of the pain and invasion than of what I was actually doing. The doctor had been quiet, steady, slow. "I'm removing the products of conception," he'd said in his soft, flat voice. "Breathe slowly. It won't hurt."

It hadn't hurt much then, but it hurt now. I looked at the jar, and as I did my right side was stabbed with a pain so sharp and startling that I fell to the floor.

I woke to a ring of faces above me. Students, the department chairman, Page. Walter. "Grace," Walter was saying. "Grace?"

"I think it's my appendix," I said weakly. It might have been; the pain was in the right place. But I knew it wasn't. It had to be my ovary, struggling to pass another egg through the tangled web of tissue. I would have welcomed appendicitis: let it rupture, let it burst. Dark poisons spreading through me, an operation and a stay in the hospital between cool white sheets. No classes, no tests, no labs. I fainted again.

What I got for my pains was an evening in the Emergency Department at Cooley-Dickinson, just long enough for the doctors to rule out appendicitis, a strangulated bowel, gallstones, pyelonephritis. Just long enough for the resident gynecologist to examine me and to announce gravely, in Walter's presence, that I had chronic pelvic inflammatory disease that had probably damaged me already.

"Is that serious?" Walter said. His face was tired and drawn in the cruel hospital light. He'd left a class behind, I knew. And a grant that was due, and a ringing phone, and a thesis committee. I'd never been sick before, in all our time together, and I was surprised how much I'd frightened him. "I hate hospitals," he'd muttered, as we waited in the curtained cubicle. He'd rubbed his fingers along my arm, stroking, smoothing, soothing. Soothing himself as much as me.

"It's not an emergency," the doctor said. "She fainted from the pain of a cramp, and there's nothing acute going on. But these chronic inflammations are serious enough. She needs long-term antibiotic therapy, and frequent exams. But she doesn't need to stay here now."

"Thank you," Walter said. He let go of my arm and stood to shake the doctor's hand.

The doctor smiled and turned to me, and Walter moved away to gather my clothes. "Have you ever had an abortion?" the doctor asked.

I made a face at him, trying to signal that yes I had and no, I didn't want to discuss it. The doctor read only half my face. "It's no crime," he said gently.

Walter looked over his shoulder at me. "I had one a long time ago," I muttered. The white paper drape in my lap was as stiff as a placemat.

"What?" Walter said carefully. He looked from the doctor to me.

"Before I knew you," I said.

The doctor made some notes in a chart. "Have you had trouble conceiving since then?"

I answered yes again. Walter dropped into an orange plastic chair and buried his head in his hands. He was so upset that he couldn't spare a word to comfort me, and when I was discharged we drove home in silence. He put me in bed and draped a heating pad over my sore side, but he wouldn't look me in the eye. "I can't believe you never told me," he said hours later.

I thought of all the other things I'd never said. "It wasn't your business," I said. "I didn't even know you then."

"So?" he said. "So what else don't I know about you?"

"I hate school," I said. "I'm not going back." I pressed my hand to my mouth as if I could stuff those words back in. They surprised me at least as much as they did Walter.

He didn't believe me at first. He thought I was sick, that I had a fever, that I was just run-down, and when I went to drop out he made me take a leave of absence instead. "Health problems," I wrote on the withdrawal form, and Walter chose to believe that. Perhaps I believed it in part myself. Certainly I grew pale and queasy when I thought of returning to that lab and that row of jars, and I had as much trouble as Walter facing the idea that all that had drawn us together was falling apart. When I told him embryology reminded me of medieval cosmology, all description and airy theory, he looked at me as though I'd set a flag on fire.

"I want us to visit another doctor," he announced, after a week of uneasy silences and bitter meals. "A fertility specialist."

"Why?" I said. "It's only been a year. And the doctor didn't say I *couldn't* conceive—he just asked if we'd had any trouble."

Walter drew himself up and tucked in his chin. "The implication was clear," he said. "You had this abortion. You had an infection. You didn't take care of yourself. We need to know what our chances are. And somebody here has to take some responsibility."

I was in no position to argue with him. I'd left school, betrayed him, lied to him; after I'd been taking antibiotics for six weeks, I went to the new doctor as meekly as a lamb. I had test after test, each more humiliating than the last, and after the laparoscopy the doctor finally said, "Your left ovary's dysfunctional. But your right one doesn't seem to have been affected at all. You're producing viable eggs."

"So?" I said.

"So, you've been having unprotected intercourse for—what? A year now? You should be pregnant. Let's check Walter out."

"Walter?" I said. "But Walter's fine."

"Just to be sure," he said.

We had tested my urine, my blood, and my tubes; now we tested Walter's urine and blood and finally his semen. The doctor spent two weeks trying to convince Walter to submit to this indignity. A magazine full of naked women, a darkened room, a small plastic jar. A sperm sample. A week later, Walter and I returned to the doctor's office and sat in upholstered chairs pulled up to a broad teak desk.

"Grace's infection has responded well to therapy," the doctor said. "Her left ovary is scarred, but her right one is fine. There's no reason she can't conceive in time."

Walter turned to me and touched my arm, a light tap meant to indicate his forgiveness and to erase all his silent accusations.

"Unfortunately," the doctor said. He cleared his throat and turned to Walter. "Unfortunately, your sperm count is extremely low. But there are still possibilities. We can chart Grace's ovulations carefully, to maximize the chances of successful intercourse. And there are some techniques we can explore to increase the number and motility of your sperm . . ."

We left the office in a gray, dazed silence. Outside, the streets seemed filled with parents and children, pregnant women, young men proudly carrying infants in canvas pouches pressed against their chests. Two boys flew by on skateboards and Walter, clipped by a set of rear wheels, stumbled and fell to the ground. He tore his trousers and skinned his knee, and when I tried to help him up he batted my hand away.

"I'm sorry," I said, as gently as I could. "It'll be all right."

"Just leave me alone," he shouted. "Just leave me be."

All around us people turned and stared curiously. Walter lay crumpled on the curb, dabbing at his knee with his handkerchief. I leaned over him, pale and troubled, while the leaves in the gutters moved gently with the wind.

A Yellow Tie

After that fall, the balance of power in our household shifted slightly. I had betrayed biology and the academic world; I had concealed my abortion and my failure to love science. But. But. But it was Walter's body that kept us from making a child. We had come to a joint in our marriage, a sort of elbow where all that we'd wanted and been took off in a new direction, and nothing was easy between us after that.

Walter called me deceitful. I called him cold. He was hurt that I didn't want to be his assistant and student forever, and I was hurt that all he wanted of me was that, and we weren't able to make the child who might have bridged our differences. And we never talked about any of this, because Walter became famous that year. The work that made his reputation had actually been completed at the Quabbin, where the bats had driven us together. But in the two and a half years since then, Walter had published ten papers with my help, and the media people seized on him as acid rain became hot news. It turned out that Walter's sharply boned face and expressive hands looked good on TV.

I'd drawn the elegant graphs linking reproductive cycles and lake acidity. I'd translated his scribbled notes into clean, clear sentences, deciphered the cryptic instructions each journal gave for the preparation of manuscripts, typed the final drafts. When Walter practiced his talks, I'd been his audience, following his retractable pointer as he traced his way through the figures projected on our darkened living room wall. I'd been the kind of assistant every scientist dreams of—docile, diligent, cheap—and I stood aside as Walter was tenured, promoted to full professor, and placed in charge of a laboratory with six graduate students, three postdoctoral fellows, and a budget that ran into hundreds of thousands of dollars each year.

All through our marriage I'd kept Walter's house warm and welcoming, cared for his clothes, paid his bills, dealt with minor repairs. I'd shopped and cooked and cleaned and entertained his students, made feasts when scientists visited from other countries. I'd been Walter's wife before, but I hadn't been *only* his wife—although Walter's colleagues had gossiped (I was young, I was blond, I wasn't Eileen, whom most of them had known), while I was still in school they had treated me with the same fond encouragement they gave their own students, tempered with the extra respect due Walter's mate. But after I dropped out, no one seemed to know how to handle me. Walter became a power just about the time I gave up science, and his colleagues assessed the situation and adjusted their attitudes accordingly.

Oh, my social stock plummeted that year. Suddenly I was just a wife, just a second wife at that, and our guests gently condescended to me when a quirk of dinner seating or party movement forced them near me. "But what are you *doing?*" the bolder ones asked.

"Resting," I answered sometimes. "Recuperating. Taking a break."

When I felt less sure of myself, I said, "I'm looking for a job."

When I'd had too much to drink and felt snippy and cross, I lied and said, "I'm trying to get pregnant."

That always shut people up, and as the year wore on they seemed to get used to my idleness. I painted the living room and redid the downstairs bathroom; once in a while I helped Walter prepare a manuscript. I threw elaborate dinner parties and tried recipes I'd gotten from library books: Moroccan Chicken. Moussaka. Pot au Feu. In March, Walter said, "You know, you only took a leave of absence. You could reapply for the fall," and he frowned when I told him I wasn't ready yet.

"I have a lot to think about," I said.

"Like what?"

"Like what I'm going to do with the rest of my life. If we're not going to have kids . . ."

He paled, and I knew he felt reproached again. "We could adopt," he said. "If there's nothing else you want in this world . . ."

But I couldn't imagine how any child not our flesh and blood could fill the gap between us. We set that question aside, and as Walter's life grew even busier, we stopped talking about it. Finally Walter arranged for me to see a therapist at the University Health Service. "I'm worried about you," he said. "I'm worried about us. We need to work out this baby thing, and you need to decide what you want to do . . ."

I went, but I hated it. My doctor was a woman, dry and aloof, whom I couldn't warm up to at all. Dr. Amadon sat in a swivel chair, her short legs neatly crossed, and she asked me where I saw myself in twenty years.

"On the street," I told her bitterly. And that was true,

that was all I could see. When I thought of Page, whom I no longer saw, I imagined her sailing through graduate school, through a fellowship somewhere, finally off in a lab of her own and running a part of the world the way Walter did. But when I pictured the life ahead of me, I saw nothing. "Wearing all my clothes at once," I said. "With everything I own in a shopping bag."

"That's what you want?" she said. "To be a bag lady?"

"That's what I see," I told her. "I'm twenty-seven already. I'm not trained to do anything. Everything I have belongs to Walter."

I never told her about the voices I was beginning to hear inside my head, or about the sense I sometimes had, walking down the street, that my skin had turned permeable. I felt myself leaking out my pores, and I felt other lives leaking in, and it scared me so badly I threw all my energy into finding something to do. Work, I thought. That was what I needed. Any work, anything that would catch me the way Walter's work had caught him and provide that crisp glaze of purpose and separateness.

On my third visit, Dr. Amadon asked me why I stayed with Walter, and instead of answering I left her for good. I went out to the car Walter had bought me, a new orange Subaru with a flashy white stripe down the side, and I turned up the radio and headed for Belchertown, for the tip of the reservoir. Since the doctor had delivered his bleak news, I'd taken to keeping secret foods in the car, which I used as a mobile diner; as I drove I ate my way steadily through a box of chocolate-mint Girl Scout cookies and thought how even the girl who'd sold them to me had something to do.

Who could answer the question Dr. Amadon had asked? I parked in the woods near the reservoir and remembered all the nights Walter had traveled, when alone in our bed I'd touched myself and come coldly, silently, my small shudder damped by my blanket of flesh. When we fought we fought in silence, never speaking what we meant, and whatever glue held us together couldn't be named. Three crows argued in the trees near me, their harsh calls echoing against the car windows, and two deer emerged into the clearing and then froze. On the blank margins along the back of the cookie box I wrote down their names: *Odocoileus virginianus*. Then I wrote down the crows, *Corvus brachyrhynchos*, and the names of the trees and the ferns and the small mammals and the geese passing overhead. All the names I could remember, all I'd learned, and when I was done I drove home and didn't tell Walter for weeks that I'd stopped seeing Dr. Amadon. I left our house each Tuesday at the appointed time, and then I drove to the Quabbin or to the Chesterfield Gorge and I made species lists. I grew calmer, even a little slimmer. It wasn't much of an occupation, but it was something. Walter said the doctor must be doing me some good.

"She's all right," I told him. "We've been talking about what I might do for work."

Which was not completely false—I had been thinking about that, thinking hard. I spent hours poring over the "Help Wanted" sections of the Springfield and Northampton papers, trying to think what I might do. There was secretarial work, always possible—I'd survived the Swedenborgian accountants in Philadelphia. The phone company—during high school, I'd spent a summer trapped in a room full of hot, fat women, plugging cords into black panels, pulling them out, timing calls, and I knew I could do that in my sleep. I could do laboratory work for Walter, who'd offered to bring me back into his lab as a salaried technician, or I could try for any one of those gray jobs that required no obvious qualifications. Receptionist, waitress, sales clerk, assistant of one sort or another. The ad that finally caught my eye early in January was encouragingly vague:

> Are you bright, creative, talented, energetic, and under-employed? Have you had trouble finding a career that suits your unique capabilities? I'm looking for an assistant—preferably female, 25 to 40—and you could be the singular person I want. P.O. Box 6046.

I spent three days writing a flashy letter. I mentioned my art background and left out Randy; mentioned my biology training and the work at Quabbin but left out Walter. I said I was a spectacular cook, an avid reader, an appreciator of Oriental art and antiques (I left out Uncle Owen), and a former graduate student who'd left school to explore the universe on my own. I exaggerated wildly and appropriated talents belonging to the men I'd known, and a week later I received a bright yellow envelope in return. Inside was a single sheet of heavy, electric-pink letterhead. **A L I V E** was stamped across the top in bold black letters, followed by the outline of a lightbulb in place of an exclamation point. The message read:

> Dear Grace—
> Certain I am that this isn't (real!?) news to you, yet I'll say it again—You must be described as a *phenomenon*, and not in terms known to the average being (alive!) in this Universe. We are the source of our knowledge—I have no choice but to follow my intuition and reach for a certain passing (flashy!) star. Contact me at the number below, and we'll arrange a (stellar!) meeting. Which will be (I'm certain!) for our mutual best.
> Live!
> Rollo Carlson

Printed below was a California address and an italicized line in quotation marks: "*You are the source of all thought.*"

I called, of course. Who could resist? I reached a smooth-voiced woman, who told me to meet Rollo Carlson in a restaurant in Northampton. "He'll be wearing a dark suit," the woman said. "Pink shirt, yellow tie. An unusual pin in his tie." Somehow I knew the pin would be in the shape of a tiny lightbulb.

"I have long blond hair," I told the woman nervously. "I'll be wearing . . ."

"Don't tell me," she said. "He'll know you by your aura. Be there at one."

I wore a flashy teal dress with a white linen collar and cuffs, long silver earrings, low shoes. Some combination, I thought, of the exotic and the practical. At twelve-thirty I walked into the restaurant and took a table in the far corner from which I could see the door, promising myself I'd slink away if Rollo looked too strange.

The restaurant was almost empty. Two Smith girls tore at croissants and discussed their love lives in shrill voices. A woman in her early forties held hands surreptitiously with a man in his late twenties. In the back, two of the waiters read the paper and the bored hostess sat at the cash register, filing her nails.

My heart was pounding with excitement. I ordered a turkey club sandwich, just to calm myself, and then an ice cream soda to wash it down. In the opposite corner, a pudgy woman with an unlined face and startling white hair mashed her spoon in a brownie covered with vanilla ice cream and hot fudge sauce. She glanced at her watch; I glanced at mine. She pulled out a compact and checked her careful makeup and adjusted the beads at her neck. I looked at my reflection in the back of a spoon. The Smith girls left; the middle-aged woman at the front table withdrew her hand from her companion's and bent her head and wept. At one, the door opened and a swarthy man with a big nose and a mane of swept-back hair walked in.

Dark suit, pink shirt, yellow tie. I smiled, half rose, upset a glass of water. Across the room, the woman with the white hair smiled, half rose, twisted her fingers in her beads. Rollo walked to a table in the center of the room and beckoned to both of us. "Connie," he said in a low voice. "Grace. Come sit, my dears."

We made our way nervously toward him, eyeing each other. Rollo introduced us. "Grace Hoffmeier," he said. "Meet Connie Chrisman." He beamed at us, revealing huge white teeth. "Two phenomenal women in one place," he said. "Remarkable! We're all *alive!*" Then he folded his arms across his chest and waited.

We didn't say anything. We sat; he sat. Just when the silence was becoming truly uncomfortable, Rollo said, "Well—you know who *I* am—I'm sure you've read my books and familiarized yourself with the A L I V E! movement."

Connie and I shifted in our seats. The A L I V E! movement? Rollo's books? "Time is precious," Rollo said. "Time is *alive!* I was so impressed with both your applications that I decided to learn about you by listening in as you talk to each other. Let me see the spirit within you. Let me see how you exist in the Universe! All that lives is *alive!* and you are the source of all life. Begin."

He was so dark, so strange, sitting there in his hot pink shirt and his yellow tie and the tiny pin proclaiming his Alive!ness. I looked at Connie and Connie looked at me, and then she rose and slung her purse over her shoulder and picked up her coat.

"If you're *alive,*" she said to Rollo, "I'd rather be dead."

Briefly—as I had when I'd first met Page, when Page had mocked Professor Tinbergen—I thought of Zillah. I looked at Connie and saw, not a middle-aged woman whose life had somehow reached a point where she was interviewing for a job in a dark restaurant, but a girl who'd tried to counter the world by growing wings. Before she could vanish, I grabbed my things and followed her. Once we were outside we leaned against the door and laughed together.

"Christ," Connie said, wiping her eyes. "Did you know?"

"I never *heard* of him," I said. "Or his books, or the movement—I was just trying to find a job."

"Me too," Connie said. "I should have known from the ad . . ."

We laughed some more, and then she asked me if I wanted an ice cream. When I said yes, we drove to Friendly's and ordered enormous sundaes, consoling ourselves for our lost hopes. Connie was Walter's age, but we had so much in common that our age difference hardly mattered at first. "My kids are teenagers," she said. "They're done with me. They think I'm a fossil. And my husband—he's over in History. Full professor, tenured. Reformation."

"Oh?" I said.

"Zwingli," she said airily, waving her plump arm. "Melanchthon. All that stuff."

She told me her hair had turned white when she was my age, and that she had a degree in home economics from a Baptist college in Texas. "I taught junior high for a while," she said. "But I had to quit." She leaned over her mocha praline sundae and peered through her heavy glasses. Her eyes were large and startling, almost violet. "I have this little weight problem, and all that cooking in class . . ."

"I failed Home Ec," I told her. "In seventh grade. My teacher wore false eyelashes and spent all her time trying to show us how to use lip pencil and waggle our butts like the models do. Doreen Sandowsky and I brought a shoebox full of field mice into the kitchen and let them loose, and Mrs. Kriner broke her ankle trying to jump up on the windowsill. She flunked us both. I weighed a hundred and eighty-five pounds my junior year of high school. Then I got thin, then I was fat again, then thin again. Now this."

Connie laid her soft hand over mine. I guessed her weight at a hundred and forty. Small shoulders, large breasts, most of her weight in her hips. "Diets," she said. "I've tried them all."

"Who hasn't?"

"You're married?"

I told her about Walter. "Zoology," I said. "Lake ecology, acid rain . . ."

"Children?"

"We can't. Walter . . ."

"School?"

"I quit," I said. "More than a year ago. I've been trying to figure out what to do since then."

She smiled at me fondly and pushed up her glasses. "So," she said. "We're bright, not bad-looking, educated. We live nice lives. Why are we chasing after stupid jobs? Why aren't we having fun?"

"Because we're not doing anything?"

"That's right," she said. "What we want is something to *do*."

What we did, in the few months we had together before Connie got a job in a New Age bookstore, was to get together twice a week for lunch. We took turns cooking; we turned out exotic meals and then ate them secretly, in the middle of the day. While we cooked and ate we picked our lives apart, as if going over our old tracks would show us where to go next; and so when I was browsing through the *Times* one Sunday and came across a review of Randy's first one-man show in New York, it seemed natural to save it and show it to Connie. She dipped her finger in the sauce that had enveloped our Thai chicken, and she said, "You were *married* to him?"

Together, while the coffee burbled and plunked in the pot, we studied the photo of Randy and of one of his pictures: an abstracted, wildly skewed view of the block of rowhouses where we'd lived. He'd turned the people who walked our street into cockroaches, earwigs, city bugs; the sky was a jagged field of blue and green. "What a nutball," Connie said. "You sure know how to pick them."

"It's true," I said. "I really do." Randy had earrings in both ears and hair so long it fell over his shoulders; beneath a leather vest his chest was bare. His thumbs were hooked in his belt and his fingers pointed toward his groin. He looked dangerous, even deranged, wholly improbable as a candidate for fatherhood—but the article said he shared a loft with a set designer and their infant daughter, Persia.

"Persia?" Connie said. "What kind of a name is that?"

"Maybe her mother picked it," I said. The woman had nerve, I thought. Enough to pick a name like that; enough to force Randy to keep their child. She had everything I lacked.

A Bowl of Neon Tetras

I ended up with a cheap aquarium full of fish. I bought them to comfort me after Connie found a job and we had to give up our lunches, but my first tank was a disaster. The plants died. Algae flourished. The fins of my angelfish molded and tore within days. A sleek black-and-silver creature, which I'd been unable to resist at the pet store, turned out to be a fierce and undiscriminating predator. After I bought him I woke each morning to find one fish gone, two, three, until finally I had only him, cruising sullen and big-eyed in my tank. I gave him back to the pet store and tried again, and my second time I bought only neon tetras, which were harmless and easy to keep.

Walter was writing a textbook then, the *Introduction to Ecosystems* that would seal his fame, and while I drew the figures for his manuscript I watched my fish swim back and forth and waited for them to tell me what to do. When I saw Page at departmental parties, when I ran into Connie at the store, I came home and told my fish how outcast I felt. When my family visited and my brother's twins snapped the stems from my wineglasses, I whispered my rage to the fish. I bought new copies of the books Chuck and Mark and I had once read together, and on the nights Walter worked late I sat by the tank and read out loud. But the books had gone dead and had nothing to say to me.

Uncle Owen died that February. He went out one morning to pick up a paper and a blood vessel burst in his head, felling him before he reached the street in front of his Cambridge house. By the time Dalton, his current companion, reached him, he was already gone.

"He died an easy death," Dalton told me over the phone. "We have to be happy with that." But it was hard to be happy with anything. At the funeral, Dalton laid his head on my shoulder and cried, and I cried too. I sobbed, I gasped, I moaned. The two of us made a spectacle in that quiet church, where all the rest of my family sat dry-eyed and stony-faced. Walter made comforting noises and passed me his handkerchief, but I turned away from him.

Five years of Christmas dinners had not made Walter

and Uncle Owen friends, and so each time I'd visited Uncle Owen and Dalton I'd left Walter in Sunderland. Which had never been a hardship; Uncle Owen and Dalton had treated me like a princess. We had strolled down Newbury Street together and window-shopped. We'd had tea at the Ritz-Carlton. I'd had my hair done in fancy salons while the two men looked on and gave advice. We'd gone to auctions and bid on Sarouks and Tabrizes and fine old Isaphans, and then returned to Uncle Owen's tiny shop and consoled ourselves for the bargains we'd missed. Back at his house, he'd shown me some of the priceless objects he'd bought so cheaply during the siege of Beijing, and then we'd sat in his living room, drinking port and eating the savories Dalton had made. We had danced to Judy Garland records, and when it was late enough, when we'd had enough to drink, we had sometimes talked about Walter and about my inability to carve out a life of my own.

"You're so *smart*," Uncle Owen used to say to me. "There's a million things you could do . . ."

He and Dalton proposed handfuls of job ideas and I rejected them. "Too easy," I said of some; "too hard," of others. Too dull, too repetitive, too much travel, too much work—what I was, although I couldn't tell Uncle Owen, was too scared. Walter's wild success, now that our lives had fractured, seemed somehow to guarantee my failure, and I couldn't imagine finding work that wouldn't seem trivial next to his.

After the funeral, we all went back to Uncle Owen's house. Dalton had done his best, laid out Scotch and sherry, cheese straws and scallop-stuffed pastry shells, homemade angelfood cake. But no one was comfortable. No one in my family seemed to know what Dalton was doing there. They thought of him—they wanted to think of him—as someone who had worked for Uncle Owen and no more. My mother asked him point-blank what he was doing there.

"I *live* here," Dalton said, and then his kind face crumpled. He was thirty-five then but looked ten years younger.

"You used to," my mother said. "I mean, live-in help is one thing, but . . ."

I wrapped my arm around Dalton's waist and watched as my mother moved away and toured the living room, fingering the heavy drapes and the jade animals and the celadon bowls and jars and the lovely old rugs. "All this stuff," she said, almost to herself. Dalton and I looked at each other and winced when she picked up a willowy porcelain figurine. "And then all that stuff in the shop . . ."

We knew what she was thinking. My father was Uncle Owen's only nephew, and my mother had every reasonable expectation that all this—the house, the shop, the furnishings—would fall to my father and her. Finally she'd be able to live the way she thought she'd always been meant to. Finally, my father was going to come through.

I don't think my father even thought about it. He'd been as dry-eyed as my mother and Toby throughout the funeral, but his face was creased with grief and I knew he was mourning the end of his real family. Mumu gone, now Owen; me as distant as if I'd married an Arab and moved to Abu Dhabi. Him in that house in Westfield with only his bitter wife for company, and once each weekend a visit from Toby and Linda and the kids. He sat heavily in a green Victorian chair much too small for him, and while the sun set he stared out the window and ate cheese straws absently.

I wouldn't have minded if everything had gone to him, but Uncle Owen surprised us one last time. Months later, when the estate was settled, we found out that Uncle

Owen had left ten thousand dollars to my father and an equal amount to Toby. The rest, the bulk of the estate, he'd split between Dalton and me. Dalton got the house,

> in which I hope you live (Uncle Owen had written), long, happily, with the companion of your choice. May you be as lucky as me.

Dalton also got the shop and all its contents. I got everything stored in the warehouse in Natick—all the pieces Uncle Owen had accumulated over the years, which he'd used to restock the shop whenever he ran low—and a fair bit of money he'd salted away.

> I would invest the money (he'd written to me). Although of course you may do as you wish. But I hope you invest it wisely, in your own name, not Walter's, and that you use the proceeds to get on your feet. Consider a visit to China—I have always regretted not returning. You would be happy there. If you go, visit the Forbidden City for me.
>
> Keep the antiques if you can—you know which ones are good, and their value will only increase. Remember that I have always loved you.

"He meant that," Dalton told me, when I made my last visit to him. "You were always his favorite."

"But I never did anything," I said. "I only got to college because he sent me, and I made a mess of that—and then Randy, and Walter, and look at me now . . . I never know what it is I want to do."

"You're a late bloomer," Dalton said. "Owen used to tell me how he'd been the same way, thrashing around for years before he finally figured out who he was."

"I wish I'd known him then."

"He always had faith in you." Dalton smiled and

touched my hair. "There's something here in the house I know he wanted you to have." He went into the living room and returned with a big glass bowl I'd always admired. Narrow-mouthed, melon-shaped, with a filigree silver rim; Uncle Owen had always kept flowers in it.

"It's a fish bowl, really," Dalton said. "He picked it up in Hong Kong years ago. It was meant to house one prize goldfish, but we were laughing together one night after you'd told us about your first aquarium, and Owen said we ought to give you this. It's older than the three of us put together."

I drove home with the precious bowl cradled in styrofoam and the lawyer's list of my inheritance in my purse. The bowl was thick and slightly uneven and rested on a carved rosewood base, and when I walked in the door with it, Walter's mouth dropped open.

"That's beautiful," he said. "That must be worth a fortune."

"It's for my fish," I said. I filled the bowl with distilled water and scooped my flock of neon tetras from my ugly aquarium into it. Immediately the fish looked serene and proud.

"What a nice thing for him to leave you," Walter said. And he meant that, I think; there was no greed in him. He'd always been proud of his ability to provide for us.

"Wait," I said. I showed him the lawyer's papers. Those sums of money, invested here and there; the catalog of rugs and screens and vases and bowls and dainty figurines, all labeled and numbered and waiting for me in Natick.

"I want to invest the money," I said. "That's what Uncle Owen asked me to do. I want to move the antiques here."

"Here?" Walter said.

I looked around and saw for the first time that we might have a problem. The house was full of his and Eileen's things. We had room to add a bowl of fish, but hardly more than that.

"We'll get rid of some things," I said firmly. "*Make* room. I want Uncle Owen's stuff near me."

Walter puffed up. "This is *my* house," he started, but then he backed down when he saw my face. "I mean, it's *our* house, but you know—we're all settled here. We don't need anything. We're comfortable."

We argued long into the night and all the next day, and when we got nowhere we retreated into our customary silences. Walter won, in the end: he refused to have the house cluttered up with what he referred to as "all that Oriental stuff."

I smiled at him when he said that, because I'd already hatched a plan. "Fine," I told him. "If that's what you want." I took the money Uncle Owen had left me, and I bought another house.

A Light Like a Laser

My house was run-down, almost falling down, with a leaky roof and a crumbling chimney and ancient wiring. But it sat on a ridge overlooking the river, and it was clean and cheap and spacious and had pleasant lines and a dry basement. It couldn't be lived in right away, but I didn't care; I never had any intention of living there. The house was for my furnishings, not for me, and at first I only meant to use it as storage space.

I had all Uncle Owen's treasures shipped there from the warehouse in Natick, and as the men carried the crates to the basement I checked them off against my list. The rugs were rolled in brown paper, the screens were boxed, the fragile porcelains and vases were double-crated, and the furniture was draped with white canvas. I couldn't see what anything was and could only match the numbers on the parcels to the numbers on my list. I'd started the day in a hum of exhilaration, but as the parcels vanished into the basement, their contents unseen and unappreciated, I began to wonder what the point of this had been. That night, when I returned home, I was depressed.

Walter was already furious—he hated the house, and hated that I'd gone and bought it without him. He hated the time I'd spent arranging the closing, seeing lawyers, passing papers. His book was due at the publisher's that summer, and I'd been less and less able to help him; and when I came home that night and said, "This isn't what I wanted at all. I can't even see what I've got," he blew up.

"What did you expect?" he said, scratching at his neck. He'd just finished writing a huge grant application, and he'd developed eczema from the stress. "What difference does it make whether the stuff's in a warehouse in Natick or in a basement in Whately? If you'd listened to me in the first place . . ."

I told him what I'd been thinking in the car. "I'm going to renovate it," I said. "Fix the whole thing up, decorate it, and then furnish it with the stuff in the crates."

"That's good," he said. "That's great. Then what?"

"Then I'll see what I feel like," I said. "Maybe I'll turn the house into a shop like Uncle Owen's. Maybe I'll sell it. I'll see."

Walter hardly spoke to me for a month. He was writing about food chains, coprophages, nitrogen-fixing bacteria; he'd hung the walls of his office with scribbled flowcharts and food webs that were screaming to be redrawn. When I went to him for some plumbing advice he looked meaningfully at the walls and refused to help me.

"*I* don't know," he said. "How would I know these things? Eileen and you have always taken care of whatever broke."

"But this is interesting," I told him, turning the pages of a home-repair handbook. "Remember when you first started teaching me biology, and I was so excited? This is just as interesting. We could learn it together."

"You're ruining your life," he said. "First you drop out of school. Now you won't help with my book. Before you know it, you'll have blown everything your uncle left you and you'll have nothing to show for it."

I was hurt by Walter's lack of interest—as he, I suppose, was hurt by mine—but I went ahead with the renovation anyway. At a small dinner at the Faculty Club, I overheard two women I'd always avoided discussing shingles, and when I asked them if they knew a good roofer they looked at me with sudden interest. We pulled our chairs together and talked about slate and cedar shakes, detabbing, nails, cements. They gave me a name, the roofer came; the roofer suggested a man who could refinish floors. The floor man knew a good painter. The painter knew a good electrician. The electrician knew a plumber and a mason and a carpenter, and by the following winter, after nine months of delays and reversals and small disasters, the house was almost done. It stood clean and sturdy and functional, the oak floors smooth and bright again, the moldings and woodwork refinished, the roof and chimney tight. The outside was white with black shutters and trim, the way it had been a hundred years ago. When spring came, and I had only the interior walls to refinish, I started bringing up Uncle Owen's things.

As I unwrapped and uncrated the objects, bringing up treasures one by one, I was amazed again by Uncle Owen's eye. Lacquer tables, black and silky; gilt mirrors carved like bamboo. Twelve fret-back Georgian dining-room chairs. A bronze Japanese wind god, cases of blue-and-white export ware, carved cinnabar floor screens, red-lacquer panels inset with hardstone and jade. A Japanese folding screen with a flock of sparrows and leafy twigs scattered on gold foil, a pair of Victorian slipper chairs, an eighteenth-century marquetry chest. An umbrella stand painted with dragons and scrolling flowers. A celadon lamp with an ivory silk shade, more and more. I bought books and read about what I had and learned the vocabulary: urn finials. Scroll-carved chamfered corners. Plinth bases, dentil-molded cornices, trellis-diaper borders. Names I learned as easily as I'd once learned the names of birds and fish.

At night I came home and tried to explain this all to Walter, but I couldn't interest him. I sat in one chair, flipping through the latest issue of *Antiques and Collectibles Guide* and murmuring magic words to myself. Cloisonné. Coromandel lacquer. Underglaze. Across the table from me, Walter wrote about the forests of the southern Appalachians. "Food webs are enormously complex there," he said. "The black bear, at the top, rips up trees and logs and digs out honeycomb and eats acorns and berries and drops seeds in his scat that spread the vegetation."

"Balloon-back side chairs," I said. "Would you look at these?"

"Nurse logs," Walter replied.

We spoke in different languages and couldn't seem to translate for each other; we lived like well-bred roommates. I worked, he worked, we cut deals on separate phones; he spent a few evenings a week in the lab and I spent a few at my house. When we crawled into bed at night we were tired but satisfied, and we had things to tell each other and excuses—reasonable, adult excuses—when our lovemaking didn't go well or didn't go at all. We were tired, we said. We were getting older. Our bodies were altering. And after a while it hardly mattered that we wore pajamas to bed and hugged in ways that brought only innocuous body parts together. Our bodies took care of themselves. Sleep made us strangers to each other, and when I woke sometimes, trembling and hot, from nightmares in which my new house burned and collapsed into a steaming cellar, I could often stroke my unconscious husband into surprising life.

Once in a while I stopped to wonder what this was, to worry about what happens to couples who carry on when there's nothing left between them but a piece of paper and routine, but I pushed those thoughts aside and concentrated on finishing the house. I had nothing to furnish a kitchen or a bedroom or a bath, but I had Tabrizes and Sultanabads and Herizes and Agras, enough to strew across every room. I had vases and pitchers and platters to set in every niche and windowsill. I still didn't know what I meant to do with the house, but I painted the dining-room walls lacquer red and put pale-green grasscloth in the living room.

About then, in early May, the realtors started dropping by. Women, mostly, in low heels and tailored skirts and jackets and quiet blouses. They knocked at the door and then walked in, cards in their outstretched hands, and as the rooms fell into place, the right chairs on the right rugs, the right tables crowned with the right lamps and jars, they went from saying, "Oh—I just dropped in because I was curious," to "Oh. Would you be interested in selling?"

"I don't think so," I said at first. "These were my great-uncle's things."

"Not the things," the realtors said. "The *house*. It'd show so well with all your lovely things in it, and you've done such a great job . . ."

But I wasn't done, I wasn't ready to let it go. I was lost

in the language of things, so entranced by what I'd done that I'd suddenly realized I could do this as a career. I could do to other houses what I'd done to this: renovate, rehabilitate, make something out of nothing. I took books out of the library and pored over them, and only when I felt that I'd learned enough did I let the most persistent of the realtors sell the house. She sold it for three times what I'd paid for it, more than enough to cover the commission and the cost of the repairs with plenty left over, and that was how I began my career, how I became a small success. I plowed the money from that first house into several other properties, painting and fixing and sprucing them up and then strewing them with Uncle Owen's treasures, which seemed to induce a pleased hypnosis in prospective buyers. I did over houses in Amherst and South Hadley and Leverett, learning to translate my real desires into wood and cloth and paint, and I stopped only when Walter fell into a new project that captured me.

Walter had a colleague named Tyler Robertson, who was studying the migration routes of monarch butterflies; we were at a party at Tyler's house when I first heard Walter's idea. I wasn't paying attention at first: all Walter's scholarly friends had a passionate interest in good investments, and I'd become quite popular since I'd learned to talk about tax credits and property values. A mammalogist was asking me about the potential of an old farmhouse in Conway when I overheard Walter say to a group of students, "I've been thinking about something we could all work on together. A team project, like the one at the Quabbin."

"The what?" I heard one student whisper.

Walter must have heard him too, because he winced at the idea that his new students were already forgetting his old work.

"A new ecosystem," said a woman behind Walter. "But not a reservoir and its watershed. Something else."

Walter looked over his shoulder. "That's right," he said. "Page. It's great to see you."

Page—of course she was there. I'd hardly seen her since the day I'd dropped out of school, but Walter had always made sure that I knew of her progress. She'd returned to his department as an assistant professor, after two years doing a fellowship at Yale, and she'd cut her hair to celebrate her new job. A spiky, asymmetric cut, short and clipped on one side, swinging low across the other cheek. She made me feel old.

"Page," I said. We smiled politely at each other. "Good to see you again."

"You too," she said. She turned and reached behind her, seizing the arm of a young man who was gazing out the window. "Have you met Hank Dwyer?" she asked. "You two have a lot in common—Hank took five years off before he went to college, and then he decided to be a biologist after doing some work for Paul Glover. You remember that owl project? That's what got him started. Hank's a senior this year."

I felt the blood rushing up my neck. Where did Page find these men? Hank had huge hands and a big nose but was gorgeous anyway: twenty-five or so, tall and blocky, with streaky hair and thick straight eyebrows and green-gold eyes shot with copper, like a cat's. But it wasn't his features that got me—he sent out a force, a beam, some light like a laser that caused everything to well up in me, all the longing I'd tamped down since Randy. All I'd missed with Walter, which I thought I'd learned to live without. A voice in my head, just above my left ear, said, *This, this, this. Him.*

I managed to stutter hello and then looked at Walter, and when I did I saw something interesting: Walter was uncomfortable. Walter was twisting the buttons on his shirt. "Page," he said, clearing his throat. "This is your student?"

"Maybe," she said. "With some luck. Hank's still an undergraduate, but I'm hoping to snag him for our program."

"Wonderful," Walter said, still gazing at Hank. "Can I get you a drink?"

Hank edged closer to Walter. "Dr. Hoffmeier," he said shyly. "I've read all your papers. I'm very interested in your work."

The surest way to Walter's heart. "Why don't you join us this summer?" Walter asked. While the other students shifted places, Walter told Hank about his plans. "We need an untouched environment," he said. "Preferably not too far from the university, preferably with some water. We'll do a more complex model than we did at the Quabbin. More factors, more data. Better algorithms. A much better computer."

The rest of the students chimed in then, suggesting various ecosystems. Swamps, forests, urban environments, another lake, a mountaintop. Someone started taking notes on a cocktail napkin. Hank listened to everyone, turning his head from voice to voice and tugging occasionally at his turtleneck. I stood at the edge of the group, wondering what he'd look like without his clothes.

"I know a great place," Hank said. "If you'd be interested. There's this swamp where I used to live—my family's place is at the tip of it, and we own part of the acreage. And I'm sure we could get permission from the families that own the rest. It's just sitting there, worthless land. Completely unspoiled."

"Really?" Walter said. I could almost hear what he was thinking. *Completely unspoiled*—that was Hank, the kind of student Walter hadn't had in years. He often complained how his current students worried about jobs and grants and salaries. "They're all so petty," he'd say. "We never worried about those things." Never remembering how he'd never worried because he'd never had to. His generation of scientists had come up when money flowed like water and universities were expanding, when anyone halfway good had a job and a lab for the asking. Five-percent mortgages, easy tenure, automatic grants; Walter and his peers could afford to be idealistic. They could afford to look puzzled when their students dropped out or left for higher-paying jobs. "If they'd worry less about money," Walter would say, "and more about science . . ."

And here was Hank, as innocent as if he'd lived his life on a raft. They bent their heads together then; Hank gave directions to his swamp and Walter wrote them down. I took another look at Hank—a long, hard look—and I moved closer to Walter and said in his ear, "You know, I've been thinking."

"What about?" he said. Cool, stiff. He couldn't imagine I'd be interested.

"This new project?" I said. "If you decide you want to do that swamp, I could help you, like in the old days. Remember?"

"Of course I do," he said. He softened instantly and moved his hand in a slow spiral down my spine.

"I could take a little break from fixing up the new house," I said. "I could help you instead. Really pitch in."

"You'd do that?" he said. "For me?"

"Sure," I said. I felt strangely sad that he'd forgiven me so easily. Had that been all he wanted? A little attention, a little concession to the importance of his work, an offer to bend my life a bit toward his? I hated myself for all the times I'd withheld it.

What I didn't understand at first was that Walter was

also enamored of Hank. Not that he would have admitted it; not that anything happened, or would ever happen, between them. The chemistry that flowed between them was intellectual, not sexual, but I had seen Uncle Owen and Dalton together and I knew that smile, that quickening of the eyes. I knew, from my days at the Quabbin, how irresistible Walter found an eager student.

The project came together more quickly than Walter could have dreamed, and soon we were making field trips almost every day to the swamp that Hank had offered. Page and Tyler Robertson were both involved, as well as Hank and two of Walter's students and three botanists Walter had recruited. And me: I kept my promise to Walter and I set my latest house aside for a while so I could be part of Walter's team. In the afternoons we gathered at the lab and then traveled out to the swamp, Page and Tyler in one car, the students piled in a red van, me and Walter and Hank in my Subaru. Walter drove and Hank sat next to him. I sat in the back with a stack of field guides, brushing up on my taxonomy and listening to Walter's enthusiastic comments. They were directed toward Hank, not me.

"We'll divide the area into sectors," Walter said. "Since it's so complex. Work in concentric circles, from the water through the cattails, then up through the drier land to the limestone talus. We'll run some percolation tests, define the boundaries of the microclimates and determine how the communities overlap. Then see how they change with time and rainfall and changing pH and the nitrate runoff from the fields . . ."

He was thinking out loud, noodling with words, and Hank sat openmouthed and listened. I thought I knew how Hank felt. Excited that all this knowledge was opening to him; flattered at Walter's focused attention; determined to deserve it. Walter was seductive in high gear, and I was so jealous of what was passing between them that I felt sick. One afternoon I leaned over the car seat and touched Hank's arm, interrupting Walter's monologue.

"What are you going to start with?" I asked Hank.

"The birds," he said shyly. "Because that's what I know. I'll do a census for each sector, then determine the nesting sites while the birds are breeding. Then I guess I'll work on capturing some specimens so we can determine the food web. Figure out who's feeding on what and when—there's so much stuff I want to do."

He was beginning to talk like Walter already. He looked at Walter for confirmation and Walter nodded happily and said, "The botany students can analyze the buds and seeds in their crops. Page can check out the insects they're eating. Bob Jenkins says we can use his instruments for the pesticide analyses and the calorimetric data. And Tyler's going to follow the larval hatches while I'm working on the fish."

No mention of me at all. "Well," I said. "Since Hank's new to this, why don't I start by helping him? It sounds like he could use another pair of hands."

Walter looked at me in the rear-view mirror. "I thought you'd help me," he said.

"I will," I said. "Later. But you'll be busy coordinating everyone else at first and trying to make sense of the data. I'll just get Hank started."

"That'd be great," Hank said, before Walter could object again.

I told myself Hank said that because he wanted me. I ignored every twinge of common sense I felt, every flash of reality, and I began to spend all my time tromping around with Hank. I traded in my silk dresses and linen jackets for old chinos and rubber boots and long-sleeved shirts, and I followed Hank like a faithful dog, my knapsack weighed down with binoculars and topographic maps and notebooks and specimen bags. Hank, who'd been uneasy at first, seemed to grow used to me. We established a rhythm and worked in circles as Walter had suggested, from the pond with its herons and ducks and geese to the marsh surround with its bitterns and snipe and then the thicket with its warblers and hawks. Hank made the sightings and called out the numbers and species to me, and I recorded whatever he said.

I might have grown bored if I hadn't had Hank to watch. Or to listen to—when we weren't slinking through the reeds, Hank amused me with bits of local lore, which he probably didn't mean to be funny. He called the least bitterns thunder-pumpers, from the weird noise they made. Great blue herons were shitpokes, from their habit of poking through garbage, and pied-billed grebes were water witches, sinking slowly beneath the surface when startled and vanishing like submarines. He seemed to take particular pleasure in crows.

"My grandfather kept a crow as a pet," he told me one afternoon. We had taken a break so I could strip off my boots and patch my blisters, and three crows near us were arguing over a gum wrapper. "Corvids are cool," he said.

"Crows, ravens, jays," I said. "Is that right? Those are the corvids?"

"That's right," he said, pleased. "But crows are the best. They're smart. They're monogamous. They court. Some of them get to be twenty years old. My grandfather swore his was twenty-two."

"I like crows," I said; I would have said anything to please him. We'd spent four weeks together by then, and the closest I'd been to him was this. Our whole group often gathered on evenings and weekends, but then Hank was glued to Walter's side with the other students, listening wide-eyed as the conversation tumbled from computer modeling to evolution and reproductive strategies. One night I listened, tired and bored, as Page and one of the botanists argued over the relative energy costs of viviparity and oviparity while Tyler made a case for parthenogenesis.

"Gall midges, weevils, aphids," Tyler said. "Who could be more successful?"

I remembered why I'd dropped out of school.

"That's one strategy," Walter said. He sat in the rocker his students always reserved for him, which was quarter-sawn oak with fluted spindles and an oval back and carved, curved arms. A nice chair; I'd bought it myself. Somehow it had turned into Walter's throne. "The most generations in the least time," Walter continued. "But then consider the other extreme. Semelparity."

Hank blinked. The others nodded; they knew what Walter meant. Walter leaned down and explained this bit of jargon to Hank. "Living long," I heard him say. "Breeding only once, enormously—the organism's entire energy budget goes into this one reproductive fling. Then dying. Pacific salmon."

Those evenings made me frantic, but Walter was happier than he'd been in years. The swamp was teeming with his people, working on his project; Hank applied to Walter's department for graduate work and asked for Walter as his advisor. Page was furious—she'd lost whatever hold she'd had on Hank, and now she'd lost him as a student as well. She drew away from the project, claiming she had a paper of her own to write, and Hank was so caught up with the work and with Walter that he hardly seemed to notice. Sometimes I let myself think that he didn't miss Page because he had me instead.

I should have understood, if anyone did, that it was Walter who was pulling Hank. I'd been through the same thing, falling into the field of Walter's excitement like a rabbit falling down a hole. Walter knew that he had Hank charmed, and he thought he had me as well—I was working for him again, neglecting my own business while I cooked huge dinners for everyone, and he was as smug as a cat because the change was so clearly good for me. Everyone remarked upon my new shape: I was slowly, steadily losing weight, which Walter attributed to clean living and exercise and lots of fresh air. Privately, I thought the cause was much simpler; I had no time to eat. Between working outside all day and collecting data at night, then lying sleepless in bed and plotting how I could get Hank to touch me, I was melting away.

One day in September I took drastic action. I'd already tried everything else I knew—I'd spent all the time I could alone with Hank. I'd flattered him and been helpful to him and listened to him. I'd sat next to him on rocks so small that they crowded us together. I'd baked special treats for our field lunches and watched him eat them; I'd unbuttoned the top of my shirt and then bent low over broken nests on the ground. Nothing had worked. Hank's idea of getting personal was to ask me about Walter.

"You worked on the *Quabbin* project with him?" he said. "You were so lucky."

"I was just a girl," I said.

"That's what's so amazing. Even when you were an undergraduate you got to be around him all the time, watch him work, hear him think. You must have been so excited. Did you work with him in graduate school?"

"I quit," I said, wondering how to explain why I'd left the charms of Walter and science for a career that was bound to sound frivolous to Hank. I tried to make the change sound accidental. "I was sick for a while," I said.

"And afterwards I wasn't in any shape to do field work. And then my great-uncle died and left me his things, and I had to do something with them . . ."

So I stretched the truth a little. I stretched the truth, I changed my clothes and adopted the student uniform as shamelessly as Tyler had; I wore my hair long and flowing again; I stopped wearing jewelry and makeup. After years of trying to look older I tried to look twenty-two again, and it didn't work. Nothing did.

The day I chose was unseasonably hot. Hank and I were both wearing shorts, and while my legs were not nearly so wonderful as Hank's, I thought I didn't look too bad. We climbed up a limestone outcropping at the swamp's far end, searching for evidence of hawks, and when we reached the top I sat down and spread our lunch on a cloth. Below us I could see the transects the botany students had laid from the edge of the water through the reeds, stakes hammered at one-meter intervals. I gave Hank the cans of beer I'd smuggled in and he drank them gratefully. When he was done he took off his shirt and stretched himself out on the rocks.

"God," he said. "This weather's the best."

"It's nice," I said. I lay down next to him and pretended to enjoy the sun, which was making me sweat.

"This is great," I said. "Do you mind . . . ?"

He lay on his back with his eyes closed. "Mind what?"

I took off my shirt. He opened his eyes, blinked, looked at me again. Smiled. "Hell," he said. "Why not? It's not fair, the way women always have to wear tops." He closed his eyes again.

I lay next to him, no more exposed in my taupe satin bra than I'd be in a bathing suit. I moved my arm so that it brushed his.

Still nothing. He moved his arm away and smiled at the sun. I moved my arm again. He moved his. I moved my leg until our thighs touched. This time he shifted a little uneasily. Of course I should have left things there, moved away, pretended disinterest. Given up. I rolled over heavily and kissed him, my unclothed chest mashed against his.

He threw me off as if I were a rabid dog. He pushed me off, sat up, rose to his knees. "Jesus, Grace," he said. "What the hell? You're *married*. To *Walter*."

I kneeled next to him, a sharp stone pressed into my shin. "Forget that," I said. "Forget Walter." As if either of us could. I reached out and rested my arm on his shoulder. "Don't you want me?" I said.

His mouth opened and closed and he flushed dark red. He shrugged off my hand and stood up. "Let's just forget this whole thing happened," he said. "Okay?" His voice quivered with his effort to stay calm. "Let's just get back to work. We don't want to wreck this project."

But of course I did. I wanted to wreck this project, wreck him and Walter, tear apart this life I found myself floundering in. I was so humiliated and disappointed that I started crying. Hank looked at me for a minute and then grabbed his shirt and ran down the rocky path. He left me alone, hot and sweaty and half-naked, brokenhearted, and that's how Walter found me an hour later when he passed by with his gill net and happened to hear me crying.

"Hello?" Walter called from below me. "Who's up there? Are you all right?"

I couldn't answer; I couldn't stop crying. Walter left his gill net by the transects and sprinted up the slope.

"Grace?" he said. He kneeled down beside me and wrapped me in his arms. "Grace?" he repeated, completely bewildered. "What is it? Are you all right?" He checked me quickly for cuts and bruises, his hands pausing over the sweat and dirt and gravel stuck to my back.

His face darkened. "Did someone . . . ?" he asked. "Has anyone . . . ?"

"Hank!" I wailed. Perhaps I meant Walter to understand that the only way he could. Perhaps that cry simply tore itself from my heart.

"Hank?" he whispered. "Hank did this?"

I never contradicted him. I let him dress me, lead me back to the car, think what he wanted. I let his own heart break, half with rage at my supposed violation, half with a pain he could never admit, and I didn't care. I knew I could never face Hank again, never survive unless Hank was out of my life. I could never stand to watch Hank and Walter together. I brought our world crashing down around us, the end of another life.

A Refuse Heap

No one could have missed the changes that occurred in Walter after that. Over the years, five horizontal lines had carved themselves across his forehead, which folded into neat corrugations when he lifted his eyebrows. Now a pair of vertical lines sprang up above his nose, crossing the horizontals in a ragged checkerboard. The web of fine diagonals around his eyes darkened and deepened, and two furrows cut from the wings of his nose to his mouth. His face cracked into a complex map, as if I'd carved it with a razor; and at night, when he thought I was sleeping, he groaned. Not once or twice, on falling asleep or awakening, but all night long. Each time he rolled or moved he let out a low, broken sound, as unforced and unstoppable as breath. In the mornings he lay in the tub, quite defeated, and he couldn't get out until I'd brought him coffee. Through all this he could never say what was hurting him so: as if, by his not saying, I wouldn't know.

I knew. Walter had confronted Hank and Hank had refused to defend himself; all he'd ever said to Walter was, "I didn't touch her." Walter turned all his frustration and hurt into anger and cut Hank off completely, and still it wasn't enough for me. I was seized with a sense that I'd lived my whole life wrongly, falsely, badly; and all I could think of to do was to thrash at the world around me. Walter's project collapsed and his group disbanded and Hank transferred to Page's lab, and I congratulated myself on how well I'd punished everyone, even me: Walter was perfectly kind and sympathetic, but he could no longer make love to me. Perhaps he knew more of the truth than he knew he did.

As the fall wore on, Walter threw himself into the plans for an international conference he'd been invited to organize in Beijing, for the following September. He grew tired and anxious, drowning in a sea of visas and invitations, travel agents and hotel brochures, but I couldn't make myself help him or even show any enthusiasm for the trip. This was my chance to follow in Uncle Owen's footsteps and see what he had seen, but I had never meant to go like this: a forced march on the arm of an angry husband, who refused to allow me to stay at home alone. Our living room filled with papers and abstracts and I grew guiltier each day, until finally I roused myself enough to write Dalton and tell him some of what was happening. I described Hank and what had happened in the swamp, and what I had done to Walter; ". . . and now he wants me to go to China with him," I finished. "What am I supposed to do?"

"Whatever you have to," Dalton wrote back. "But just *go*."

His note lay on top of a big box of Uncle Owen's things, all his diaries and dictionaries and maps, and despite myself the box roused my interest a bit. I compared Uncle

Owen's things with the guidebooks Walter brought home, and even that brief acquaintance was enough to tell me that the China Uncle Owen had visited was gone. The walls around Beijing had vanished; broad streets cut through the old alleys; concrete towers had replaced the low houses. Even the language was different: *Beijing*, not *Peking*. *Cixi* rather than *Tzu Hsi*.

I tried to take an interest in that. I buried the knowledge of what I had done, I buried everything, and I tried to forget Hank and to warm toward Walter, to show a little enthusiasm for this trip he was working on so hard. I tried to believe we might enjoy traveling together; we had in the past. But meanwhile I had nothing to do but eat.

When my mother visited early in December, she turned white with horror at the sight of me. She turned white and then laughed and then frowned and then smiled, and then she tore a sheet of paper from a pad and started outlining a diet. Slim as always, she wore a straight navy skirt and a white blouse with a boat neck, beneath which her bra straps showed. For my birthday, she'd brought me two bras that resembled armor, boned and thick-sided and fastened with long rows of hooks and eyes, as expensive as a good pair of shoes. Neither of them fit.

"Grapefruit," she said firmly. "Grapefruit after every meal—burns up the calories. High protein, no fat, no carbohydrates, ten glasses of water a day—how did you let this *happen?*"

I looked at the floor. Letting had nothing to do with it—I had done it on purpose, eating with all the stealth and steadiness of a prisoner of war. Since my escapade in the swamp, I'd gorged as I hadn't done since Mumu's death, gaining ten pounds, fifteen, twenty. At twenty, Walter had noticed. We ate our meals in silence then, he reading scientific journals while I flipped through Uncle Owen's China diaries, searching for solutions to my life.

Walter had frowned at me one night, after I'd taken a second helping of mashed potatoes and then a third.

"Are you sure you want that?" he'd said, sounding exactly like my mother. "A third helping—you look like you're putting on a little weight."

"That's my business," I'd snapped. But after that I'd taken to eating in secret, concealing my habits from Walter the way I'd concealed them from my mother as a child.

In the basement below us, our washer and dryer stood against adjoining walls, leaving a small corner of empty space between them. I'd always kept our clothes hamper there, but after Walter's comment I began keeping our dirty clothes in plastic bags and I used the hamper for hiding food. I kept flat tins of anchovies there, jars of jam and peanut butter, bars of dark chocolate, nuts and sourballs, cookies in tins, fruitcakes and canned pâté and maraschino cherries. At night, when Walter groaned beside me, I crept downstairs in my robe and slippers and headed for the hamper.

I ate like an animal, ripping and tearing the food from the packages, greedy, furtive, fast; half-asleep while the night passed by like a dream. The emptiness in me was so deep I could never fill it, and each time I found myself in the basement, my mouth smeared and my stomach so taut it hurt to touch it, I hardly recognized what I was doing. The food hit my brain like a club, sedating my confusion and pain until I could lumber back to bed. Night after night I'd done this, making something of myself. But when my mother asked how I'd let this happen, I looked at the table and said, "I don't know. My metabolism must be changing."

"How's the latest house?" she asked me then.

"I'm selling it," I said. Nothing about my business seemed interesting anymore. By then I'd had fantasies of living in one of my houses, away from Walter, away from our lives, but I went ahead and sold the last one and then, instead of buying another, put the money in the bank. I was tired. I couldn't understand what I was doing. Walter was so glad to see me out of the rehabbing business that he threw a New Year's party.

Because I couldn't manage much of anything then, Walter's colleague, Tyler Robertson, made most of the arrangements and brought over most of the food. I cleaned up a little and then wrapped myself in a new dress: white, soft, cut low and tight around my breasts but floating gently elsewhere, obscuring (I thought) the weight I'd gained since September. Page showed up; since Hank had returned to her lab she'd forgiven Walter for trying to steal him, and I think she even felt sorry for him. Stuck with this idle, crazy wife; she and Walter were colleagues now, and had more in common than she'd ever had with me. She'd shed her girlish shell somewhere, when I hadn't been paying attention, and she'd turned into a formidable woman. Where once she'd made me feel old and sedate, now she made me feel like a child.

She took one look at me and said, "What's happened to you? Are you pregnant?"

"I wish," I said.

She raised her eyebrows and looked me over more carefully. "So?" she said. "What in the world is wrong with you? Can't you pull yourself together?"

"No," I said. I couldn't tell her what had happened. "Not right now."

Her disapproval was so strong that I could smell it. She moved toward the bar Walter had set up in the kitchen, and I forced myself to circulate among the other guests. Tyler was so drunk he was prancing around in a rhinestone tiara. His shirt was hiked above his pleated pants, displaying six inches of freckled paunch. His third wife,

Elena, a Hungarian graduate student four years younger than me, kept rubbing her fingers on his stomach. The two of them circled our living room together, filling glasses from a big jar of something they referred to as glog.

"Scotch, brandy, spices, lemons, sugar, gin," Tyler recited gaily, pushing his tiara into his thinning hair. Elena had crowned him King of the Night and he was taking his role seriously.

He and Elena smooched and fondled each other, stuffing food into their open mouths; they'd been married for less than a year and Elena had cooked goulash and pierogies and potato pancakes, onion dumplings and a huge ham, shaming me completely. Tyler had invited all his students to the party, as well as his ex-students and postdocs and protégés, and all Elena's foreign friends, Russians and Indians and Pakistanis, Chinese and Koreans. Almost everyone there was dependent on Tyler in some way, and so he was a happy man and this was a happy party for almost everyone but Walter.

While the party bubbled and tumbled and roared, Walter sat in a corner and sulked. He was wearing a hat shaped like a giraffe's head, with ears and painted eyes and a long, quivering nose that seemed designed to express his slights. My own hat bore pink stuffed hands that clapped when I pulled a string; Tyler had crowned us all earlier and now the headgear he'd brought as party favors bobbed as our guests sweated and jiggled to the old Motown tapes he'd also brought. It was Tyler's party, almost completely; only the house was ours.

I got trapped against the wall with a clump of comparative-literature types, Elena's friends, and I stood there miserably. I wanted to dance with the students. I wanted to wear, as one girl did, a spaghetti-strapped green cotton undershirt and black Lycra pants. Instead, I stood in my white tent and listened to a discussion about folktales and the wish-fulfillment of barren couples.

"This occurs so often," one black-haired woman said. Her hair was swept in a complex knot below a pale blue, Carmen Miranda-like hat sprouting blossoms and fruits—one of Tyler's favorites. The woman spoke as if she'd forgotten she was wearing it. "A woman begs an old witch for a tiny girl and then finds a baby in a tulip: Thumbelina. A woman beneath a juniper tree pleads for a child and then eats some berries and is granted her wish, but then she dies. A queen pricks her finger sewing and then begs for a daughter as red as blood and as white as the snow. The wish is always granted, but there is always a twist."

She smiled at me; she had lipstick on her front teeth. I turned and stared out the window, at the snow lying over the grass, and I thought how I could prick my finger with the marcasite brooch Uncle Owen had given me. The drops might fall, harden like sugar-on-snow, leap up as triplets. Life might leap up in my womb. I had had too much to drink but I thought I knew how the women in those fairy tales had felt: yearning, burning, brooding, dreaming, wishing, wanting. Despairing, sometimes. Lost in an inner world. I still dreamed that I might get pregnant somehow; that I might, like a marsupial, have a baby no bigger than my thumb.

A man wearing a silver alien's helmet said, "Remember the man who said, 'I want a son so bad it could even be a hedgehog'? And then he gets one who's half hedgehog, half boy?"

The people around him smiled knowingly and their voices rose and fell, confident, self-satisfied, dry. Here at a party where all was permitted, even encouraged, they could find nothing better to do than to talk about their work and insinuate that if I was finally granted a child

I'd either die or bear some sort of monster. Two girls were dancing near us, eyes closed and hair flying, ignoring us completely. I tapped my feet and longed to join them but knew I couldn't; I was too old, too heavy, too respectable. I had just turned thirty, and I thought no one would ever dance with me again.

As I moved away from the folklorists I bumped into a plump Pakistani who lowered his lids and confided that his astral body could fly. "I fly over mountains and deserts," he said, waiting for me to be impressed.

"Desserts?" I pricked up my ears.

"*Deserts,*" he said. "Dunes, oases, date palms . . ."

"Great," I said. "Watch out for D.C."

"Excuse me?"

"Missiles," I told him. He looked so disappointed that I told him not to worry. "Never mind," I said. "Probably you fly too fast."

"Oh, very fast," he beamed. "Several millions of miles per hour. And also I fly when everyone else is asleep."

I wished him well and excused myself and moved on. A Russian woman, a prominent biophysicist, tried to tell me about her theories of the arctic soul. "Cold climates," she said. "The long nights, the temperatures, cause a darkening and deepening of the soul. Korlovsky clearly demonstrates . . ."

I excused myself again.

"The parthenogenetic whiptail lizards of the Southwest," a pale man said.

"Wulfric of Haselbury," a tan girl said. "You've never heard of him?"

Two biochemists were slandering their brokers, a political economist was proclaiming the perils of not studying Latin, a sculptor was trying to buy an old Dodge from a girl with remarkable legs. I drifted through all of them to the corner where Walter, still crowned with giraffe ears, sat surrounded by his students. The students cast yearning looks at the dancers, at the group watching the physicist who was demonstrating the laws of surface tension by blowing bubbles through a straw into other bubbles, at the thumb-wrestling finals and the limbo contest and the crowd throwing Velcro darts toward a target fastened to a woman's bottom. But they knew better than to abandon Walter, who was trying to reconstruct a colony from the rubble that I'd left him. He'd told everyone he'd had to abandon the swamp project because of his other commitments. Now everyone wanted to know what those other commitments were.

"China," he kept muttering. "I'm arranging this big meeting in China . . ."

Tyler Robertson danced by just then, his tiara glimmering. "Outside, everyone!" he called. "Two minutes to midnight!"

We tumbled out of the house and into the clear, cold night. Tyler pranced along the snowdrift at the edge of our driveway, setting out sparklers. "Ten seconds!" Elena called. Tyler struck a match. "Nine, eight, seven, six . . ." Tyler lit the sparklers. "Five, four, three, two, *one!*"

"Happy New Year!" Tyler shouted. He lit a cherry bomb and threw it over his shoulder. The noise echoed off the windows; the sparklers sent out silvery trails; people clinked glasses and kissed. I was standing by myself, watching the swarming crowd. Walter pecked Page on the cheek. Tyler and Elena mashed themselves together and Tyler's glasses fell into the snow. The fair-haired man who'd told the hedgehog story slipped his hand down the black-haired woman's pants, his silver alien antennae entwined with her Carmen Miranda fruits. The students were knotted like pollywogs and the Pakistani I'd met in the hall had his eyes closed and was, presumably, flying

above us all. The girl in the green cotton undershirt whirled a string attached to a tuft of burning steel wool, sending sparks flying in all directions, and when I turned a woman I didn't know smiled at me and asked if I were pregnant.

"No," I said.

"Oh," she said.

I smiled with sealed lips and walked inside. Of course I looked pregnant, I looked like a cow, and something snapped inside me after I left her. I slunk out of our white-fenced yard and down the stairs into our basement, and once I was there I wept for my lost child, my lost lives, for the houses that had given me only a stack of money in the bank. I wept, and then I ate, and when Page called my name from the top of the stairs and then turned on the light when she heard the crackle of cellophane, I cowered in my corner like a trapped opossum.

"Grace?" she called, already moving down the stairs. "Is that you? Walter's looking for you, he wants to know if the champagne's down here . . ."

She came around the corner, past the water heater, muttering something about scientists who couldn't remember their names, and then her mouth dropped open in shock. She couldn't see the hamper behind me; I'd blocked it with my body. But she could see all too clearly the refuse heap beneath the soapstone sink. Candy wrappers, empty bottles, torn boxes, open tins, foil and cellophane, fruit skins, jars I'd cleaned out with my fingers and tongue. Page kicked at the pile with the toe of one red shoe.

"Jesus," she said. A stranger's voice, cool and academic. "What are you doing?"

My hand was trapped in an open sack of glazed pecans. "Nothing," I said. "I don't know. What do you want?"

"There's all that food upstairs," she said. "All the stuff Tyler brought. Why would you eat here?"

Why indeed. The basement was dark and damp and smelled of mold and spiderwebs. The pecans were stale. I couldn't explain to Page or to anyone else why I needed to eat alone; for weeks, since I'd blown up again, I'd eaten like a mouse in public. I was huge, grotesque, enormous. I had no right to eat.

I stared at Page, my eyes dull and my hands dirty. From the head of the stairs I heard Walter calling. "Page?" he said. "Is she down there?"

I froze. "Tell him I'll bring the champagne up myself," I said. "I'll be right there."

"She's here," Page called instead. Her voice was puzzled, frightened; I don't think she meant to be cruel. She probably assumed that Walter already knew what was going on.

But Walter didn't know. He came down the stairs with Tyler and a student named Larry, all three of them laughing and ready to lug up boxes of liquor in their strong arms. When the three of them came upon me and Page, they stopped quite suddenly. All of them had cornered animals in the woods.

"Holy shit," Tyler said. He moved closer to Page.

I hunched over my bag of glazed pecans and glared at them. Walter reached behind me and lifted the lid of the hamper and then drew a deep breath.

"Grace," he said. "What's going on?"

"Nothing," I told him. "Leave me alone."

I drew back against the hamper, aware that I was acting bizarrely but unable to stop myself. That corner had been my place, the only place I could call my own since I'd sold my other houses, and it was ruined now. My place, my food, my trash. I growled, I couldn't help it. And when Page squatted down, her face inches from mine and her hand extended, I leaned over and took her hand in my mouth and held it there dumbly, like a dog.

▪ IV ▪

The Cultural Revolution

September 1986

Patient: *I sudenly got a pain in the chest on both sides since yesterday after supper.*

Doctor: *Any shortness of breath?*

Patient: *Yes, very difficult breathing.*

Doctor: *Have you grown angry with somebody?*

Patient: *Oh! Yes, I had a quarrel with my husband just before supper yesterday.*

Doctor: *Are you still angry?*

Patient: *Yes, he is a stubborn fellow. He never accepts other people's advice.*

Doctor: *In Chinese traditional medicine we say there are seven kinds of emotions: joy, anger, melancholy, brooding, sorrow, fear, shock. Each of them is related to one organ. For example, anger attacks the liver and joy hurts the heart. I'll give you a prescription for your liver, and in the meantime please be happy all the time.*

—*adapted from* A Dialogue in the Hospitals

Incense Burner Peak

> There are no straight roads in the world; we must be prepared to follow a road which twists and turns and not try to get things on the cheap.
>
> —Mao

Zillah's voice vanished with my pneumonia, which left as quickly as it had come: a drenching sweat and a plunge in my temperature, and suddenly the pain in my chest was gone and I could breathe again. I woke, hungry and thirsty and worn, to find the room cool and quiet. The flowers on my bedside table were only flowers. The blinds hung sedately over the windows, and the only sounds in the room came from the other patients. I drew the air into my lungs and slept, twenty-two hours of dreamless rest. Then I woke and ate everything Dr. Yu gave me—she was there, as she'd been all along—and I had a bath. Then I slept again, another full day and night, dreaming this time of Dr. Yu and her life.

I dreamed of her and her husband and children, exiled to the countryside; I dreamed of famine; I dreamed of war. The war against the Japanese, the civil war, and then the smaller battles Dr. Yu and her family had survived. I dreamed of peasants planting millet on small strips of land, and then I dreamed the land gathered up and bound into communes, hoes and rakes replaced by tractors, houses carved up into rooms, backyard gardens replaced by common fields and the sun overturned in the sky by the Cultural Revolution. Without understanding why, I dreamed Dr. Yu and her family spinning like pollen on a river, every motion of their lives determined by the current.

When I woke for the second time, I felt well but very confused. Dr. Yu told me what day it was. "A week," she said. "You've been here for a week. Unusual vacation." She guided my feet into my shoes, my arms into my blouse. My limbs felt airy and weightless. I looked down at the rest of me and marveled that there was anything left. The fever had pruned me but my body was still mine, and I stroked my hips with new affection.

"How do you feel?" Dr. Yu asked.

"I feel good," I said. "I feel fine."

I was as weak as a newly hatched chick, but I knew that my body was healed. Beneath my slack skin and softened muscles I could feel my body rebuilding itself, although my heart was puzzled by what Zillah had brought me: the chunks of my past I'd ignored for years as I tried, each time I changed my life abruptly, to forget who I'd been before. Zillah had made me look at my life as if it belonged to someone else, and when I looked at it clearly, I was ashamed.

"My husband has arranged for your discharge," Dr. Yu said. "And Walter arrives from Canton today. We are to meet him at your hotel."

"Today?" I said. "He's coming today?" Suddenly I wanted very much to see him.

"So he says—he, two others he travels with . . ."

She dressed me carefully and gathered up the food and utensils and bedding she'd brought. I concentrated on moving myself. My blouse was loose. My skirt was baggy. Even my shoes felt too big. I wondered if I would have simply vanished, had I gone into this illness thin.

"You can walk?" Dr. Yu said. She took my elbow and raised me and then, after I'd stood for a minute, she let me go. I took a few tentative steps across the polished wooden floor. The grain swirled mysteriously through the layers of wax and varnish, forming faces and landscapes and words. The sunlight fell in a wide wedge that solidified part of the air.

"I can walk," I told Dr. Yu. "Absolutely. I feel almost like myself."

"We took good care of you," she said. "But it is nothing. It is of no consequence. You are our guest."

When she spoke I remembered something else from my lost week. "You were talking to me," I said hesitantly. Another voice besides Zillah's had been whispering in my ear, feeding me the material that had powered my last dreams. "You were telling me things," I said. "Weren't you?"

The nurse moved to the end of the room and began changing some dressings on a patient's chest. "I maybe said a few things," Dr. Yu said quietly. "Just to tie your mind here while you dream. You remember this?"

I closed my eyes and concentrated. What had she said? Her sister, her father, her mother's work, a time when she'd gone to school—there was nothing I could hold onto. Nothing concrete. I'd listened so hard to my own life that I'd lost hers. "It's gone," I said. "Whatever it was. What was it?"

"All in good time," she said. "Perhaps some will return to you."

I reached back to straighten my collar, and as I did I touched my hair. Dr. Yu winced when I pulled the tangled rope over my shoulders. Knots, mats, nests, snarls—I held the mass in front of me and examined it. A muddy tan, gold no more, lusterless and dry. My hair had been my chief vanity.

"I'm sorry," Dr. Yu said. "The nurses and I tried all week to keep it combed and washed. But your hair tangles so easily. It is nothing like ours."

I smiled as best as I could—it was only my hair—and I let the ruined rope fall behind me. "We will cut it," Dr. Yu said. "It is the only cure. We will give you a modern style, very short and light, like my daughter's."

I nodded docilely and followed her out of the ward. We stopped at a wooden desk downstairs, where I found that Walter had already taken care of the bill. I signed a few forms and Dr. Yu signed a few others, and then we stepped outside into the cool, smoggy air. A clean white Datsun waited for us.

"I arranged for a cab," Dr. Yu said. "Walter sent some extra money for your care, along with payment for the bill. We'll go to your hotel and make you comfortable. One quick stop on the way."

So Walter hadn't forgotten me. Somewhere in Canton, in a room I couldn't imagine in a city I'd never seen, he had taken the trouble to wire money, make arrangements, think of me. This, after all I'd done to him. An image of Hank, which I'd buried for months, floated by. I pushed it away. I leaned back against the slipcovered seat and rested my head on the antimacassar while Dr. Yu talked to the driver. The driver smiled in the mirror at me. The image of Hank floated back.

"We'll stop at the market on Wangfujing," said Dr. Yu. "For one minute only."

"Fine," I said. The sidewalks were covered with peddlers: boys selling freshly popped corn and rice, an old woman squatting over a tray of roots and herbs, a young man selling tapes of Taiwanese pop singers. When the cab stopped, Dr. Yu darted into the covered market and I rested and watched the crowd. The driver turned around and spoke to me, but I couldn't understand him.

"I've been sick," I told him, patting my chest with my palm. "I had pneumonia."

He wore a gray tunic, crisp and starched, and a flat blue cap. He patted his own chest in response. "Nermone-ee-yar?" he said, and then he laughed at the alien syllables. I laughed with him and then tried to mime a cough, a sore chest, a fever. By the time Dr. Yu returned, we were gesturing like monkeys.

"Success!" she said. She brandished a pair of scissors and then spoke briefly to the driver, who tried to repeat the strange word I'd taught him. Dr. Yu nodded. "*Shi*," she said. Yes. "*Ta hao le.*" I think she told him I'd be all right; I recognized *hao*: good. Dr. Yu turned back to me as the driver wove his way through the crowded streets. "You rest," she said. "We will be there in one hour."

I fell asleep, completely secure in her care.

At the hotel, the manager greeted us as if I'd been gone for a year instead of a week.

"You are well?" he said anxiously. "You are cured?"

"I'm fine," I said.

"We have greatly apologize for your disease," he said. He led me up to the room Walter and I had left the week before. "We cleanse everything, very completeness, for death to all germs. Hoping you are not blaming this inadequate guest house."

He was visibly nervous, as if he feared his job hung in the balance. I told him his hotel was fine, and that it had nothing to do with my illness. He relaxed a bit.

"Hot water here," he said, pointing out a large flowered thermos. "Tea, drinking cups, boiled cool water . . ."

"Laundry?" I said. "Do you think I could get some clothes washed?" My clothes lay where I'd left them, but they'd been folded in my absence: picked up carefully, shaken out, the surfaces beneath them cleaned; then replaced with the arms and legs bent and crossed. A blouse on a chair, a skirt on the floor, dresses marching down one bed and shoes neatly upright here and there across the rug, reproaching me. My mother had always said to leave strange rooms just the way I found them, as if each time I closed the door behind me might be my last. For once I wished I'd followed her advice.

"Our great pleasure," the manager said, and then he waited while I gathered an armful of clothes and tucked them into the laundry bag. "All was respected," he said gently. He seemed to sense my discomfort. "None was disturbed. We cleanse by two hours. Three at latest."

He closed the door behind him and left me alone with Dr. Yu. She wandered around the room, fingering the white drapes, the tan upholstered chairs, the beds and the metal console between them, which had taken me hours to figure out. She pushed one button and lights came on over the beds. She pushed another and the radio blared. "Most amazing," she said. I realized this was the first time she'd seen one of the guest rooms. She drifted into the bathroom and ran the taps and flushed the toilet.

"Where do you think Walter is?" I called.

She emerged from the bathroom wiping her hands on

a thick towel, which she then refolded carefully. "Amazing," she repeated. "Extremely hot water on demand, at all hours of day. And such a deep tub. And visitors' soaps . . ." She held out a stack of smooth pink soap bars wrapped in creamy paper. In his house in Cambridge, Uncle Owen had kept round Spanish soaps wrapped in pleated paper and tied with flat ribbons. "We cannot stay here," Dr. Yu said. "Even if one night's room did not cost one month's salary, even if Foreign Exchange Currency was not needed for payment. It is completely disapproved."

"Who's 'we'?" I asked. "You mean you and me?"

"Us—Chinese citizens. Some places like this, even overseas Chinese are not allowed."

"But the staff is Chinese."

She shrugged. "They select those of good background and loyalty, then teach them to guard against foreign influences. 'Spiritual pollution,' they call it. We had a campaign against this several years ago, which Deng launched. 'Guard against corrupt and decadent ideologies of exploiting classes,' he said. 'Guard against stinking bourgeois life-styles.' " She laughed. "Guard against this soap, he means. But you are here, smooth pink soap is here, tourists are here with clothes and cameras. Some of us go to meetings in places like this. Of course we see. Of course we want." She shook her head. "Anyway, the government pulled back when the campaign interfered with business. We were told to take from the West what is good and leave the bad behind. Take technical knowledge. Leave ideas."

She put the soap down with a sharp crack. "So," she said. "Enough politics. Walter should be here in two or three hours, but first we will get some air—fresh air is curative. We will go for a walk and I will show you something from when I was a student."

"That sounds good," I said. "Let me take a quick shower first."

"Wet your hair," she said. "Do not dry it. We will fix it before we go."

When I came out of the bathroom she wrapped a towel around my neck and shoulders and cut off my hair with the scissors she'd bought. Snip, snip—she left it all one length, pushed behind my ears and level with my chin. Then she toweled what was left and combed it and smoothed it with a drop of conditioner until it came alive again and began to gleam. I watched in the mirror, interested despite myself. I hadn't worn my hair short since Zillah's death.

"There," she said. "You like it?"

"It's good," I said. No pins, clips, barrettes, or scarves; no fuss. Just a smooth blond cap that made me look young. "I like it," I said. "Maybe I should have done this before."

"Could be," Dr. Yu said. "You are regretful?"

"Not at all," I said.

Because it was daylight, and because I was with Dr. Yu, the park that had rebuffed my nighttime exploration ten days earlier opened to me now. We walked on winding paths through the park, past dusty flower beds and tiny houses and small pavilions and pagodas. Many of these were in ruins, chipped and shattered and plastered over with notices I couldn't read, but a few had been restored with gold leaf and paint and one was under construction that afternoon. Three women on rickety ladders were repainting the stylized chrysanthemums and the decorative borders and the tiny landscape scenes, and a man was repairing some broken tiles while another scraped layers of handbills and notices from the lower walls. I stopped to watch, amazed that they were doing everything by hand, but the sight made Dr. Yu impatient.

"What is the point?" she asked. She gestured toward some old graffiti. "Earnestly Carry Out Struggle, Criticism, Reform!" she said in a mincing voice. "Put Politics in Command, Let Thought Take the Lead!" She made a disgusted sound and turned away. "They ruined all these old places during the blood years," she said. "Now they are embarrassed for foreign visitors to see. So they paint to make them nice again, but it means nothing—it is only for show."

"You think?" I said.

"Better they should leave ruined," she said. "For remembering. Come. I will show you something good."

She led me down another path, to a small shabby building wrapped twice with a long line of people. "Cablelift," she said. "I hoped it was still here. It climbs up Incense Burner Peak."

Double chairs hung from a rusty cable and moved slowly up the hill that blocked our view. The chairs swung around a huge wheel sheltered by the eaves of the building, and they scooped up squealing couples from a square of cracked concrete. Babies giggled at me as we waited in line. Men pointed and women smiled and then covered their eyes. I was the only Westerner there.

"They didn't tell us about this at the hotel," I said. "It's not even on the park map."

"People who live here know it," Dr. Yu said. The line moved slowly toward the lift, which resembled an old ski lift back home. "Families take the bus here from Beijing, for afternoons off. It is inexpensive, provides fresh air and famous views from the top. Meng used to bring me here in the old days, when we were courting. I am very pleased it is not destroyed."

She had to buy our tickets when we finally got to the counter; the ride cost ten *fen* and the smallest note I had was a five-*yuan* FEC bill, which the ticket-taker pushed back to me. Ten *fen*, as best as I could figure, was worth about four cents; my five *yuan* could have put fifty of us on the swaying chairs. When we climbed on, I realized that the lift brought people down as well as up. Every fifteen seconds or so, a couple facing us passed by our chair.

"Ni hau," Dr. Yu said to each couple who passed. The riders dissolved into giggles as they stared at me and tested their English across the air between us. "Hal-loo!" one would call; "LAA-dee!" the next. Most often we'd hear an excited guess at my nationality. *"Meiguo ren! MEIGUO REN!"*

"Ni hau!" I called back to them. I didn't mind their stares; I was happy to be outside. As we rose I could see the pagodas scattered beneath us like colorful stones, the rolling hills worn old and smooth, the narrow dark paths and roads ribboned in every direction. Small pools dotted the landscape, as blue and artificial as the pond in Boston where the swan boats sat. Dr. Yu led me through the smiles and stares to a quiet, sheltered rock that overlooked the entire park. "You are enjoying this?" she asked.

All around me were faces as singular as stars; if I could memorize them, I thought, they might unlock my life. "It's wonderful," I said. "There's so much to see. I could watch all day."

"The world was not put here for you to watch it," she said. Her voice was tart, and her comment so out of character that I opened my mouth in surprise but then closed it again. Somehow her words seemed to link to what I'd felt in the morning, when I'd first woken up.

"Randy, Walter, Page, Hank," she continued. "Even your Uncle Owen—you can't just watch these lives and then try them on for size like clothes. You must make your own."

Below us, some bright birds dipped and swooped through the trees. "How do you know those names?" I asked.

"You talked in your sleep," she said. "We talked together. You were dreaming, I think. Or something. Do you remember this?"

I stared at the trees again, and then I tried to tell her what had happened to me. How I hadn't been dreaming, not exactly; how Zillah's voice had come to me and bent Dr. Zhang's description of his memory palace to her own ends. "I was a house," I told Dr. Yu. "The parts of my body were rooms. This voice—the voice of a girl I knew when I was small—made me remember things I don't usually think about."

Things, I heard Zillah say. Of course. My life was made of things; my language was the language of things. I was drowning in things, devoured by my possessions, and that couldn't have been what Uncle Owen had meant. *Invest it wisely*, he'd written. Instead I'd invested my inheritance sensibly.

"Yes?" Dr. Yu said. She fixed her eyes on mine. "Your memories came very detailed, like hallucinations? Smell, sound, place? You heard this voice actually speak?"

"Yes," I said. "How did you know? It was just like that, the voice was so real—it was like I was living those scenes again. I felt everything."

She nodded slowly. "Meng knows about this," she said. "Years ago, before the bad times, he studied this. What happened to you is something special, which usually happens only in those having seizures. The place in your brain where memory lives—when it is stimulated, your memories come back entire. As if life is lived again. Sometimes this can happen with high fever."

"Chinese medicine?" I asked.

"No—Western doctors know about it too. But one doctor here in Beijing became famous when he showed that gentle electricity applied to certain brain parts causes memories to pour out and voices to be heard. Meng did postgraduate training with this man. But then the Red Guards seized the institute and burned all the books and files and locked the doctors away."

"I'm sorry," I said. "Is that what made your husband so bitter?"

"That is some of it," she said. "The rest he did himself." She paused for a minute, and then she said, "What did you get from your memories?"

"I'm not sure," I said. "They were so *real*—it was like my whole life was given back to me. But I'm not sure I wanted it. When I look at what I've done, the ways I've lived . . ."

Dr. Yu rubbed a few pieces of gravel between her fingers. "Yes," she said. "That is always the way. That is what happened to Meng on the farm, when he put all his heart into making his palace and ignored everything around him. Then he compared what is then, and now, and he sank into sadness. That is the way with old things. Not that you should forget them—but to make a palace of them? No."

"Did that ever happen to you?" I asked. "Did you ever get lost in your old lives?"

"Never like what happened to you," she said. "And I never did on purpose what Meng did. If I made anything, it was a palace of dreams—what I wish for. What I want. What I hope. I remembered my life before, and then I dreamed of life to come. You understand?"

"A palace of dreams," I said, turning the idea around in my mind. And then I heard Zillah's voice again, gentle, persistent, and low. *Sally Ferguson*, I heard. *Nancy Knauf. Cece Rubin*. The names of the realtors who'd haunted the first house I'd redone.

"What is it you wish for?" Dr. Yu continued.

"Right now?" Those women had entered my house and gazed at it with calculating eyes, congratulating me on my skills. I had let Cece sell the first house for me, and then I'd let her sell the others. There was nothing left for me to do but repeat myself, and suddenly I knew, more strongly than I ever had, that I wanted something else. "Right now I wish I could stay here," I said.

"Here on this hill?"

"Here in China." The wish crystallized even as I said it. "I like it here. Everything interests me." The faces, I thought. The surge of people surrounding me; the way a disconnected string of figures would suddenly form a shape in the crowd, standing out like a piece of sculpture. The chaos. The noise. The sense that every person I spoke to held the end of a thread that tied into the web of life I'd been too lost to perceive.

"So stay," Dr. Yu said.

"How? Walter . . ."

"Walter," Dr. Yu said impatiently. "Forget Walter, for now. Forget all things at home that call you back for bad reasons. You want to stay?"

"Yes," I said. "But . . ."

"Here are ways," she said. She raised a finger with each one. "You could teach English—everyone wants to learn. You could tutor students for examinations. If you wanted to, if you wanted to do science again, you might even be able to work for me. I have wonderful students, and you would be a help to them."

"You make it sound so easy," I said. "But what about Walter?"

"Walter could stay," she said. "Any university would be happy to have him—visiting famous scientist, absolutely. But also he could go, and you could stay alone.

Visas, all could be arranged if you did work useful to serve the people."

"I haven't felt useful in years," I said.

"No?" She looked at me skeptically. "Maybe not. What about those houses you did?"

"I made some money," I said. "That's all."

"You can do things with money," she said. "If my children had money, if I had money to give them . . ."

We rose and strolled around the hilltop, drawn by the clamor beyond a small ridge. A crowd of people clustered around a young Chinese woman and four tired horses draped in embroidered blankets and crowned with glittering headpieces. An old camera mounted on a tripod stood next to the woman. Dr. Yu laughed. "Watch," she said. "Family pictures. Oh, this *never* would have been permitted before."

The parents of a small girl handed the young woman a few *fen*, and then the woman gravely dressed the girl. A red velvet cloak, silver ornaments, an enormous crown dripping baubles and fluffy red balls. Four-foot feathers stuck up from her crown like ears. The woman posed the girl on the horse, against the panorama below. The girl grimaced fiercely, her best imitation of a Mongol warrior, and the woman shot several portraits. The parents beamed.

"So silly," Dr. Yu said. "But so nice to see." Young men posed with their sweethearts, and girlfriends posed together. The photographer put her fees in a small metal box and wrote out receipts for the pictures to come. Dr. Yu looked happier than I had ever seen her.

"What is it *you* want?" I asked her curiously. I didn't doubt anymore that we'd talked in the hospital, but I'd lost her half of the conversation and it was odd, now, to feel that she knew so much about me when I knew hardly anything about her.

"What do I want?" she repeated. She tucked her rumpled blouse in while we watched the photographer. "Not so much for myself, now—it is almost enough to have my life back, my work. It is almost enough to watch this. But I want for Zaofan. I want him to go to the U.S., to study there, to work. I want more than anything that he make his life there. He is not safe here, I think—someday he will land himself in trouble. There is some way, perhaps, that you could help him leave?"

Zaofan; Rocky. We hadn't mentioned him before and I had managed not to think about him. I remembered our cab ride together and I trembled so violently I had to sit down.

"You are sick," Dr. Yu said. "Oh, this is all my fault. I have taken you outside too soon."

"I'm just hungry," I said. I ducked my head between my knees. "I think."

"I should not have asked you," Dr. Yu said. "Forget Zaofan."

"It's not that," I said. "I'm glad you asked." I thought of Rocky, his gentle hands and the lilt of his voice and the drawings I'd tucked in my purse. "Show to Walter?" he'd said; I'd forgotten completely. Where was my purse? I'd had it at the hospital; I thought I'd seen Dr. Yu pick it up. With any luck it was back at the hotel.

"We have to go," I said.

"Of course." She led me to the platform, where a small crowd waited to ride down. They gaped at us as we spoke in English.

"Why do you want him to leave?" I said. "Your oldest son . . ."

"It's hard to think about," she admitted. "But I know it is best for him. Anything could happen here again. And already he has begun to forget what the bad years are like. He made some of those *dazibao*, those posters, that the students put up on Democracy Wall. That wall is covered now with advertisements for soap and cosmetics and refrigerators, but people remember these things. Some of his friends were arrested then, and his name is known. And Zaofan has no *caution*—this business of his, these things he wants . . . he does well now. But who is to say what comes next?"

We got on a chair and began our ride down, once again greeting the couples who passed us on their way up. Far away, beyond the green park, three smokestacks belched black clouds. We sat silently for a while, and then I said, "What about you? Maybe you should come—you could study with Walter. Or with someone like him."

Dr. Yu shook her head. "It would be hard for me to get permission," she said. "I was classified as a 'stinking ninth element'—an intellectual—also as the daughter of one and the wife of another. Even though Meng and I have been officially rehabilitated, I think I would still have problems. And also I would not want to go. This is my home. Did you notice, at the conference, how you have seen old and young scientists but none your age?"

I hadn't, but I realized she was right. The scientists I'd seen with Walter had all been Dr. Yu's age and older, or almost absurdly young.

"All the people your age had to do other things," she said. "When the schools were closed. I have students now, finally, and so has Meng. We have work to do, so we stay. But Zaofan—oh, Zaofan is young. He has his whole life before him."

I didn't tell her about the drawings; of course I didn't tell her about the cab. I prayed that I hadn't spoken of Rocky during my stay in the hospital. "Let me see what I can do," I said, and for the rest of our ride down the peak, swaying gently in our fragile chair above the scarred, eroded earth, I sat silently and let the air flow into my newly healed lungs. I thought about my mother-in-law embroidering pew cushions in the Fargo airport: *For nothing is secret,* she'd patiently stitched. *Nothing is hid that shall not be known.* The wind played delightfully with my new short hair.

Walter was waiting for us when we returned. We walked into the hotel room and there he was: shoes off, feet on the bed, looking happier than he'd looked in years. I smiled at him; I had so much to say. But we were not alone.

Lou, the CAST guide I thought we'd shed a week ago, stood near the doorway and nodded coolly when we came in. He seemed unhappy that Dr. Yu was with me; he placed his hand on her elbow and started whispering fiercely to her in Mandarin. She pulled her arm away and glared at him, all the good humor she'd gained on the mountain vanishing from her face. The hotel manager stood behind Lou, listening to the conversation and grinning in embarrassment. In the soft tan chairs Dr. Yu had admired sat the people with whom Walter had traveled: Katherine Olmand and a fair young man with a bushy gold moustache, whom I had seen often during the conference but never met. Someone had opened the windows and the smell of flowers filled the room.

"Grace," Walter said. "Welcome back. This is Quentin Bradley, the limnologist we've been traveling with."

I caught the 'we,' and my smile faded as I tried to read what was going on in that room. Something; something that had to do with Katherine and Quentin and Walter traveling for seven days without me. I was tasting the air and the taste was sharp and strong. Walter didn't rise to greet me and Katherine stared at me, frankly curious, which made me wonder what Walter had told her. For an instant I saw myself through her eyes, heard how

Walter might describe me in an unguarded moment. *My wife doesn't understand me*; the old plaint of married men. *We used to work together, but now she doesn't even know what I do. She's let herself go. She's not interested in me. Once she bit a colleague's hand.* He wouldn't have told her how, during our early years, we had driven to New Hampshire and North Carolina and the Blue Ridge Mountains, bound by the plants and animals we examined into something which was, if not love, at least a pleasant companionship. He and I had parted on distinctly bad terms, and he might have told Katherine anything. Had, probably; but I was just as guilty as him. I had told Dr. Yu things that would have shamed him, and the fact that I'd done so in my sleep was no excuse.

I reminded myself that Walter had no way of knowing what had happened to me or how I was feeling now, and I forced myself to smile at him and to greet Katherine and Quentin. Then I turned to Lou, who was still snapping at Dr. Yu. "What's the problem?" I asked.

Lou bit off his last phrase and then looked at me, his face completely expressionless. "This esteemed scientist and her husband have been most thoughtful," he said. "Supervising your care. But now you are well, and returned to your husband. It is preferred that she leave now."

Dr. Yu and I looked at each other and I picked up the stack of pink soaps that she'd left on the table earlier. "Preferred by whom?" I said. The hotel manager shifted uneasily and fixed his eyes on the floor.

Lou lowered his eyes. "Simply . . . preferred," he said. "Her work duties no doubt are calling."

"No doubt yours are as well," I said. I had had enough of Lou; I filled his hands with the bars of soap and eased him toward the door. "For your family," I said, when he stared at the soaps in surprise. "Thank you for all your help. Dr. Yu has scientific matters to discuss with my husband, and she'll be staying here for a while. Thank you for your concern."

I shut the door behind him and turned back to the company. No one was smiling except Dr. Yu. "See what I mean?" she said, and then she shrugged and moved closer to Walter and welcomed him back from his trip. This was the first time they'd spoken face to face since their disastrous meeting at the banquet, and I was impressed by her calmness and poise. She waited politely for Walter to introduce her to his friends, and Walter flashed me the signal we'd used for years at cocktail parties: left forefinger rubbed on the skin just in front of his left ear. *Help,* that meant. *Help me out here.*

I couldn't believe he'd forgotten. He'd met Dr. Yu at the banquet; he'd left me in her care. Now he couldn't remember her given name. "Dr. Olmand," I said, as smoothly as I could. "Dr. Bradley. Let me introduce a colleague of yours—Dr. Yu Xiaomin, lake ecologist from Qinghua University."

Walter's face relaxed. "Dr. Yu and her husband took care of Grace while she was sick," he said. "Her husband's on the staff at the main hospital here. They've been very generous."

"It was nothing," Dr. Yu said. She looked at the floor when Katherine and Quentin praised her kindness, and she changed the subject as quickly as she could. "I heard your presentation," she said to Katherine, and then she turned toward Quentin. "But not yours, I am sorry. What is your field of special interest?"

Quentin answered her and then asked about her own work. As she described her research, Walter and Katherine listened as well, and for a few minutes Dr. Yu basked in everyone's attention. "It was a small study," she said modestly. "Money and equipment are limited, so I designed this to rely on human labor. I tried to take advantage of what we have. We analyzed the stomach contents of many fish, from samples taken over fifteen years . . ."

While she talked, the hotel manager sidled up to me. "Our washing machines your clothes have destroyed," he whispered. "No one of us understands how. We offer largest apologies, and arrangings for compensations of the future will occur." He held an empty laundry bag in his hands.

"Can we fix them?" I asked. "Patch them up, somehow?" I had given him almost everything I had.

"Oh, completely not," he assured me. "Completely, they are destroyed to bits."

He pleated the bag in his hands until it was no bigger than a belt, and I thought of the way my mother used to stand in front of the closet she shared with my father, coldly fingering the clothes she bought off-season in bargain basements. *A belt,* she'd say. *If I just had one good belt to tie this outfit together* . . . There was a broom closet off the kitchen, where a lightbulb hung over a metal chair, and when my mother was disgusted with all of us she'd retreat to that paneled box and browse through stacks of old *Vogue*s with a cold, unblinking eye.

"You will be reporting this incident?" the manager said anxiously.

"Of course not," I said. "Please don't worry about it. The clothes wouldn't fit me now anyway. I lost some weight in the hospital."

He broke into a radiant smile. "Oh, absolutely," he said. "Anyone this could see. You have great kindness. My wife, my children, will all have gratefulness—this job only has been in my possession for several months." He looked over at Dr. Yu and his face darkened again. "But your friend . . ."

"Why would she care?" I asked. He dropped his eyes and I looked at him sharply. "Did *you* call Lou?" I said. "Did you tell him Dr. Yu was here with me?"

"Oh, no, *no*," he said in dismay. "You guide, he alerts himself. I am complete discreetness."

He wrung his hands and apologized again and then he left, murmuring a few words to Dr. Yu as he passed her. The day was unraveling around me faster than I could knit it up again. My clothes were destroyed, my hair was gone, Dr. Yu had been insulted; a suitcase I didn't recognize sat next to Walter's brown leather bag, which we had bought together in Vermont. Walter's friends talked on and on and didn't seem to understand that they should go. Katherine had somehow turned the conversation to her family's long involvement with China.

"My grandfather made a famous translation of the *Book of Changes*," she told Dr. Yu. "And he translated many of the works of Li Po and the other Tang poets. And also many of the classics of Chinese traditional medicine—he used to drive my grandmother crazy, cooking up potions in the kitchen of their summer home. Boiled licorice root and scallions, dried lotus buds and dogwood and orange peel and ginger . . ." She laughed musically. "He was such a crank," she said fondly. "Yin and yang, hot and cold, wet and dry—he had arthritis. What he needed was an aspirin. And then my father studied Chinese history—his specialty was the Opium Wars and the Taiping Rebellion. And two of my uncles—my family has been involved with China for years, but none of them ever made it here. I'm the first."

She said a few phrases in Mandarin, with an accent so pure that I felt a pang of jealousy. Dr. Yu complimented her on her pronunciation.

"My father taught me a little," Katherine said modestly, her face lit up with pleasure. "But you know, it's the strangest thing—since we got here, I've discovered that I can't understand what anyone's saying. I can't seem to distinguish any words. Everyone speaks so fast, and with such an accent—all I can hear is noise."

"Well," Dr. Yu said, "no doubt we sound different than your family who taught you. Since they learned only from books, since they never came here . . ."

Everyone paused at the same time. "The laundry destroyed my clothes," I announced.

Quentin smiled and moved his sneakered foot away from Katherine's brown pump. "We know," he said. "The manager was just telling us when you walked in."

Katherine frowned and tapped Quentin on the arm, and in that instant I thought I understood the tension in the room. Katherine and Quentin must be sleeping together, or they had, or they would—they had that slyness about them, and that set of shared gestures. I moved toward Walter. I had so much to say to him—everything that had happened while he was away, everything I'd thought about. All our history, which suddenly seemed worth preserving. "Dr. Yu and her husband took such good care of me," I said. "I had this fever . . ."

Walter smiled and nodded but made no move to touch me. "I heard," he said. "I called the hospital every day." He turned toward Dr. Yu and said, "Really—I'm so grateful for your help." Katherine dug in the suitcase I didn't recognize and passed a small package to Walter, which he offered to Dr. Yu. "Please accept this token of my thanks," he said.

Dr. Yu moved forward reluctantly. "There is no need," she said. "Your wife has been my close friend."

"Please," Walter said. I was proud of him then, proud of his thoughtfulness. I prayed that he'd brought something useful and good—a cassette player, perhaps, or even something for Dr. Yu's lab, a pH meter or a micropipette.

Dr. Yu unwrapped the package slowly. Inside lay a black silk Qing-style jacket, with a mandarin collar closed by a red frog. The silk was coarse, the embroidery rough; the style was a crude imitation of an American's idea of imperial elegance. I had seen work like this at home, in shops that aped Uncle Owen's Oriental taste but couldn't tell good work from bad. Tired peddlers had hawked trays of these jackets to us at every tourist spot I'd been dragged to my first week.

"Thank you," Dr. Yu said slowly. "That is most kind."

"Try it on," Katherine said. Her voice was high and clipped. *Cream?* I could imagine her saying. *Weak or strong?* I saw her pouring at a proper tea, ironing sheets and storing them with lavender sachets. Her shoes were excellent, sturdy and expensive.

Dr. Yu put the jacket on. The sleeves hung four inches below her fingers, and a chain of small white holes dotted the shoulder seam.

"A little big," Katherine said brightly. "But surely the sleeves can be hemmed. Any good seamstress . . ."

Dr. Yu and I looked at each other, trying to shut out Katherine's voice. But Katherine seemed compelled to tell us how the jacket had been bought.

"Xian," she said. "What a place. Our hosts took us to the tomb of Qin Shihuang—you know the famous emperor? The one who built the Great Wall and buried all the pottery armies around him?"

Dr. Yu and I nodded politely. Everyone had heard of the Xian tombs. Even us.

"After we left the museum we got funneled through this market set up outside the exit. Two rows of stalls, us forced down the middle . . ." She smiled at Walter and Walter smiled back. Quentin made a face at his shoes. "Wasn't it amazing?" she said.

"It was something," Walter agreed. He wasn't looking at me.

"Sort of third-world," Katherine said. "We didn't expect it after the majesty of the tombs. These little boys kept plucking our sleeves and saying, 'Hello, hello, lady hello, you buy?' and then pulling us over to their parents' stalls. And then they had all this stuff, pottery replicas of the buried soldiers and horses, and lapel pins and embroidered runners and carved jade and shoulder bags. Some people were selling fruit, and someone had homemade Popsicles—instant hepatitis, if you ask me—and a few people had some silk, and they were willing to bargain."

Dr. Yu had taken the jacket off and was rolling a corner of it between her fingers. "Yes," she said quietly. "They would bargain. It's a poor city."

My chest was hurting again and so was my head. I wanted Katherine to shut up, get out of my room, get out of my life. She went on talking.

"So anyway," she said, "Walter found this jacket and said it was just the thing for you, and so we bought it. And I bought one for myself, and then when we turned around we found Quentin surrounded by all these kids trying to sell him clay animals. He bought this whole flock before we could stop him. And then he had to leave them at the hotel because our baggage was overweight, which was too bad, really—they would have looked stunning on a mantelpiece."

"Oh, stunning," Quentin said sarcastically. On the mantelpiece in Uncle Owen's house, the *netsuke* Dalton collected had been ranged in ordered rows.

Katherine paused to catch her breath, but it was easy to tell she had more to say, that she might go on forever.

She spoke with the enthusiasm of someone just escaped from a cloistered life, as if everything she'd seen had printed itself on her eyes but hadn't made its way to her brain or her heart. I wondered how she'd lived her life.

"You had an adventure," Dr. Yu said softly. Quentin laughed.

"We did," Katherine said. "A real adventure."

"You really saw the country."

"We really did."

"I hope you like the jacket," Walter said. "And if there's ever anything I can do for you . . ."

Rocky, I thought. I still hadn't had a chance to look in my purse, which I'd spotted on the floor beneath the window ledge. "I am only glad I could help your wife," Dr. Yu said. "And now I must go."

"So soon?" Walter said. "Will we see you at the banquet?"

"Perhaps." She backed out of the room, her face closed to all of us, and I felt a sudden panic. We were due to leave the country in four days, and I didn't know how we'd manage to see each other again.

"What banquet?" I said. I moved toward Dr. Yu.

"Tomorrow night," said Quentin. "Most of the other scientists stayed here in the city while we went away. They've been visiting labs at the universities and seeing some of the sights. All of us, and all the Chinese scientists who participated in the conference, have been invited to a formal banquet at the Great Hall of the People."

"We rushed back to be here for it," Katherine said.

Dr. Yu looked at Walter. "You rushed back for Grace, I think."

"Of course," Walter said. And then he looked at me again, really looked for the first time, and he said, "Grace. What happened to your hair?"

"We had to cut it," Dr. Yu said shortly. "Her fever

weakened it." She nodded in my direction. "I will see you tomorrow night. With luck."

I followed her into the hall and closed the door behind us, just in time to see her crush the silk jacket into a ragged ball. "That *woman,*" she said fiercely. "These *people*—how can you live?"

"I'm sorry," I said. "Please come tomorrow—I'll wait for you, we don't even have to sit with Walter. And I'll talk to him about your son, I promise. Something will happen."

"Something will," she said. "I have no doubt at all about that."

The Summer Palace

> If you want knowledge, you must take part in the practice of changing reality. If you want to know the taste of a pear, you must change the pear by eating it yourself . . .
>
> —Mao

That night was one of those nights that never ends. Katherine didn't leave us—on and on, all the way through dinner, she regaled me with tales of their traveling hardships. "Roaches," she said. "Worms in the dumplings. Spiders the size of birds. We got sidetracked to Kunming, four hundred miles out of our way, because some general *had* to go there . . ." And even after dinner, when I thought Walter and I might go to our room and talk, he walked me upstairs, touched my hand lightly, and left me behind while he rejoined Katherine and Quentin in the bar. I leaned over the railing, unable to think of the words that might have made him stay, and I watched him move through the central atrium, past the jade plants, the goldfish pool, the reception desk. His feet were light; he was happy to leave me. During a pause at dinner, when Katherine had turned to Quentin with some remark, I'd asked Walter how he'd managed to forget Dr. Yu's name. "Oh," he'd said lightly. "Half the people here have names that sound alike."

I had told myself that that was Katherine talking, not him, but after he left me and went to the bar I was no longer sure. Our room was neat, sterile, sheltered; perfectly receptive and completely anonymous except for our few traces. Walter's brown bag sat on the carpet like a dog. Some lecture notes from his trip were stacked on the table. Five pairs of my shoes—shoes were almost all I had left—stood neatly on the closet floor. My purse sat below the window ledge, where I had left it, and in Walter's absence I dug through it and finally looked at Rocky's drawings. My purse was enormous and the drawings were small and somehow they hadn't been damaged; they were as beautiful as I'd remembered. Clean, precise, articulate, they spoke more about Rocky than anything he'd said, and I thought how, had the situation been different, Walter would have recognized their value instantly. But there was no way for Walter to see them without my explaining how I'd come by them.

Walter had once made me love him by crying out in his dreams, but I knew less about his dreams now than I ever had. I knew his work dreams and only those, and those were only his ambitions. He knew even less about me. If I wanted anything different for us I'd have to tell him about Hank, and about the years after Mumu had died, and then what had happened between Randy and me and why I'd had that abortion; and if I told him all that and he told me anything real in return, then I'd have to tell him about Rocky. I could blame it on the fever, my state of mind, the strangeness of a dark night in China, but none of that would help; there was no avoiding the mess my confessions would make and no predicting which would upset him most. I liked the parts of my life to be separate: one vase on a white table. One rug on a smooth wooden floor. My parents separate from Uncle Owen, my husbands separate from my family; I liked that, I needed that, and I was pretty sure that Walter did too. No one could have lived with me for six years and known so little of my real life without wanting not to know. There were reasons Walter sat downstairs, ignoring me; reasons he'd married me and then allowed our lives to move on parallel tracks, side by side but never intersecting except in small daily ways. I knew other couples who lived as if a fistula connected their separate skins, but nothing oozed like that between Walter and me. We had rules in our household: we said what we meant, we meant what we said, if we didn't say it, it wasn't so. If I never admitted what I'd done, I hadn't done it. If Walter never said what he wanted, he didn't want.

I fell asleep, missing the nightgown the laundry had shredded, missing Walter, and then I dreamed that I stood on the cliff at the gravel pit, overlooking the flat spot where Zillah and I had played. I dreamed that I jumped, not from the lower ledge where I'd broken my arm, but from the cliff itself, a hundred feet above the ground. I jumped and Zillah jumped beside me, and this time our arms did what we'd always wanted: we held them out and they turned into wings. Our arm bones shortened; our fingers lengthened enormously and splayed like spiders' legs; smooth skin spanned our bones in flexible folds. We grew the wings of bats, the leathery membrane stretching back to our legs, and we sailed over the gravel pit in silent flight.

There was an epidemic in Westfield the year Zillah and I got sick: she caught it from one of the children her grandmother cared for each afternoon and I caught it from her. On the last day I saw her, she'd drooped over the village we were building from Popsicle sticks and said her throat was sore. I meant to visit her the next day, when she didn't come to school, but by then my own throat was aching and burning and I had a headache so bad that the sunlight pained me. And so we were sick in our separate homes, which wasn't entirely my fault: I was nine and the world was run by adults, and I had no power to force my mother to take Zillah in or to park myself at Zillah's and refuse to leave.

I had lain in my own bed, in my own room, and my mother took care of me as I'd known she would although we didn't get along. I was bundled off to the doctor, given medicine, packed in ice; I was sponged and changed and bathed and fed, held and sung to and comforted. My father sat by me at night, when he came home from work. Mumu sat there in her wheelchair and stroked my hands. Our house was worn and we were pinched for money and my parents fought, but while the skin peeled off my hands and feet and the soft covering of my tongue dissolved, my parents suspended their differences and they took care of me. Meanwhile my fever soared so high that I heard Zillah's voice, which is how I know the way her illness went.

I hadn't understood until then that Zillah's life differed from mine. She was miserable at home and so was I, and I had thought our situations were equivalent. A false empathy: I imagined that my life was actually as bad as Zillah's. As if there were no difference between having no food I liked and having no food; between having a grandmother in a wheelchair who lived with us because my father wished it and having a grandmother who lived there because she had no place else to go. I had been in the place where Zillah lived, but I hadn't understood it, any more than I'd understood how relatively safe I was. Zillah lived in the corner of a long, low, concrete project, where the apartments were stacked like building blocks. The stairs ran up the outside and led to outdoor walkways, onto which the apartment doors opened. The door to Zillah's place was red, and inside were uncurtained windows and cardboard boxes spilling clothes, scuffed linoleum and a green shag rug and a dark line across the wall where the children Zillah's grandmother cared for—four of them, plus Zillah's sister and two brothers—ran their fingers. Zillah had no father; her mother worked at the corrugated box plant and was never home. Her sister had a cleft lip that had never been repaired. All those children got sick, passing streptococci among themselves like toys, and there was no space in there for Zillah to rest, no person able to devote himself completely to her.

There in my hotel room in China I dreamed I'd done what I'd wished: that I'd rescued Zillah and healed her so we could fly away. But actually I'd done no such thing. The morning my own illness left I lost Zillah, and with her any brief understanding I'd had of her world. I was left with the knowledge that I'd been lucky and she had not, but I was nine and couldn't make the next connection: I lost the glimpse I'd had of the idea that good luck was an accident of birth. Two of us had gotten sick and one of us had died, and I thought what had spared me had only been blind chance. That the doctor, the proper medicine, the food and care and shelter I was given had nothing to do with my recovery; that whatever had stricken Zillah might strike me. In the absence of Zillah's voice our lives seemed equivalent once more, which I took to mean that her luck would be mine if I didn't take drastic steps. And so I laid on the padding that would insulate me from the world, and later on I ran away from everyone and every situation that made me think my life was like Zillah's. I ran toward safety. I stockpiled stuff, as if I'd stay lucky if I owned enough. And yet in my dream, Zillah and I flew naked and unburdened. While she lived, what we had sought was always light.

I woke when Walter came to bed, and when he slipped beneath the sheets I crept from my bed to his and then clung to him as I hadn't done in months. "I want," I meant to say. "I know," he was meant to answer. Almost a year since we'd made love. I pressed my skin to his as though I could dissolve the membrane between us. I ran my hands along his thighs and felt them firm and lean and strong; I licked his neck and tasted familiar salt. "Make love to me," I murmured, but he was still and cold against me. He wrapped his arms about me obediently, he threw his leg over mine, but there was no pressure, no warmth, he never grew hard. When I took him in my mouth he felt cool, smooth, small, dead, his penis just a piece of flesh like any other, soft as the skin on the inside of my arm. He pulled away from me. He said, "I'm sorry. I'm tired." He rolled over and fell asleep, his ribcage expanding with each breath and then falling silently, the air moving gently in and out of his mouth. I watched him sleep and I thought about Zillah, who had known that my life was blessed with all I'd ever need, and whose voice had returned with the news that I'd thrown it all away, that I'd squandered near everything.

I rose from the bed an hour later and dressed quietly. This time I didn't make the mistake of leaving through the lobby; I crept down the stairs and along the back hall to the door that led out to the gardens. The air was cool and fragrant and a fountain splashed. I walked along the gravel paths, past flowering bushes and trees someone had pruned into artful shapes, and I watched the clouds move over the surface of the moon. If I'd been at home, or in any other place, I would have found a phone and called Rocky. I would have taken a bus or a cab to his place, borrowed a car, sent a telegram, but none of that was possible here and there was no way for me to reach him. I sat down heavily on a rough stone bench and wept for Zillah and Rocky and Walter; for my own frustration; for my inability to understand the smallest part of the world. My mother-in-law kept a shoebox in her closet, in which were all the letters her husband had sent her from France, during the war. Mumu kept a clumsy doll her husband had carved from a lobster buoy. Even my mother, unsentimental and sour, had dried roses from her wedding bouquet in a small glass box. Walter and I had a house full of his things and a storage room full of mine; a textbook full of his words and a few of my drawings; a handful of papers from our early days together. That was all.

When I looked up, I saw a man across the pond at my feet. His size and shape were enough like Rocky's that I almost called out before I caught myself. He gave no sign that he'd seen me, although the moon was nearing full and lit the garden palely. He bent over the water and set down two long pieces of bark on which he'd placed some petals and twigs. As I watched, he took two scraps of paper from his shirt pocket and laid one on each piece of bark, and then he said a few soft words and struck a match and set the rafts on fire. He crouched down lower and blew the flaming rafts away from the shore and toward the center of the pool. The rafts flared, burned brightly for a minute, and then disappeared. When they did, the man stood up and brushed his hands on his pants and looked directly at me. He didn't look like Rocky at all.

"Nice night," he called across the water. "Isn't it."

His face was Chinese, but his voice was absolutely American. He walked around the edge of the water, apparently unembarrassed by the scene I'd just witnessed, and when he reached my bench he asked if he could join me.

"I thought you were a ghost," he said.

"So why did you come over?" His face was lean, high-cheekboned, clever. He wore a short-sleeved shirt that left his smooth forearms bare.

"Needed the company," he said, and then he smiled and extended a hand toward me. "James Li," he said. "You must be here with the conference."

"Just a wife," I said. "Just one of the scientist's wives, tagging along."

He smiled as if I'd said something funny. "Just-a-wife," he said. "What brings a wife out here by herself in the small hours of the morning?"

"I couldn't sleep."

"Me either." He gestured toward the pond, where his rafts had sunk without a trace. "As you can see."

"What were you doing?"

He shrugged and looked over the water. "A little love charm," he said. "Something my mother taught me. You know how it is—love makes us stupid."

Perhaps because it was dark and late and we were strangers, we talked easily after that. I told him his rafts reminded me of things Zillah and I had made as children. He told me his parents were Cantonese but that he'd been born in New Jersey and taught at Yale. "My father's an epidemiologist," he said. "Very westernized. But my mother still keeps to the old ways. She was a midwife here, but she can't practice in the States. Her English is still terrible. And she's very superstitious." He paused and then laughed. "Not like me," he said. "Not much."

His voice was low and peaceful, but despite that he seemed to burn next to me, as if he had a fever. "You were visiting?" I asked.

"These last two months," he said. "Giving some lectures in Fujian—my first time over here. I went to see my grandparents in Canton last week. All these places I'd only heard about from my mother. All these relatives. Everyone thought I was rich and all of them wanted something. I had to get out of there after a week, so I came up here."

"What's here?"

"Good question." He threw a pebble into the pond and we watched the rings spread from the center to the shore. "What's here," he said, "is an old college love of mine I haven't seen in years. Working this conference. I came to give a couple of lectures at one of the universities, and when I registered here I saw the conference program with Tinnie's name on it. Who I haven't been able to track down at all—and tomorrow I have to give two more lectures, but I heard there's some big banquet tomorrow night and I got myself invited to that. Maybe I can hook up with Tinnie there."

"Pretty long shot," I said.

He nodded. "Hence the rafts. I'm as nervous as a girl."

His feet sat square on the ground, his legs were completely still. "You don't look like the nervous type," I said.

"Everyone is—sooner or later." He plucked a few strands of grass from the ground and rolled them between his fingers. "So why were you crying?" he said.

He seemed so kind, so gentle, so open, that I told him, or at least I tried. In broken sentences, digressions, allusions, confusions, I tried to describe how I'd met Dr.

Yu and her husband and Rocky and what had happened between us. "And then I got sick," I finished. "And now everything's so complicated." I never mentioned Walter or the troubles we were having, but despite that James's face darkened and grew thoughtful as we talked.

"How did you get so involved with this family?" he asked. "So fast?"

"I don't know. It just happened."

"What do you think they want from you?"

"Do they have to want something?"

"Of course they do," he said gently. "Your friend, this Dr. Yu—why do you suppose she's gone to all this trouble?"

I thought back to our first meeting. "She wanted to meet my husband," I said. "He's sort of a big wheel here. And she was too shy to talk to him, so she tried me instead. But that was just at first."

"And after that?"

I shrugged. "We like each other."

He plucked at the grass again. "People here," he said, "believe very much in the importance of personal connections. Everything works through this network of favors and obligations. You do me a favor, I do you one—when I was at my grandparents, I accepted meals and hospitality from all kinds of people, and I didn't realize what I'd done until I was getting ready to leave. And then everyone wanted something—letters of recommendation, help emigrating, foreign exchange certificates, help buying a television set from the Friendship Store. You name it. And no one thought it was unusual to ask. I owed. Dr. Yu has done you a lot of favors, and now she may believe you owe her in return."

"I wouldn't mind that," I said. "What's the harm?"

"No harm," he said. "As long as you understand. But these connections aren't casual, the way they can be in the States. My parents still get letters from people they knew thirty years ago, fourth cousins needing help, children of old friends needing a sponsor for a visa. And they'd never think of disregarding those obligations. All I'm saying is that you should be careful what you accept."

"It's too late to be careful," I said.

"Then be fair. Make sure you honor your debts."

He stood and straightened the crease in his pants. "This Rocky," he said. "Are you in love with him? We could make another set of rafts. My mother swears by them."

I thought about Rocky once more. "No," I said slowly. "He's lovely, and I'm glad we met, but I'm not in love with him."

"One thing you don't have to worry about, then. No love charm?"

"No," I said. "But I hope yours worked."

"Tomorrow will tell," he said. "Wish me luck."

"Luck," I whispered. He vanished into the garden, following one of the paths that led to the top of a small hill with a view. Perhaps he meant to wait for the sunrise there. I sat alone for another few minutes, thinking about what he'd said and wondering if I could trust the advice of a man who called love to him with spells.

Walter and I woke so uneasy with each other that I almost welcomed our continued lack of privacy. We'd be alone together soon enough, and I dreaded what would happen once we boarded the plane home and left all this behind. All the noise, all the people, all the sights. All the buzz and clamor Walter had been swimming in. He'd be miserable when we got home, I could see that coming. Whenever he returned from a conference he went through weeks of withdrawal, and this time he'd have more to miss than usual and less to welcome him. But meanwhile we had Katherine and Quentin to distract us from each other. Katherine and Quentin had breakfast with us; they also had lunch with us. And after lunch, when the afternoon began to weigh so heavily that I suggested to Walter that we visit the Summer Palace, Katherine and Quentin came along as easily as if they'd been invited.

"What a good idea," Katherine said. "We were so busy working when we were here that we hardly saw Beijing."

I got stuck in the cab's front seat while the other three nestled in back. *"Ni hau,"* I said to the driver. The others seemed inclined to let me take charge of this expedition. *"Ni jiang Yingyu ma?"* Do you speak English?

The driver smiled—a nice smile, although his teeth were cracked and stained. *"Wo shi Meiguo ren,"* I said.

"You are, American," he said slowly. His smile widened. "My English, *Yingyu,* very poor. Hello."

"We want to go to the Summer Palace," I told him.

He frowned and looked puzzled. I opened my guidebook and showed him a map of the palace grounds. *"Yiheyuan,"* I said.

"Sights-seeing!" he replied. His face lit up and he nodded vigorously, and then he hurtled us through the hotel gates, thumping his horn at the horse-drawn carts in the road. We passed through fields and past a brickmaking plant and the low barracks of a military school, heading for a distant hillside studded with tile-roofed buildings. I'd seen these each time I'd passed between the Fragrant Hills and the city, but always the driver had followed a road that swung in a wide loop around them. This time we took a different route, passing hamlets I'd never seen before. On the outskirts of one was a vast, shallow pond completely covered with white ducks.

"Roast duck factory," Quentin said as we passed. "All that Peking Duck that gets served to tourists in the city . . ."

"Remember *our* duck?" Katherine said. "The one we had in Canton?"

I pictured her and Quentin at a small table, rolling crisp duck skin and scallions into pancakes spread with sauce. But when I looked over my shoulder I saw that Walter, not Quentin, was smiling at Katherine in shared memory.

The entrance to the palace grounds was packed with tour buses, bicycles, and cabs, and our driver muttered under his breath as he snaked the car into the lot. He honked his horn at a slow-moving cart. "These, these . . . *nongye,*" he said indignantly. "These, from *nongcun* . . . " Peasants, I finally understood. Farmers from the countryside.

A wave of people pressed Katherine against the wall when we got out. "My goodness," she said. "Where did everyone come from?"

"They're tourists," Quentin said. "Just like us. They're visiting the sights of their capital. Like people from North Dakota visit Washington."

Walter flushed; his hometown was always a sore spot with him. "Listen," he started. "You'd be surprised what people from Fargo do . . ."

Quentin raised his hand and cut him off. "Just kidding," he said. "Really."

I asked the driver to wait for us and he slouched down in the seat and pulled his cap over his eyes, preparing for an afternoon nap. The sky was completely clear and still, blue with a slight brownish cast where the smog lay over the city. The air smelled, even out here, and the lake to our left was turbid and dark. We stepped into the stream of people heading through the east gate toward the Hall of Benevolence and Longevity, where everyone seemed to be snapping pictures of everyone else. Gap-toothed fathers posed with their sons in front of the roped-off throne and peered at the labels, which I couldn't read.

I felt Uncle Owen's presence everywhere. He'd come here often, I knew, with friends who had sat with him by the glittering lake, which was blue then, and completely clear. The buildings the Dowager Empress Cixi had planned had lapped at the low hills, wave after wave of brightly colored pagodas and pavilions and halls, and below them islands linked by ornate marble bridges had floated in the water. Uncle Owen and his friends had tempted each other with the food they'd carried in—yellow wine, chickens baked in lotus leaves, roasted suckling pigs and spicy sausages. The grounds had been almost empty then, except for a few visitors like themselves, and they'd recited old poems to each other and had made up new ones, praising the harmony of the landscape. They had told tales of the *huhsien*—the male fox-spirits who love to create mysteries and perpetrate stupid practical jokes—and of the much more dangerous *huliching*, the vampire-fox who often assumes the shape of a beautiful young woman and then sucks the life from young men. Once, a girl with a lute and a beautiful voice had sat in a rented boat with them and sung folksongs as they floated across the water.

If there were spirits here now, I couldn't find them; the crowds of people were overwhelming. We wandered aimlessly through the cool pavilions and then we split up, not as I would have expected—me and Walter, Katherine and Quentin—but just the opposite. Katherine glued herself to Walter's side and marched with him down the Long Corridor, leaving me to follow with Quentin.

The covered walkway stretched before us, a mile and a half of tiled floor, painted pillars, wildly decorated canopies and open sides, which separated the lake from the hill. Each curve presented us with a new view, framed by the carefully placed pillars. I stood in the openings, trying to imagine what Uncle Owen had seen, but I was distracted by my feet; I had chosen a foolish pair of shoes and my toes were pinched. Katherine and Walter quickly left us behind.

"Do you believe this?" Quentin said. I thought he meant the palace, where the emperors had once come to hide from the epidemics and the heat, but he tilted his chin toward the couple vanishing before us.

"It's my feet," I said. "I wore stupid shoes." Katherine's shoes were perfect, soft brown oxfords with crepe rubber soles, and I wished I'd worn a similar pair. "I don't mean to hold you up," I told Quentin. "You go ahead, if you want." Beads of sweat had sprung out along his hairline, darkening the crest that sprung up from his forehead, and his nose was already starting to burn. "You should have worn a hat," I said. "You're getting fried."

Ahead of us, Katherine and Walter strolled like the Dowager Empress and her chief advisor. A yellow butterfly flew past, followed an instant later by a little boy in hot pursuit. "I'm in no rush," Quentin said. "If you don't care what's going on, why should I?"

"What's going on?" I asked. I was just making conversation, just killing time. Somewhere during the previous night I'd given up trying to control anything around me, and now I was determined just to let what had to happen happen. The day was very warm, and I was tired.

Quentin gestured toward Katherine and Walter. "What do you think?"

I followed them with my eyes. They were looking at each other and talking so quickly their words must have overlapped. Some birds I didn't recognize darted and swooped around them—swallows, maybe, something sharp-winged and fast. Katherine was shorter than Walter but much taller than me, which allowed her to look him easily in the face. And she was younger than Walter but not so young as me, and she knew Walter's work very well. She'd read his papers. She'd done similar experiments. She'd studied the effects of acid rain on the northern lakes of England in much the same way Walter had studied the lakes at home, and of course they had lots to talk about. Of course Walter was completely absorbed with her.

"You don't understand," I told Quentin. I steered him toward the shade. "Walter's always like this when he's around someone who shares his work. He thinks it's this big conquest for him to capture their minds. He likes to pick their brains, and share his. That's all."

Quentin took out his handkerchief and dabbed at his face. "Whatever you say. Do you suppose there's someplace here we could get a drink?"

"At the end of this walkway," I said. "I think there's a restaurant."

"If we make it that far," he said. He rolled his sleeves above his elbow and I loosened the collar of my blouse.

"I thought something was going on between you and Katherine," I continued.

He laughed then, loud and long. "She's ten years *older* than me," he said. "And anyway—Jesus."

"Walter's twelve years older than me."

"So what's your point? I don't think I've ever seen such a badly matched couple."

His voice was sour, and suddenly I was tired of him. Watching, judging, grading, his mouth always set as if he'd bitten something bitter. He was as fair-skinned as I was but twice as frail, the skin on the back of his hands already dotted with heat rash. I couldn't imagine how he'd survived his tour of the southern cities. A woman holding a tray full of lukewarm juice in paper containers approached us, and Quentin stopped to examine her wares. "Rose hips, apple, orange," he read. The labels were printed in English as well as Chinese. "Rose hips? Do you have any ice? Do you have a straw?"

I left him to his negotiations and strode away, ignoring the pain in my feet, and a few minutes later I came around a bend and found Katherine and Walter sitting on a marble bench, much as I had sat with James Li just a few hours ago. I reminded myself that Walter always talked endlessly to anyone who flattered him; that James Li and I had also talked and smiled and it had meant nothing. The sun was so bright, the reflection off the lake so brilliant, that Walter's head seemed almost black against the background of the water.

I sat down on the bench across from them and stripped off my shoes and then pretended to admire the view. Katherine and Walter went on talking, but they weren't discussing their work.

"Remember when we first saw the White Swan Hotel?" Katherine said. "Like a piece of home, right there?"

"We were so hot," Walter said. "And then all that glass and white concrete . . ."

"And *air-conditioning*," Katherine said.

"And iced drinks," Walter replied.

They knew I was there; they smiled at me. But their conversation excluded me completely, and when they kept on talking I felt a stab in my temples that might have been jealousy. The memories they were sharing were supposed to have been mine; if I hadn't been sick I would have gone on that trip. I listened hungrily, my eyes half-closed against the glare, and I tried to imagine what they'd seen.

"That ferry," Katherine said, and they both laughed.

"What ferry?" I said. I tried to imagine it—low, with a

roof and open sides, square and steel-floored and crowded. Or maybe it was small and made of wood, with glassed-in sides.

They stopped laughing. Walter composed his face and said, "I'm sorry, Grace—you don't even know what we're talking about. This was in Canton. We split from our guide for the afternoon and went wandering around on our own. And it was ninety-five degrees out, and we got lost . . ."

"You and Katherine and Quentin?" I said. I struggled to focus on what he was saying, but I was distracted. By half closing my eyes, half dreaming, I could see simultaneously all the palaces that had occupied these grounds. The palace the Emperor Qianlong had built and the ruins left after the Opium Wars, the Empress Cixi's renovation and the rubble left after the Boxer Rebellion, the new renovation that Uncle Owen had seen, and the new destruction and the even newer repairs . . .

"Me and Katherine," Walter said. "Quentin stayed in. He had diarrhea from something he'd eaten in Shanghai." I turned my head and saw Quentin in the distance, moving slowly from one patch of shade to the next. "Katherine and I had been walking along the river," Walter continued. "She found a bridge over to Shamian Island. And then we found this amazing hotel, so we went in and had lunch."

"A BLT," Katherine said. "With ginger ale. And *ice cubes*."

There was real pleasure in her voice, and I focused on her face. Good teeth, straight nose, light brown hair, and wispy eyebrows. The kind of face that looked well outdoors. Her hands were small and sinewy. "You must be very homesick," I said.

"The food here," Katherine began, and then she shook

her head and smiled. "The sights have been wonderful, but the food . . ."

"That lunch was *great,*" Walter said, as if I'd questioned it. "After lunch we found this ferry across the river and we took it just to be adventurous. There was this amazing market on the other side, all these animals being sold for food—snakes and eels and frogs and sparrows. Snipe, even. Monkeys. Owls."

"Live?" I said. Uncle Owen had told me that Cantonese restaurants were famous for their exotic dishes. Once, when he'd been visiting our family, he and my father had roasted a saddle of venison from a deer a friend of my father's had shot. The meat had been dark and savory and strange, and the two men had made a pungent sauce for it.

"Live," Katherine said. "It was so outrageous. But we did what we could."

"It was Katherine's idea," Walter said. "We bought as many of the birds as we could, and as soon as we'd paid for them we let them go."

"Right there," Katherine said. "Right in front of those cruel men. Selling wildlife like that—who ever heard of such a thing?"

"It's part of their culture," I said mildly. "They've always eaten those animals." Uncle Owen had eaten snake there, and wildcat and bear and more.

"What culture?" Walter said, and then he looked around the grounds when I made a face. "Oh, this," he said. "All this, I know it goes back thousands of years—but where's the culture now? They're thirty years behind us, and they're destroying their own environment, killing off everything but the people."

Katherine nodded in agreement. "In the fifties, they ried to kill all the songbirds here," she said. "They thought the birds were eating too much grain. And I've heard they kill dogs and cats in the cities for food."

That seemed to be what she disliked about China—not the politics, not the bureaucracy or the legacy of the blood years or the reappearance of paupers and thieves, but a lack of respect for wildlife and pets. "You probably ate some during your trip," I said. "And didn't even know it. My great-uncle ate cat here—he said it tasted like chicken."

She paled and gripped her thigh with her hand. She was as thin as Walter, and their thighs on the bench looked identically long and bony. A shadow fell across my lap and I looked up to find Quentin hovering over us, the paper container that had held his drink suspended from one hand. He was damp all over and his lips were pale.

"Aren't you all hot?" he said. "It's so hot here, there's no breeze . . ." He sat down heavily next to me. A limnologist, I remembered. At home in cool lakes. Here he was like a fish on the shoreline, hot and scalded and sick.

"We were telling Grace about the wild animal market," Katherine said. "In Canton."

"The great liberation," Quentin said. "The rescue of oppressed wildlife by the noble foreigners."

"Very funny," Walter said. "We did the right thing."

"The world's staunchest cultural imperialist." Quentin crossed his ankles and stared over the lake for a minute. "I should have brought sunglasses," he said. "I can't believe I forgot."

"I saw a kid selling some," I said. "Back at the east gate."

Quentin ignored me and looked at Walter. "Did you tell her about the project yet?"

Katherine reddened and Walter shifted uneasily. "Not yet," Walter said.

Quentin turned to me. "Katherine's going to spend her sabbatical in Massachusetts," he said. "In Massachusetts, at your university. Walter's department, actually. Walter's *lab*."

The heat had made him mean. Walter glared at Quentin and folded his arms and Quentin copied the gesture. "It's not for certain yet," Walter said.

"Your house," Quentin continued. "That extra room over your garage—Walter says Katherine might as well stay there, she'll be perfectly comfortable."

My old room, the place where I'd first holed up when I returned to Massachusetts. The sloping walls, the neat bed, the desk in front of the window; I wondered how my life would have gone if I'd stuck to that room, treated it as shelter and nothing more. I couldn't imagine Katherine there.

Katherine was very pink by then, but Walter stood his ground. "We want to do some work together," he said, and then he took a swipe at me—intended? unconscious?—while I was trying to picture them dissecting fish together in a trailer by the lake. "Since I can't finish the project at the swamp," he continued. "I was telling Katherine what happened there, how things fell apart right in the middle of our work, and she said I ought to put the research team back together and go to the Quabbin instead. It's a great idea—I don't know why I didn't see it. A better model, more refined than the first one, a follow-up study looking at the changes over the last ten years . . . we got so excited planning it that Katherine volunteered to help."

Something clicked into place in my brain, the way a jigsaw puzzle piece which has always appeared to belong to a mountain suddenly reveals itself as part of a cloud. *Everything is related to everything else,* Zillah said; Walter's first law of ecology.

"Isn't that nice," Quentin said. "That she's willing to help?"

"She has a huge grant," Walter said. "We can use the Quabbin data for a comparative study with her work in Sheffield."

An old man in a blue coat passed by, carrying a duffle bag and smoking a long pipe. He wore a small white cap and walked as if he'd come from the sea or was heading back to it. Two boys in miniature green army outfits watched me and giggled when I caught them at it. Someone had carved dragons over all the walls and pillars; someone else had pruned the trees for decades into gnarled and amazing shapes, so there was something to look at in every direction. Out on the lake three small boats floated, no bigger from this distance than the rafts James Li had floated on the garden pond.

"I was thinking we could stay here," I said to Walter quietly. I already knew what he'd say, but I wanted the words out in the open. "You could teach at one of the universities, and I could tutor people in English, and we could live in one of the dormitories."

"*Here?*" Walter said. "You're kidding."

"Not really," I said.

"I hate it here," he told me. "I mean, it's interesting for a few weeks, but all I want right now is home."

"Hot water," Quentin said helpfully. "Air-conditioning. Decent restaurants."

"That's right," Walter said. "And I'm not ashamed to admit it."

"I love it here," I said.

Katherine laughed nervously and Walter made a disgusted face. "You think you do," he said. "Because you don't understand it. You don't see one real thing that's going on here. All you see are your fantasies."

That was Walter; full missionary position. I shrugged

and rose and headed down the long smooth path, leaving him and the others behind as I tried to imagine China the way Walter did, as it might be. Just a big dirty country. Just a lot of people. Snarled up, unworkable; not a romance, not a story, not a myth. Maybe Walter was right and all I saw here were my dreams. Above me the glazed tiles of the Temple of the Sea of Wisdom glittered in the sun. *I made a palace of dreams,* Dr. Yu had said to me. *What I wish for. What I want. What I hope.* Everyone had one; maybe everyone had two, the way we had two ears, two eyes, two lungs, two hands, a pair of kidneys, and a pair of feet. One palace for the past and one for the dreams to come. I felt the way I once had in Massachusetts—as if my skin had grown suddenly permeable, as if the world were leaking in.

Walter saw a sea of things too broken to fix and I saw, below me, hundreds of people near the edge of the lake, enjoying the sun and the gentle breeze and dreaming their own dreams. I leaned against a carved stone lion and emptied my mind. *Listen,* Zillah said. *You can hear if you try.*

My boy has red cheeks and fat arms.

Four babies sit at my feet.

In a field green with new wheat, two rocks sit.

From our houseboat, floating down the river, we hear tigers call.

If only that man would move his arm.

If only I had a new bike.

He lifts his hand, which is creased along the back, and he takes my chin in his warm fingers.

That woman by the water there, beneath her clothes her skin may be like ivory.

Suppose I had just two young pigs.

I walk into the office and I am firm, I am perfectly clear, I do not apologize.

In the old garden, the stones shot straight from the earth. The trees might talk.

I opened my eyes. Maybe I'd heard the people below me; maybe I'd only guessed. Somewhere my mother dreamed of being rich, not understanding that no amount of money would ever fix her life. My father dreamed of small rare stamps, a face printed upside down or a boat with its sails reversed. My brother dreamed that his children might be wholly unlike him and that his wife had turned into a model. My mother-in-law dreamed of her son and my father-in-law dreamed of peas. James Li floated rafts on a puddle and dreamed of his lost love. Rocky dreamed of shopping malls and unrationed pork, his father dreamed he could live his life again, and Dr. Yu dreamed that her sister and parents were still alive, that her students had not been lost, that her lab gleamed with new equipment . . . for a minute, just a minute, I heard her voice in the hospital, telling me the story of her life.

I walked down to the marble pleasure boat the Dowager Empress had bought with the money meant for the Imperial Navy, and as I did I saw the first house I'd bought with Uncle Owen's money. *Which was the more useless purchase?* Zillah said. *Which more cruel?*

I couldn't answer her. The Dowager Empress had had an answer for the people who criticized her purchase: she told them she *had* used the money for shipbuilding, and she invited them to visit her boat. I had never asked Walter to visit my first house. He'd come twice, uninvited, only to stand silently in the lacquer-red dining room, and only now did I wonder what he'd thought. Perhaps he'd looked at my careful arrangements of screens, chairs, and porcelains, and had seen, not a woman combining and recombining objects into a pleasing pattern, but a woman getting ready to leave.

In the distance I saw Walter standing near his bench,

waving his left arm at me in broad, slow strokes. Years ago, in Fargo, he'd once waved across space like that to me. He and his father had gone for a walk and were returning across the rutted fields; from the window above the kitchen sink I'd seen them emerge from the trees and move our way. The wind caught at their jackets and puffed their sleeves. Walter had turned toward Ray and then Ray had taken a little twisting step and sunk to his knees, as if he wanted to demonstrate to Walter some property of the soil. Walter had turned toward the window where I stood and had thrown his left arm up in the air, moving it slowly back and forth.

I had waved back, and then Walter had cupped his right hand around his mouth and shouted something. I'd thrown open the window. "What?" I'd called. I couldn't understand him. "What?"

His left arm beat at the air: up, down, up. "Geese!" he'd cried. And when I'd raised my eyes to the sky above him, I'd seen an enormous flock of geese in the air, winging their way south.

"*Geese!*" he'd shouted again.

"Wonderful!" I'd called back, touched that he'd thought to point them out to me. I'd shut the window and gone to find my mother-in-law, meaning to show her the spectacle, but Lenore was folding sheets in the basement and I got caught up in helping her, left corner brought to right, left brought up again, the two of us moving together for the final folds. By the time we returned to the kitchen, Walter had already led Ray inside. Ray was ashen-faced, leaning on Walter's arm.

"What *happened?*" I asked.

Walter packed crushed ice in a towel and then wrapped it around Ray's leg. "His knee," Walter said furiously. "He twisted his knee out there. Couldn't you hear me calling you?"

I had heard him, but I'd misunderstood him completely; I couldn't be sure what he was saying now. His arm still waved at me, broad and slow and strong. He cupped his hand to his mouth and shouted.

"Grace!" I heard this time. "Come on! We have to get back!" Perfectly clear, as clear as Zillah's voice.

The Palace of Dreams

> A revolution is not a dinner party, or writing an essay, or painting a picture, or doing embroidery; it cannot be so refined, so leisurely and gentle, so temperate, kind, courteous, restrained, and magnanimous. A revolution is an insurrection . . .
>
> —Mao

The sky began to darken and the kites a pair of children flew seemed to come alive over Tiananmen Square as the buses drove us in for our final banquet. One, two, three small buses, soft-seated and gray-windowed, nothing like the public bus I'd ridden with Dr. Yu. People stared into the windows at us. We were a sight, a spectacle, all of us dressed in our best clothes and giddy because we were going home. I could taste the relief in the air.

"Two days," I heard the scientists say again and again. Two days. They were making plans: what they would do, eat, buy first. The Belgians stuck close to the Belgians, the French to the French. The Australians couldn't be separated from each other. Two and a half weeks of traveling, listening to talks, visiting factories and power plants, eating unfamiliar food; all they could think about was home. They poured up the forbidding steps of the Great Hall of the People, chattering in a dozen languages and unaware of the quiet Chinese who climbed slowly beside them.

I walked up the steps alone. Quentin had abandoned me for James Li, which I should have seen coming but hadn't. James had been waiting in the hotel lobby when we returned from the Summer Palace, and as we entered he'd cried "Tinnie!" and then thrown himself into Quentin's arms like a long-lost brother, while I stood frozen in surprise.

"Tinnie?" Walter had said. *"Tinnie?"* The name didn't seem to fit the serious scientist beside us.

"We were college roommates," Quentin said, and Walter appeared to accept that. I don't believe he saw the gentle touch James gave Quentin, but I did and I felt a moment's panic as Quentin introduced us all around. James shook my hand as if we'd never met before. "Mrs. Hoffmeier," he said, rolling the name on his tongue. He gave me a small, conspiratorial smile.

"That's right," I said lamely. I'd told him so much, thinking we'd never meet again, and now I worried that he'd tell Quentin, who might tell Katherine, who would surely tell Walter. But James touched my arm lightly before he and Quentin strolled off together, and his touch told me my secrets were safe; he had secrets of his own for me to keep. Katherine stayed behind with me and Walter, and later, as we dressed for the banquet, Walter paused every few minutes to add something to the list growing on a piece of hotel stationery. The list was headed "Quabbin Retrospective: A Comparison." He was gone.

Now they hung behind me two by two, James and Quentin, Katherine and Walter, and all four of them ignored me as I greeted Dr. Yu, who was waiting for me on those wide steps. She stood perfectly still, her hands clasped quietly at her waist. She wore the same clothes she'd worn the night we first met: gray skirt, dove-colored silk blouse, black shoes, pearls in her earlobes. The partygoers streamed past her quiet figure.

"You came," I said. "I'm so glad."

James and Quentin and Katherine and Walter passed us without a word, completely preoccupied. Dr. Yu nodded. "Of course I did." She watched me watching the others, and she said, "This is interesting. They have been like this all day?"

"Pretty much," I said. Their heads seemed magnetized, locking the couples eye to eye.

"The new young man—he is overseas Chinese?"

"Born in New Jersey," I said. "It's a long story."

"I imagine," she said. She followed James Li with her eyes. "Look at his clothes—how well he wears them, how nice they are. His shoes, his haircut—all very good. He looks refined. He looks like Zaofan would look, if Zaofan got away." She paused for a minute and watched as James bent toward Quentin. "How is it these two men are so friendly?"

"They're very old friends," I said. "They went to school together."

She raised her eyebrows but said nothing more. We passed through the massive doors and into the reception hall, where we stood with several hundred people amidst the huge paintings and the crystal chandeliers and the golden moldings. A small man in a gray suit shepherded us toward another pair of doors at the room's far end. He barked something in a high voice, and then he threw open the doors into the banquet hall. The hall stretched on forever, dotted with round tables covered by crisp white cloths. Rows of white-coated, white-gloved waiters guarded the tables and stood rigid and unsmiling.

The small man came over to Walter as we stepped inside. "Dr. Hoffmeier?" he said. Walter nodded and the man continued. "Please," he said. "You, also other honored guests in your party, please to seat yourselves at one of these six front tables. For distinguished conference members."

Walter couldn't have been surprised—he'd organized much of the conference, given one of the key lectures, jetted about the country on a speaking tour. But still he flushed pink with pleasure. I sat next to Dr. Yu and Quentin sat next to me, and then came James Li and then Walter and then Katherine. The tables sat eight, and I watched the small man puzzle over how to fill our empty seats. As the scientists entered the hall he'd been separating them into two streams, Chinese and foreign, so he could recombine them properly: four or five foreigners at each table, three or four Chinese. An equal balance, very diplomatic, but I could tell he wasn't sure how to count Dr. Yu and James Li. Finally he sent over a pair of blue-suited men who introduced themselves as Dr. Wu and Dr. Shen. They greeted Walter and Katherine and Quentin and me in English, and then they murmured to Dr. Yu in their soft Mandarin. When they tried the same on James, James blushed.

"My apologies," he said in English. "I was born in America, and I speak only English and my parents' dialect. Cantonese. I can't speak the northern tongue."

The two men looked at each other. "Not at *all?*" Dr.

Shen said. His English was correct but very heavily accented, and I watched as Walter's face closed to him and Katherine's followed.

"Not at all," James said. "But of course I can read." As if to prove himself, he plucked the handwritten menu from the lazy Susan and slowly began to translate it for us. "Winter melon soup," he said, struggling over the characters. "Crisp skin fish." No one had the heart to point out the English version written on the back.

Somehow that scene set the tone for the rest of the meal. Every attempt at a general conversation seemed to fail and silences fell after every general observation. We broke into pairs, probably doomed to that from the start by what was going on among half the table. James talked to Quentin in a low voice, describing how strange this visit had been for him. "My parents' country," I could hear him say. "But it's not mine at all, although of course it is—but it isn't, really, my parents fled during the revolution . . ." Walter described Fargo to Katherine, lingering long on his hometown's quiet charms, and Katherine listened happily and agreed with him. "I love traveling in the States," she said. "Everything's so wide open, so big—it's the only place to be for a biologist. When I think of what I could do there . . ." Dr. Wu and Dr. Shen talked to each other and also to our waiter, who filled our glasses with beer and sweet pink wine and pressed plates of savory appetizers on us. Dr. Yu talked to me.

In front of us were several tables of high-ranking Chinese scientists and Party leaders, and Dr. Yu pointed some of them out to me. "President of Beijing University," she murmured. "President of Qinghua, vice president of Chinese Association for Science and Technology, head of

Chinese Academy of Sciences—and there, over there to the left, those are scientists visiting from Shanghai for special study."

"It's so amazing," I said. "For me to be here at this . . ."

One of the scientists proposed a toast, and then another. The waiter refilled our glasses. Dr. Yu said, "It is amazing for me also, to be here."

"Yes?"

"Very much," she said. "I was here in Beijing when this building was made. In 1959—everything still seemed so hopeful then. Our fathers both had escaped somehow the Anti-Rightist campaign in '57, even though many scholars were punished then. And so Meng and I were able to go to university, as we wished, and help build socialism. Serve the country. Serve the people. When the huge harvest of '58 came, our classes were canceled and all of us, we went on buses to the countryside to help. We lived in tents. We did not mind the work. We sang, danced, gathered crops. We felt like part of our own country."

"That sounds wonderful," I said, reminded of my early days with Walter. Dr. Yu's voice had a wistfulness I could recognize.

"It was," she said. "It was almost the last time like that we had. The weather changed the next year and then the famine began—you know about this? The three bad years?"

I shook my head, although it didn't sound completely unfamiliar. Her words came to me as if I'd heard them before, vaguely, in a dream.

"It's not your fault," she said. "Only now do people begin to admit what happened then. Everyone was hungry. Everyone. In the city, here, we received one-half pound of grain each day, no salt, no fat, no meat, no vegetables. We ate bark we scraped from trees and boiled. Also leaves and wild herbs. In the countryside, where two of my brothers were, they ate ground-up cornstalks and sorghum stems and bark and roots."

She ate steadily as she spoke, her chopsticks moving quickly from the platters to her plate to her mouth. Our waiter brought dish after dish and kept our glasses full, and I concentrated all my attention on Dr. Yu's voice. Some of what she was saying sounded familiar to me.

"You have known famine?" she asked.

"No," I said. "But sometimes I've eaten to fill up what seems empty, like you'd drink hot water to fill your stomach when you couldn't get anything else. It's just as useless, but that's how I got this big."

"I must tell Meng," Dr. Yu said thoughtfully. "You have eaten from sadness?"

"Something like that."

"Meng thought you had thyroid disease."

We both smiled, and Katherine looked up at us before she returned her attention to Walter. Dr. Yu pulled the red-cooked chicken over and then she continued talking. "Well," she said. "Some people blamed the weather for this famine. Some blamed Mao and the Great Leap Forward. But still we were very idealistic, and we finished our studies and became married and thought, now our lives are really beginning. I was so proud to stay and teach at Qinghua, such a place of prestige. But of course, Qinghua—there was the start, practically, of the Great Proletarian Cultural Revolution. So soon, almost immediately, the president of the university was overthrown, and then all rightist elements and bourgeois academic authorities and also those they call 'escaped from the net,' which included me. Immediately my father was attacked because of his foreign training—they said he colluded with reactionaries, secret agents, and cultural imperialists.

They said his body was saturated with evil germs of the bourgeoisie, as old meat is with disease."

She caught her breath and quickly ate some prawns in bean sauce. "Well," she said. "I told you this part before. The Red Guards came, they locked him up, they paraded him around Shanghai, he died."

"I remember this," I said. "I remember some of this."

She hardly heard me. She snipped at her food with her chopsticks while she decided what to say next. She plucked and chewed and spoke again, swallowing quickly.

"Oh," she said. "Oh, *then*—once my father was taken, all was over for me. He has escaped the net, they said; he should have been reformed in the fifties. They will not make this mistake with me. I am contaminated. I am from a hopelessly bad class background. A dragon is born of a dragon, a phoenix is born of a phoenix, and a mouse is born with the ability to make a hole in the wall—that is what they told me. So I was guilty, Meng was guilty, our children—only two of them were born then, Zaofan and Zihong—they were guilty from birth because of us. Things were done to us, and to many others. Our jobs were taken."

"And your salaries," I said.

"And we were struggled against daily," she said, nodding with approval. "In the lake at Beida, the beautiful lake you passed the night we met, floated new bodies every day of the suicides. People we knew. At Meng's hospital, the doctors were made to work as orderlies, cleaning latrines and changing sheets, while the nurses and orderlies pretended to be doctors."

"And then you were sent to the country," I said. "For labor reform. And your sister was removed from the Ministry because of her connection to you, and the school where your mother taught was burned to the ground." I could have gone on; suddenly I felt like I knew the outlines of her life. Certain scenes lay before me as clearly as the ones Zillah had brought to my long sleep, and I knew then that I'd heard two voices and both of them were real.

She looked at me. "You were listening," she said, and then she smiled broadly. "You heard me!"

"I must have," I said. "But we don't have to talk about this. I hate for you to be upset."

"I am not upset!" she said. James and Quentin and Walter and Katherine all looked up then, but they were hypnotized, they were sheep, they were as stunned as if a spell had been cast on them. They were in love, two by two; if I hadn't known it before I knew it then. Once I'd stood like that next to Jim, Page's boyfriend, and had felt my feet moving his way as if my toes had minds of their own. Once, on a stony hillside, my leg had eased toward Hank's thigh. And I had felt like that once toward Randy and maybe even toward Walter, and during none of those times had I been able to see the world around me. A child could have starved in front of me during those white flashes and I wouldn't have noticed, any more than those two hypnotized couples noticed Dr. Yu. They registered the click of her chopsticks, the rise in her voice, and then they forgot.

"I am not upset," Dr. Yu repeated. She leaned back in her chair and breathed deeply through her nose, and then she emptied her glass. "Of course I'm upset," she said, more quietly. "See what I mean? You think of these things from the past all the time, you press them to you as Meng does, living again and again each thing—of course you become upset. You become upset if the things remembered are bad, and you become distracted from your own life if the things you remember are good."

She paused. Dr. Shen, who had been watching her

curiously for some time, leaned over and spoke to her softly in Mandarin. She nodded rapidly and held her hand out to him, palm up. "It is fine," she said to him in English. "It is fine. She is my friend. She knows of my life."

Dr. Shen looked at me gravely and inclined his head in a small bow. Dr. Yu touched the back of my hand lightly with one finger.

"All this I have told you," she said, "all this, is only to say that for me to be here in this building, as an honored guest, after all that has passed before . . . well. Only I wish Meng had come."

"You couldn't bring him?" I said.

"I could—spouses were invited. But he swore he would never set foot inside these doors. And then I thought to bring Zaofan, but he laughed when I asked him. He asked me, should he come to this place where extraordinary incident occurred?"

"Did you tell me about that?" I asked. I struggled to fit the pieces I remembered into some larger shape. "I remember the trouble in the countryside, over the sweet potatoes. And the *dazibao*."

"This is something else," she said. "Zaofan was six when we were sent away, thirteen when we came back. He had almost no primary school, but somehow he had to pass the examinations for middle school, and somehow he did. But just when he started, Zhou Enlai died, and Zaofan participated with his classmates in the Qing Ming demonstrations. And—probably you know this, probably you read about this in your papers at home. It was just ten years ago."

"I know about Qing Ming," I said. "A little. When my Uncle Owen was here, he used to go with his friends to sweep the graves of their ancestors. Afterwards, they had big parties to celebrate the spring."

She nodded. "This was the same celebration. You remember pictures from 1976, hundreds of thousands of people filling the square outside this building?"

"Sort of," I said.

She smiled. "Sort of," she repeated. "A great sadness occurred when Zhou died, and then anger when the government made no official mourning for him. People my age, our lives had just been returned to us and we were too timid, still, to do anything. But young people, students especially, they made their own mourning. A bad article against Zhou appeared in the Shanghai newspapers, and this caused great demonstrations. People marched outside here, bringing wreaths and poems honoring Zhou, and some people pasted these poems to the Monument to the Revolutionary Heroes in the square. Also someone made a poem comparing Mao to the Emperor Qin Shihuang. The one Katherine visited the tomb for, in Xian."

"I thought he was a hero," I said.

She made a face. "Some hero. He made an empire, perhaps, united many peoples and guarded empire's borders. But also he ordered all books burned and many scholars killed. So to say this, to say what Mao did during the blood years is like what the Qin Emperor did—well, this is a strong thing."

"What happened?" I asked.

"What you would expect. By the second night of the demonstrations, most people had left, but the wreaths stayed, rows and rows of them. Late in the night, trucks from the government came and stole all the wreaths away, against tradition. This was seen by some, and at dawn people poured back into the square. Many were students from the middle schools, among them Zaofan. They asked that the wreaths be replaced, and when no answer came they grew angry. Several cars were burned. One building was set on fire. Foreign journalists, their films were taken."

"A riot?" I said.

"A small one. That evening, the mayor of Beijing stood on the steps to this building and he called out, 'Go home! All you boys and girls, you go home!' His voice came out of the loudspeakers on the lampposts in the square. Some boys and girls went home and some stayed, Zaofan included. Later they turned on all the floodlights and then the militia came with clubs and surrounded the students and beat them. They arrested many and hurt some, and a few were killed. Zaofan was arrested, and even though he was released the next day, this went in his file along with notes about how we, his parents, had undergone labor reform, and also the sweet potato incident when we were in the country. So of course when he applied to art institute, he could not get in."

She brushed the tablecloth with the tips of her fingers. "Always, this will be with him," she said. "The rehabilitation committee excused him after Mao died and the Gang of Four fell, and also they restored my job and Meng's and returned back salary for our lost years. But always the stain has remained for all of us. Always, these times repeat."

As the meal wound down, we drank many toasts. We drank to the heroes of the revolution, to the victories of the anti-imperialist wars, to Sino-American cooperation and the continued friendship of our peoples. We drank to the increased joint production of high-technology goods, to the weather, to the various dignitaries, and to some of the prominent scientists. Once, even, we drank to Walter, and Walter trembled with pleasure when a department chairman from one of the universities praised him for organizing the conference so well. When Walter sat down after toasting his hosts in return, he bent toward Katherine and squeezed her hand.

His smile was as clear as a poster, the light in his eyes as strong and sharp as the *mao-tai* the waiters had poured for the toasts. I felt like I held Dr. Yu's life in my head, a small glowing ball buried deep in my brain, and I heard children singing in the streets and saw a ring of people with linked arms dancing. Two steps in place, one step forward; kick with the right leg, kick with the left. Music poured from the loudspeakers in the street. I saw myself in a concrete-walled classroom here, with a stack of sticky labels inscribed with the names of things. The language of things: *chair, desk, window, wall, pencil, lamp, pen;* me sticking labels on objects and the students repeating the words. It seemed like a pleasant dream, maybe even a possible one. I had no idea that Dr. Yu had something else in mind for me.

I rose unsteadily and walked over to Walter and tapped him on the shoulder. "Outside," I said. "Now." The hand I placed on his shoulder felt dead, or his shoulder was dead, or whatever should have flowed between hand and shoulder was dead. I felt a wish just then, as strong as a kick in my chest, for a man with Walter's brains and Randy's wild anarchy and Rocky's sweetness and Hank's kind heart, and there was nothing I could do with that wish except to hold my ribs with my hands and know I wouldn't die from the wanting.

Walter followed me without any argument; maybe he knew from the look on my face that I was serious. He followed me through the endless rows of tables, along the red carpet, across the huge hall, out the massive doors to the dim broad steps overlooking the square. The square was empty except for a few people cutting the corners between one building and the next, and I saw it as it had been twenty years ago, filled with shouting Red Guards being blessed by Mao on the eve of the Cultural Revolution. I saw it ten years ago, filled with silent students laying wreaths at the base of the obelisk, and I saw Rocky there, still a teenager, risking himself while I burrowed deeper into all that hid me from my life. His mother had given me something precious, I saw, something I'd always lacked: a sense of context, a framework in which I could measure the choices I'd made.

Walter started to say something, but I stopped him before he could. "Look," I told him. "Here's the deal."

"What?" he said. He touched my forehead with his fingers. "Are you sick again?"

"You're in love with her," I said. "Anyone could see it."

He managed to smile and look pained at the same time. He hugged himself, his hands cupping his elbows. "Grace," he said. "You don't . . ."

"Never mind," I said. "It's true."

"She makes me feel young again," he said—the most honest words he'd said to me in ages. "Happy. She makes me feel *alive*, like I can start over. Do anything. Be anyone. Sometimes I get so tired of who I am and what I do, and I wish I could go back to when I was just getting started."

I tried to listen to him the way I'd listened to Dr. Yu, and when I did his words made me feel all we'd failed to build together. "There's so much stuff I never told you," I said.

"You think I don't know? It used to hurt me, the way you'd never tell me anything."

We stared at each other for a minute. I'd tried not to take anything from my mother but I saw now that I had, without meaning to or even understanding what it was: I'd assumed her desperate gentility, which had made me see my family as crude, coarse, impossible; something to be left behind. And having done that, I'd learned to leave my other lives behind me like larval skins. I had never mentioned Zillah to Walter, or my old friends, Chuck and Mark. I had never let Walter see more of my family than the bare outlines, the hard facts: if I hadn't been forced to on our first Christmas, I wouldn't have let him see even that. It was my fault, at least in part, that he didn't understand me. I'd given him nothing to work with but smoke.

"I could tell you now," I said.

"What would it change?" he asked.

We were silent for a minute, listening to the steady flow of traffic down the Avenue of Eternal Peace. Cars and bicycles slipped past the gate to the Forbidden City, and I felt such a pull that I could hardly keep from leaping up and running toward the street and blending into the flow of bodies moving through the night. *Let go of the house,* I heard Zillah say, as clearly as if she were sitting in Walter's place. *Let go of the house, let go of the yard. Let go of the blue satin drapes, the old pine table, the Persian rugs; let go of the trellis planted with purple flowers and the white picket fence. Let it go.*

I crumpled my fingers into my palm and uncurled them slowly. All the things in our house and yard were Walter's.

"She keeps these notebooks," I heard Walter say shyly. "She binds them herself, in different fabrics, and she keeps notes about everything she sees in them. I've never seen anything like it."

He looked good when he said that, he looked young. For a minute I thought of telling him that I could keep notebooks too, that I could work with him side by side at the Quabbin Reservoir. But it wouldn't have been what either of us wanted. I let him go.

That's good, Zillah said.

"So do you want to marry her?" I asked.

He ducked his head. "I might."

"So we'll get a divorce. I'll make things easy," I said. "And I won't ask for anything, if you'll do me a couple of favors."

He looked up expectantly. In the dim, kind light, he might have been thirty-four.

"First," I said, "first, you pull all the strings you can and get me an extension on my visa and whatever other papers I need to stay here. I'm going to stay. I'm going to work here."

Walter looked at me blankly.

"Second," I continued, "Dr. Yu has a son who's an excellent scientific illustrator. Hire him to work in your lab and take care of fixing his papers and getting him to the States."

"This part's a joke," Walter said. "Right? This is the kid who dropped you off at the hotel, the one with the funny T-shirt? I don't even *know* him."

"He's nice," I said. "He's bright and talented and his English is good, and he's never going to be able to do what he wants here. He needs a break." I dug in my purse and came up with Rocky's drawings, knowing as I showed them to Walter that I was giving Rocky away. But he'd never been mine; that night in the cab had only been a night in a cab, a dark place, two lost people. I needed to stay and he needed to go. "Look at these," I said to Walter. "No joke."

He squinted at the drawings, tilting them into the glow of the dim lamps. "These are good," he finally said. "These really are."

"So hire him. If you and Katherine go to work on the Quabbin again, you'll need someone to do what I used to. Draw the dissections, make the graphs, do the illustrations for the papers. And Katherine's not going to do that—she's not like I used to be."

Walter took a deep breath. "I can try," he said. "I guess. Jesus, Grace. What are we doing?" He wrapped a long arm around my shoulder and pulled me close.

"What you want," I said. "What I want." I eased away. "You take Rocky and Katherine back home, and go back to your reservoir and write your papers. I'll stay here."

"What will you live on?"

"On what I earn. Dr. Yu said she can get me some work teaching English. And if I need more money, I can always sell some of my things back home."

As soon as I said that, I knew I wouldn't. *Let go of the antiques,* I heard Zillah say. All of them had come from China; Uncle Owen had just about stolen them. I'd leave them to Rocky, who could sell them or keep them as he saw fit.

"So that's it?" Walter said. "Just like that?"

"That's it," I said, and I felt my lungs swell as if I'd filled them with air for the first time. I could let everything go. *Let go of the swamp,* Zillah said, and that was right too. That was the last thing, the largest thing, the mistakes I'd made there all that were tying me down.

"You know," I said to Walter, "nothing ever happened between me and Hank. I was just being crazy."

He pulled his eyes back from the monument in front of us. "I know," he said quietly. "I figured that out while you were sick. Once I got away from you, I was able to think over what had happened. Then I realized Hank had been telling me the truth, and that he never touched you. Did you make that up just to hurt me?"

"I don't know," I said. "I was mad at you. At him too. I was mad at everybody."

"I'm sorry," he said. "For whatever it was I did to make you that way."

"I'm sorry, too," I said. "For everything."

Dr. Yu opened the door and came down the steps to

us. "The banquet is over," she said gently. "They are making the final toasts. They would like to toast Dr. Hoffer-meierr one last time."

Walter stood and looked at me before he left. I gave him a little push, the last time I'd ever touch him, and then I watched as he galloped up the steps two at a time.

"You are all right?" Dr. Yu said.

"Better than that. I'm staying. He's going. He's taking Katherine home. And he's taking Rocky—Zaofan—with him. He's going to give him a job."

Dr. Yu smiled and pressed her hand to her chest. "This is true?"

I nodded.

"Will you work for me?" she said. "My laboratory assistant is leaving, and I would like for you to have her job. Will you accept?"

"Of course," I said.

"Then we have much to celebrate. Do you dance?"

"I love to dance," I said.

Across Tiananmen Square, down one of the large avenues and past two others, through a maze of *hutongs* and a forest of small buildings, was the cellar Dr. Yu had in mind. Inside the unmarked door was a white room with a low ceiling and an old mirror ball and a scattering of faded paper decorations on the walls. One step up from the floor, on a wooden platform, a small band played a mixture of American show tunes, Chinese folk songs, and pop music imported from Hong Kong. Rows of wooden chairs stood before the platform, but all of them were empty; some of the guests stood against the walls but most of them moved gravely across the floor, dancing dances I hadn't seen in years. Not the Loyalty Dance, not the Planting Dance, but the waltz, the foxtrot, the mambo, the rumba, the conga. Dances Uncle Owen had once taught me. Perhaps he'd learned them here, in those strained times just before Liberation. Or perhaps he'd taught some of these people, who waltzed gracefully past a sign on the wall that read:

Dream Palace
For Dancing.
Band Tonight.

The crowd absorbed us instantly as we walked in. People stared at me, at my clothes and my hair and my size, but their stares weren't hostile and they drew closer to me as Dr. Yu touched my arm and murmured, "*Pengyou.*" Friend. Then everyone wanted to dance with me. The first woman who propelled me around the room said my hair was remarkable; several other people said they wanted to practice their English with me. I danced with a little boy, with men old and young, with girls and with women my own age, because that's the way things were done in that room: everyone danced with everyone. I traded my scarf for a carved wooden comb and my pin for a string of beads. I gave away my pen. I danced until I was breathless, until my feet were sore and my cheeks were red, and as I did I listened to my partners talk. There were a hundred stories in that room, a hundred lives. When the band took a break I bowed to my last partner and ran over to Dr. Yu.

"You are liking this," she said, laughing at my flushed cheeks and disheveled clothes.

"I love this," I said. "I like the music. I like the people. I like what this place is called."

She smiled. "It has a good name," she said. "Since its new opening. In 1983, when the government tightened again, this room was closed for two months for weakening the spirit of revolution among the people. And all of us thought, oh, the bad times are happening again. But they were not. When this room opened again, the group which runs it said its existence was only a dream, that it flowers between one conservative movement and the next. And so the name."

"Well, it fits," I said. "I feel like I've been in palaces all day. You know, Walter and Katherine and Quentin and I spent the afternoon at the Summer Palace. That's where I figured out what was going on."

"You didn't tell me that," Dr. Yu said. "There is a story from that place for you, which I have been meaning to tell you. Did you see the building at the top of the hill near the lake? The one called the Temple of the Sea of Wisdom?"

"Just from a distance," I said.

"Not much is left there to look at now. But inside that building, before the blood years, were three big golden Buddhas—one in the center, almost two stories high, and two others, a little smaller, on either side. In tradition, the one in the center represents the present. Those to the left and right represent the past and the future."

"One is like your husband," I said. "Always dreaming of the past."

"You could say this," she said. "And the other is like I am sometimes, and also I think you—always dreaming of the future. Sometimes when I was working with the pigs in the country, I would have such visions of what I wanted that I could see nothing before me."

"Your palace of dreams?" I said. "Is that what you mean?"

She nodded. "All the time I was in the country, I dreamed of a five-room apartment bordering Beida, overlooking the Lake with No Name. There, rather than Qinghua, because then I thought I never wanted to return to where I had been. In this place was a room for me, a room for Meng, a room for my children to share when they were home from school. Also a living room with bookshelves, in which were all my books and those of Meng and my parents, which were destroyed by the Red Guards. I dreamed a desk near the window, and a soft chair like that one in your hotel room. Actually, I dreamed exactly that chair."

She paused and then shrugged. "Chair is chair, I suppose," she said. "Especially here. Anyway, I dreamed time, space, books, light. Privacy. A smile on Meng's face. Also maybe some small land in the Western Hills with a vegetable plot and some hens."

"That's a pretty reasonable dream," I said.

"But this is my point—there is no such thing. Even Marx says you cannot choose your dreams. What you wish for is determined by who you are, what life you come from. But you can choose how you act, how you live."

She bought two bottles of orange soda from a little boy who approached us, and then she continued. "These Buddhas on the hill, they were destroyed many years ago by the Red Guards, and all the bronze was melted down to make things useful for the people. I never saw them, but the story is that the Red Guards broke the left-side Buddha first, the one representing the past, because that was their job. Destroy the four olds, eliminate the past. They cracked that Buddha into small pieces and carted the pieces away. But when they returned, there was discussion over which of the others to take next. Which sequence was more politically correct? One boy said that to destroy the future is to make the present hopeless, so they should take the middle statue first, leaving the future to stand briefly alone. China is a country of the future, he said. The future is progress. China must move ahead.

"But another girl, she said no. She said that to destroy

the present instantly destroys also the future, and that they must take the right-side statue and leave the center one, at least for one minute, alone. That way, she said, they would ensure that the present always exists, and a present always existing in the end is all things. And she won, or so the story goes, and for a few hours that central Buddha sat in the temple alone."

The band started up again, and while I puzzled over Dr. Yu's words she took my hand and spun me out in a waltz before anyone else could claim me.

"What I mean," she said, as we twirled over the floor, "what I mean is that a middle way is sometimes best. Not too much looking back. Not too much dreaming ahead. Time you spend in the past and future is time you spend alone. But between them is a middle kingdom, both feet planted here."

The floor was filled with dancers now, all of us moving through the small lozenges of light cast by the mirror ball. Faces lit up and vanished and reappeared, and I saw a small, dark shadow flitting through the bodies, darting between the elbows and knees. A slight figure, short and airy; a nine-year-old girl sprouting leathery wings—Zillah. *You'll have a boy,* Zillah said to me. *With hair like Rocky's.*

"What?" I said out loud. I turned my head, but Zillah's shadow was gone and all I could see were my dancing neighbors.

"I'm right here," Dr. Yu said, pressing her hand against mine. "Move your feet like this."

You'll have a girl, I remembered my mother-in-law telling me, years ago. *With hair like yours.* Then I remembered the pain I'd felt the night I spent with Rocky, that sharp click as the egg in my ovary had tumbled into its waiting nest. Was that possible? That Rocky had touched that egg, that the few hours we'd spent together should have been just the right few hours? I carried his blood in me, and Dr. Yu's and her husband's and their dreams and their memories, as well as those of my parents and Mumu and Uncle Owen, and Dr. Yu's father who'd died in Shanghai, and my own and others I didn't know but couldn't deny.

Dr. Yu led me around in a fancy turn, and as she steered me into a square of light I said, "You know, I think I might be pregnant."

"I know," she said, and the smile she gave me was so complex that I couldn't tell if she'd be surprised when she first saw the face of my child. I still hadn't discovered all Dr. Yu had told me during my lost week; I still didn't know all I'd told her. But now we had some time to sort it out. We joined ourselves to the back of a conga line that was circling the room, and as we did I thought I saw Zillah's shadow again, dancing at the head of the line with her feet several inches above the ground and her wings outspread.